THE PRIMROSE SWITCHBACK

Recent Titles by Jo Bannister from Severn House

CRITICAL ANGLE
AN UNCERTAIN DEATH
UNLAWFUL ENTRY

THE PRIMROSE SWITCHBACK

Jo Bannister

This first world edition published in Great Britain 1999 by
SEVERN HOUSE PUBLISHERS LTD of
9–15 High Street, Sutton, Surrey SM1 1DF.
This first world edition published in the U.S.A. 2000 by
SEVERN HOUSE PUBLISHERS INC of
595 Madison Avenue, New York, N.Y. 10022.

British Library Cataloguing in Publication Data

Bannister, Jo
The primrose switchback
1. Detective and mystery stories
I. Title
823.9'14 [F]

ISBN 0-7278-5489-5

Typeset by Palimpsest Book Production Ltd
Polmont, Stirlingshire, Scotland.
Printed and bound by Creative Print and Design Group, Wales.

One

"Explain this to me just once more," said Dan Sale, glancing sidelong over his granny specs as he cornered the big car at roughly twice the urban speed limit. "With particular emphasis on why it has to be you rather than the SAS, and what use you're going to be to my newspaper with your throat cut."

The editor of the *Skipley Chronicle* was a spare, slightly stooped man in his fifties with a manner as dry as sticks and less hair than he once had. Those who only ever saw him behind a desk supposed the Mercedes was a status symbol. But Sale learnt his trade before mobile phones, when the ability to drive like Jehu could mean the difference between hold-the-front and a page-two filler, and when the need arose he could still burn rubber like a Hollywood stuntman.

Rosie Holland waited for gravity to return her to her seat beside him before attempting to reply. Her broad, capable hands were fisted white-knuckled in the seatbelt, and not just because of Sale's driving. She enjoyed a good roller coaster, would venture any ride whose safety bars would accommodate her ample frame. But this wasn't a fairground thrill, engineered for the maximum of terror with the minimum of danger. Sale was driving like this because, just possibly, a life depended on it. And what he wanted to know was why he was risking his licence to rush his paper's famous Agony Aunt into a battle zone when anyone with a titter of wit would be speeding in the opposite direction.

And there was an answer, even one that he would understand. It had to do with a notion as old-fashioned as Sale himself: personal responsibility.

"This is my fault," said Rosie, as calmly as she could though the frank brown eyes in the apple-cheeked face were rimed with fear. At forty-seven, five foot eight and fourteen stone – on a good day – this was not a woman who was easily intimidated, but she was worried now. "I misread the situation and now there's a woman being held at knife point in her own house who doesn't know where else to turn."

"She could try the police," said Sale shortly. "It's a police matter. The knife *makes* it a police matter."

"He's her son, and he's eighteen years old, and that makes it a family matter," insisted Rosie. "She might be sick and tired of the mess he's making of his life – sick enough to want to wash her hands of him, desperate enough to seek support from a so-called professional counsellor. But that's a long way from wanting to see him in the remand wing at Winson Green."

"That may still be the best solution for all concerned," grunted Sale. "Whatever feelings she has for him, the woman has no right asking you to risk your safety to keep a drug addict out of jail."

"No?" Rosie sounded doubtful. "I think I gave her the right when I presumed to advise her. If she'd asked her mother or her sister or her best friend what to do about young Robbie, about his drugs and his thieving and his bad friends, she might have gone on losing sleep – and money from her purse – but he'd never have pulled a knife on her. Instead she asked me; and I told her that all that was left was Tough Love. I told her to bag his gear and sling it on the street, to change the locks and take the phone off the hook. I told her he had to take the consequences of his own choices until he was ready to acknowledge her needs."

She sucked in a deep, unsteady breath. "And God help me, that's exactly what she did. Only I didn't anticipate that he'd come back armed with a sledgehammer and a flick knife, and tell her to get Aunty Rosie with her big nose and her big mouth round for a heart-to-heart. Maybe I should have done; maybe if I was as good at this job as people seem to think I *would* have done. Whatever, I can't leave Marjorie Miller to cope alone. I can't walk away now it's got messy."

"It could get messier if you don't," growled Sale. "Robbie Miller isn't really going to stab his mother. He wouldn't be waiting for you to arrive if he was. What he's waiting for is the chance to stab the woman who told her it was time to damn him and put herself first."

Rosie acknowledged that with a rueful sniff. "That's why I need you here. Or someone I can rely on, anyway, and with Matt and Alex away for a dirty weekend . . ." She shrugged. "I do have friends," she added, a shade defensively, "but not many I'd trust with my life."

"There's Prufrock." It wasn't an altogether serious suggestion – in fact Sale would have been offended if she'd asked anyone else – but the old man had taken so heartily to the role of her amanuensis that Sale was a little surprised he wasn't in the back seat right now, chipping in with his unsought advice.

Rosie snorted. "If I need help I'll need it fast. Arthur doesn't drive, and every time he uses a mobile phone he gets the weather forecast. I'd sooner not be bleeding while he's struggling with the complexities of push-button dialling."

"You mean, you'll bring in the police but only after you're hurt?" Sale's nostrils flared impatiently. "Rosie, that makes no sense. Let me stop the car and call them now. They won't stop you talking to him. If you *can* talk him out, fine – but nobody's going to get hurt if you can't."

"She is," said Rosie stubbornly. "Mrs Miller. I owe her better than that. Dan, you didn't hear her. She was terrified, but she begged me not to call the police. She'd rather deal with him alone, even in that state, than let the police have him. What could I do? – I gave her my word. This isn't some passing maniac we're talking about, it's her son. She knows what he is, what he's done. She knows she can't do anything more for him, and if she wants any life for herself she has to put him out of it. But she doesn't want to destroy him as well.

"Once the police are involved, all the options vanish. There's only one way the courts can deal with a man who steals from his mother to buy drugs and comes back with a knife when she throws him out. Whatever he's done, he's eighteen years old and she doesn't want him doing four years with the block barons selling his rectum every Saturday night!"

Rosie realised from the quality of his silence that she'd succeeded in shocking Sale. Normally this would have been a cause for satisfaction; now she felt a pang of regret. She sighed and touched his hand on the steering wheel. "I'm sorry to get you involved. If the shit hits the fan nobody'll be surprised that I was in range, but you have a reputation to lose. If you don't want to stay you can drop me at the house and—"

Before he'd been worried; now she'd made him angry. He didn't shout: his voice dropped from gruff to gravelly. "Is that what you think of me? You won't leave this woman to deal with her own violent son, but you think I'd leave you? You're willing to risk your skin for her, but you doubt I'm willing to risk my reputation for you? You're right, Rosie, you do have friends. I'm one of them. I hoped you might have noticed."

It was dirty pool, and in any other circumstances she'd have knocked him off his high horse with a raucous laugh like a bar-room parrot's. But there was just the chance, and both of them knew it, that they might regret anything they left unsaid now. She said simply, "You, Matt and the *Chronicle* are the best things that have happened to me in ten years. I know you're worried about me. I'm not sure I deserve it, but I like it.

"I'm not aiming to get hurt in there. I think I can defuse the situation. If I can't, maybe I can disarm the little sod. He's only eighteen, and junkies are mostly physical wrecks. Anyway, I have to try. For my own peace of mind, and because I want to go on doing this job and I don't think I could if you, me and the punters knew there was a point beyond which I couldn't be counted on. But if I'm wrong, Dan, there is nobody I would rather have watching my back."

If he'd thought it would do some good Sale would have kept trying to dissuade her, found other arguments, even made it an order. But he knew he'd be wasting his breath. Once her mind was made up Rosie Holland never yielded to any form of restraint that didn't have buckles on the sleeves. "At least let me come in with you."

She shook her head, untidy curls dancing on her broad brow. She affected the kind of hairstyle that most people avoid after their mothers stop doing it. "That wasn't the deal. He'll let me in if I come alone. If he sees anyone else he might hurt her. And I really don't think that's what he wants. She's still his mother, probably the only person in the world who actually cares about him. I think he was just shocked to find that even her tolerance has limits."

"He's a drug addict. You don't know what he'll do."

"He's an eighteen-year-old boy. If he gives me a hard time I'll pick him up and spank him."

Sale barked a desperate little laugh. "I don't think you've any idea of the size of eighteen-year-old boys these days!" Then, thinking again: "Ah . . . Perhaps you have."

Actually she knew more about the physical structure of eighteen-year-old boys, and everyone else from babies to old ladies, than anyone who hadn't spent twenty years dissecting them. She knew that her previous incarnation as a hospital pathologist still caused him unease, that he preferred to think of the author of the *Chronicle*'s advice page The Primrose Path as a doctor. The fact remained, the patients on whom she'd bestowed most of her medical expertise were all dead.

She bit her lip. He would never know how easy it would have been to let herself be persuaded, how difficult being this stubborn really was. "The bottom line is, I'm doing this and you're helping me. We might both wish we were spending the night some other way, but the phone went and this is it. I'm going inside, and you're waiting out here in case the thing goes pear-shaped. Give me half an hour. If you haven't heard from me by then, call the cops. If you hear screams, call them sooner."

Brindley Road was built between the wars of comfortable semi-detached houses set back behind leafy front gardens. Sale slowed the car, looking at the numbers on the gates. Then he stopped.

There wasn't much time – partly because of what might be happening in the house, but mainly because if Rosie intended to do this she couldn't afford to think about it much longer. But a few seconds couldn't matter. In the open door of the car she paused. "Dan, if this goes wrong, don't blame yourself. I didn't give you any choice. Remember that."

He nodded tersely. No one would query it; everyone who knew her had been cajoled, coerced or bullied into doing something unwise by Rosie Holland, and they all forgave her because everything she did came straight from the heart. But he wouldn't forgive this in a hurry, however it turned out.

And because he didn't know how it would turn out, he couldn't let her go without a word. He leaned across the car. "And there was nothing wrong with the advice you gave. *You* remember *that*."

The driveway in front of the house was dark. Only the glow of the street lamps, dim through the trees, showed her the way. At two in the morning there were no lights in any of the houses. Rosie took a deep breath, tasting the October frost, then set her jaw determinedly and went through the gate.

Marjorie Miller was a teacher, fifty-two, a divorcee with two daughters and a son. An ordinary middle-class family, except for one thing: the youngest child was a drug addict.

She wrote to The Primrose Path more because she needed to talk about her situation than in any hope of a solution. She'd done everything she could think of to rescue the boy but he wasn't interested. When she found an addiction clinic he wouldn't stay; when she made appointments for him with a psychiatrist he wouldn't go. He lost his job; she found him another one; he lost that too. She fed, clothed and sheltered him; she gave him pocket money. It wasn't enough: he stole from her to buy drugs. Once she came home to find he'd sold her television.

Rosie considered the dilemma at (for her) some length before asking Mrs Miller if, since she was clearly nearing the end of her tether, she was desperate enough to take the Tough Love approach.

She'd heard of it, thought it was some American fad with little relevance to the Midlands. On the contrary, said Rosie, it was increasingly being seen as an option by responsible people who'd tried everything else. Nor was it just an exercise in damage limitation. In a significant number of cases removing the safety net – 'I can always go home, I can always get money at home, they won't see me suffer' – was the jolt that made addicts, thieves and other black sheep face up to their problems. When a severe talking-to, a serious heart-to-heart, a few lost tempers and cutting the plug off the television set had failed, it was time – for some people – to start thinking in terms of Tough Love.

Robbie Miller was legally an adult, no longer entitled to be provided for as of right. He was in no stronger position in his mother's house than a lodger, said Rosie, and could be asked to leave at any time. If he refused to go, the 1988 Housing Act gave her the right simply to change the lock on the front door and deny access other than for the purpose of removing personal property.

The factor Rosie had overlooked was that the letter of the law probably wasn't much of an icon to a drug-addicted thief.

It was a little after one when Rosie's phone rang. This was not unusual: she gave her home number to people she thought needed it, was quite capable of dealing with those who abused the privilege. She would rather lose sleep talking to a desperate correspondent than have his suicide splashed across the front page of the *Chronicle* while The Primrose Path inside was advising him to stop being so pathetic and pull himself together.

Mrs Miller was certainly desperate, so desperate she was hardly making sense. It took Rosie minutes to get a straight tale from her: that Robbie had returned, had beaten in her back door with a sledgehammer and had a knife at her throat. He was demanding to see this Primrose Holland who'd splashed his private business all across her column and told his mother it was all right to sling him out.

"I'll call the police," Rosie had said, already grabbing for her clothes.

"No – please – don't do that." As far as Rosie could tell through the terror catching up her voice, Mrs Miller was not merely saying what she was told to. "Don't worry, I'll sort it out. He'll calm down soon. I'm sorry I troubled you, Ms Holland. It's just . . . well, putting him out of the house was one thing. Putting him in prison is another."

"All right," said Rosie quickly; "all right. I'll come, and I won't call the police. But you tell him from me: if anybody gets hurt he's going to do hard time. And the way they get you off drugs in prison isn't how they do it in those fancy clinics."

She'd already dialled Matt Gosling's number before she remembered he was out of town – not, in fact, for a dirty weekend but for a conference on the economics of small-scale publishing. Matt became a newspaper proprietor recently enough to think other people in the industry had a clearer idea of what they were doing and might share that knowledge with him. In another year he'd realise they were all doing it by guess and by God.

Her secretary, Alex Fisher, was at the same conference. Matt didn't have a PA, and wouldn't employ one while Alex would fill in. His first career, as a soldier, had taught him a stalker's patience: he knew about taking the high ground and waiting for the quarry to come to him. When Rosie asked Alex about Matt she said, with just a hint of surprise in her beautifully modulated voice, that they were friends and colleagues. When she asked Matt about Alex he said she was the girl he was going to marry.

So she'd called Dan, and he – to her eternal gratitude – had put the questions on hold until he'd collected her. Then, of course, he tried to talk her out of it, but that was all right – she quite liked the idea that someone thought she was being absurdly brave.

Brick walls loomed above her. She'd brought a torch: she shook it to try to beef up the weak orange beam. She found the side gate. Come to the back door, she'd been told, it'll be open. Knowing that it had been attacked by a junkie with a sledgehammer, Rosie could have guessed as much.

In the silence and the dark, she heard the frantic thud of her own heart. The doctor in her kicked in: adrenalin pumping into her blood in response to the imminent threat, readying her for fight or for flight. But she wasn't built for flight. She rounded the corner of the house shoulder first, like a Green Beret entering a Vietnamese village.

The back door was indeed standing open. Rosie frowned: less damage than she'd expected. OK, that was good, that meant Robbie'd got in without having to work himself into a frenzy.

Maybe his mother had exaggerated. Maybe he didn't have his knife at her throat either, merely in his hand; or even in his pocket. Maybe it wasn't even a knife. Was it too much to hope that it was a potato peeler from the kitchen drawer?

The time had come to find out. Pushing the fear down through her with a determination almost as solid as hands, she stepped inside. She drew a deep breath, flicked the paling torch around the kitchen . . .

And then somehow, unaccountably, the whole back of the house was filled with light and sound and people. Bright lights dazzling her, laughter and instructions she didn't understand, people she didn't recognise except that none of them was a middle-aged woman or her eighteen-year-old son.

Out of the chaos two men came into focus, one squatting in front of Rosie with a camera on his shoulder, the other cosying up to her with a microphone and that smirk that television personalities confuse with charm.

"Primrose Holland," he beamed at the camera, "women's page editor at the *Skipley Chronicle* and celebrated Agony Aunt – You've Been Had!"

Then she understood. She watched a lot of television in a desultory sort of way, had the deplorable habit of turning on as soon as she came home and letting it run like background music until she went to bed. She saw a lot of bits of programmes that way, most of them rubbish. Dick Chauncey's *You've Been Had* was typical.

She'd never have admitted to being a viewer, but in fact she'd seen him do this before – to a fireman conned into rescuing his own toddler from a supposedly unsafe building, to a dog breeder delivering her pedigree bitch of indisputably mongrel puppies, to a conductor whose orchestra was playing from a different score.

So she knew what the form was. Victims were supposed to look horrified, then see the funny side, then give the smirking Chauncey either a quick kiss or a slap on the back depending on their sex and/or inclination.

Marjorie Miller and her son Robbie? – figments of the imagination. Chauncey must have written the letters, chuckling over

Rosie's growing involvement, finally paid an actress to phone her in the middle of the night and bring the thing to a climax. He'd borrowed the house, installed his film crew and waited for her to follow the bait to the back door. He may have wondered if she would chicken out, but he wouldn't let that spoil the programme. He may have wondered how she'd react. He'd given her every reason to be afraid. She'd come here expecting to confront a dangerous young man, and if the anti-climax was enough to provoke a stream of obscene invective – Rosie Holland was not known for either self-restraint or delicacy of expression – that could only add to the entertainment.

All these thoughts raced through Rosie's mind in the seconds that followed the dénouement. She saw Chauncey waiting, that smug smile on his face, the microphone in his hand, waiting cheerfully for her to respond to the jape he'd played on her.

She met his gaze. She smiled wryly and shook her head. She chuckled. He chuckled.

Then all that adrenalin washing round her system somehow gathered in her right fist and she fetched him such a clout that he'd have measured his length on the linoleum had he not landed on the sound recordist first.

Two

They held the inquest on Monday morning, in Matt Gosling's office up in the eaves of the *Chronicle* building.

"And there never was a Marjorie Miller?" said Alex incredulously. "The letters were forged?"

Rosie grimaced. "Every word – except the address, which is Chauncey's producer's house. Everything else was a lie. And I never suspected."

"Don't blame yourself for that," said Matt staunchly. He was a big man, when he stretched his legs into the room they became a hazard to navigation. This mattered less than it might have done because one of them didn't hurt if it got kicked. "It never occurred to me we'd have to be wary of people inventing problems. What kind of a sick mind thought that up?"

Sale sniffed. "The same one that thinks up all his stunts. You've seen the programme: humiliation disguised as humour is what it's about. If it's any comfort, Rosie, this wasn't personal. You could consider it a compliment – Chauncey wouldn't have bothered if The Primrose Path wasn't so popular."

"I'd rather have had an appreciative note and a bunch of flowers," Rosie said ruefully.

Matt grinned. He thought the world of Rosie, loved her warmth, her fallibility and her sheer enthusiasm for life. A similar sense of humour, verging on the juvenile, a common sense of adventure, a shared enjoyment in the world and all its wonders made them natural allies. If Rosie had turned out to be the world's worst women's page editor – and there had been moments when that seemed a distinct possibility – Matt would never have regretted hiring her.

But the grin faded, leaving him worried. Rosie Holland was the best thing about the *Skipley Chronicle* – its heart, its soul, its conscience; and the revitalised *Chronicle* was one of the best things about Skipley. Without it the place would have been just another Black Country township in constant danger of being absorbed into the Birmingham conurbation. Its own weekly newspaper made it a community, and The Primrose Path was the main buffer between the *Chronicle* and insolvency. Anything that threatened the Path threatened the paper.

Alex was frankly appalled. She'd known Rosie for years, was the chief administrator's secretary at the West Country hospital where Rosie practised pathology until she took up journalism. Now her PA, Alex knew better than anyone that Rosie could exasperate for England. She'd undoubtedly made enemies in the short time they'd been here, any of whom might have sought redress. A smack in the eye was an occupational hazard. But this was an act of deliberate cruelty, a snare baited to trap only someone who took the job seriously and tried to do it well. To Alex, who put a high value on courage, it seemed inexcusable to use a person's virtues against them. And for what? For television entertainment.

Matt said, "What do we do about it?"

Sale was the only career journalist among them, it gave him a sense of perspective. He'd seen it all before. He knew survival was the best revenge: that if you stood long enough on the bridge, the bodies of all your enemies floated underneath. "If we complain they'll just say we've no sense of humour and Rosie's better at dishing it out than taking it. I think we have to chalk it up to experience. Just be glad that, however scared we both were, she was never in danger."

Alex said diffidently, "We could ask them not to screen it."

Rosie looked up sharply. "We're not asking them any favours. If Chauncey wants to make me look stupid, fine – he's not the first to try, or even to succeed. I can take criticism, I can take mockery, but I'm not going to apologise because I did nothing wrong and in the same circumstances I'd do the same again. Including decking the creepzoid." She glared around, daring them to contradict.

"I'm with Rosie," Sale said calmly. "We've nothing to explain. Someone with an odd sense of humour abused a service we offer and got a black eye for his trouble. I'm going to do a story for the front page. By the time the broadcast goes out it'll be old news and the only thing viewers'll want to see is Dick Chauncey getting his just deserts."

Alex raised a dubious eyebrow. "It's a gamble."

"Life's a gamble," snorted Rosie. "Dan's right, we've nothing to be embarrassed about. Let's go for it. I'll pose for a photo." She gave a sudden, evil leer. "Tell you what – let's ask Chauncey if we can do an action replay."

The gamble paid off. The *Chronicle* switchboard was juggling calls of support from when the paper went on sale on Thursday morning until the offices closed for the weekend. The people of Skipley who'd adopted the fat woman as mentor and champion had no doubt where their sympathies lay. They were like small-town people everywhere: not very imaginative but with a strong sense of fair play. Asked to choose between a woman who did what she believed was necessary though it scared her witless and a man who thought that was funny, they voted with their fingers. The phone at PVF TV, home of Dick Chauncey's *You've Been Had*, was busy too but the messages were less supportive.

Dan Sale had been in this industry a lot of years and had made a lot of contacts. He learned all kinds of things by roundabout ways. He learned that a crisis meeting similar to the one at the *Chronicle* had taken place at the television studios. He learned that, even if the newspaper was prepared to draw a line under the episode, PVF were not.

He called to tell Matt he was on his way upstairs.

Matt wasn't sure what to expect. He enjoyed a good relationship with his editor, each taking care not to trespass on the other's territory. What went into the *Chronicle* was Sale's responsibility: getting it on to the street was Matt's. It wasn't often that the editor felt the need to consult his proprietor.

"I've heard a rumour," said Sale, "that we might not have seen the last of Dick Chauncey, and I don't know whether to warn Rosie or not."

Matt's eyebrows rocketed. "Of course you have to warn her." Then, more cautiously, "Don't you?"

"I don't want to make her twitchy. She can't do the job with one eye over her shoulder."

"Rosie?" said Matt doubtfully. "*Our* Rosie?"

"You think she's immune to criticism? No one is. Some people cope with it better than others, but everyone feels a knock pretty much the same way. I don't want her handling every query she gets from now on with kid gloves. The Path works as well as it does because she fires from the hip. Yes, most of the time she's right, but she's always entertaining. If she loses her nerve The Primrose Path'll be just another advice column."

Dan Sale had changed his tune in the last nine months. When he sent Matt to see Rosie all he wanted was a weekly column on health matters. He was stunned when Matt admitted sheepishly that he'd promised her a full page and a largely free hand as to what to do with it. When Rosie arrived at the *Chronicle* Sale was deeply uneasy; when he saw the first week's Path he was ready to fall on a specially sharpened blue pencil.

But he was wrong, and he was generous enough to admit it even before sales started to climb. Now he was almost as big a fan as Matt, and his support was even more valuable because he knew this business inside out.

Matt knew that the *Chronicle*'s fortunes were tied up with The Primrose Path, that anything which threatened it also threatened the paper's survival and with it his family's investment. Matt's mother was one of six sisters whose response to the culvert bomb that invalided him out of the Army was to finance his new career.

But the old one had taught him not to be scared into making bad decisions. "I think you're wrong, Dan. I think she can cope with the uncertainty as long as she trusts us. I don't think Chauncey can do a fraction as much damage as *we* will if we start keeping secrets from one another."

Sale was persuaded. "All right. If you want to tell her, tell her."

Matt's eyes flared in alarm. "We'll both tell her."

* * *

Arthur Prufrock had spent his professional life among boys aged between seven and thirteen years. It had left him uniquely well qualified to understand the mentality of those working in television.

"Oh yes," he said with conviction, "they'll try again. As it stands, you beat Chauncey at his own game in front of his gang. The only way he can save face is by giving you a bloody nose in return."

"That's what I thought," nodded Rosie. She didn't seem too troubled; not enough to spoil her appetite anyway. She helped herself to another hot buttered crumpet. "I just hope he'll take his best shot and get it over with. I have more to worry about than whether a TV personality in the throes of the male menopause is lurking behind every tree."

Prufrock eyed her over his cup with that mixture of affection and irritation Rosie inspired in all her friends. He was a small, round man with a puff of cotton-wool hair fringing his bald pink pate and a little white moustache. He looked just what he was – a retired housemaster from a minor public school – until you met his eyes, which were sharper and brighter and much more intelligent than anything else about him suggested. He was Rosie's senior by twenty years.

There were those among Prufrock's neighbours who entertained ideas about him and Rosie. She thought the talk was hilarious and refused to deny it. Prufrock was inclined to a certain umbrage. He had never married so this wasn't the first time he'd heard his name romantically linked with that of another. But always previously he'd been able to send the rumour-monger to bed without his supper.

He smiled under his moustache. "Such as what?"

"Such as . . ." She failed to come up with a single pressing concern. "Such as whether I should get my bellybutton pierced. Such as whether I should have Shad plant me a knot garden." Shad Lucas was Prufrock's gardener when they first met; recently he'd accepted responsibility for taming the jungle behind Rosie's house. "*I* don't know. Anything has to be more important than Dick Chauncey's punctured ego and what he might do next. I don't care, Arthur. I'm not wasting another minute thinking about it."

His diamond gaze was mildly disapproving. "That may be a mistake."

Rosie shrugged. "He's a pathetic little man who makes a living embarrassing people. Let him do his worst. He can't hurt me."

"Perhaps he can't. If he takes you on again and you beat him again he's finished; if he bests you he looks like a bad loser. As far as walking into another ambush goes, I imagine you are safe . . ."

He left a little row of dots hanging in the air to indicate there was more. Dutifully, Rosie cocked her head at him. "*But* . . . ?"

"But there are other ways. What if he targets someone close to you instead? Hurts them, makes a fool of them? Not everyone's as resilient as you, Rosie. Most people would be mortified at being held up to public ridicule."

"Most people who are close to me are used to ridicule." But her hollow tone betrayed concern. She'd thought she could handle anything Chauncey could throw at her. It hadn't occurred to her that he might find a softer target more rewarding.

Prufrock smiled fondly. "So we are. Still, it's something to bear in mind. Alex, for instance. She's younger than us, Rosie, and she's nicer – she cares what people think of her. She might be wise to watch her step for a while."

Impotent anger was not a sensation Rosie was familiar with. Mostly she dealt with anything that made her angry. Sometimes she made things better, not infrequently she made them worse, but she never sat by and let them happen around her. This time there was nothing she could do. If she tried to have it out with Chauncey, he'd feign innocence and quietly note that this was something that bothered her.

And maybe Prufrock was wrong. Maybe Chauncey hadn't thought of any such thing. But he would if she marched round to his office and told him to leave her friends alone.

"There's you, too," she said, only half in jest.

Prufrock chuckled. "What can he do to me? I'm sixty-eight years old, for all Chauncey knows there's only the battery in a pacemaker standing between me and the Grim Reaper. If he leaps out from behind a rhododendron and says 'Boo' he could have a corpse on his hands. No, I'm safe enough. Look after Alex. If he wants to get at you, he'll do it through her."

Across Skipley, in the researchers' room at PVF TV, Jackie Pickering returned the phone gently, quietly, to its cradle and hoped no one would speak to her for the next minute or so. If they did she would be unable to disguise the massive, burgeoning satisfaction that she felt, and then they'd know she had it. The big one, the story that would make her name and her fortune. They'd know it was the big one because all her colleagues were looking for a big one of their own, and they wouldn't rest until they found out what she had.

Soon she'd be happy to share it with them. Hell, she wanted to share it with the whole damn country, and for that she'd need her producer's help. She'd get it; she knew she'd get it. Maybe tomorrow, certainly before the weekend, she'd talk to Ms Frank, put her cards on the table, set out her stall and start selling. Once it was safe; once it was real; once there was no danger of it slipping away.

And after she'd talked to Debbie. More than anyone, Debbie would understand what it meant to her. People here would see it as a bold career move, admire her dedication and skill and envy the success it would bring her. But Debbie would recognise it as a personal triumph as well. For that reason, and others, Debbie should hear it – had the right to hear it – first. She'd call her tonight,

So Jackie kept her head down and waited for her heart to stop pounding; and to avoid her colleagues' gaze and the casual questions that would undo her, she pretended to be updating her notes in the light of the conversation she'd just had. In fact she hadn't taken any notes. She didn't need to: she'd remember every word both of them had said until she died. It was that important. The moment she agreed to a meeting, and heard the trap she'd set so carefully, so patiently, snap shut, ranked among the chief moments of her life.

Things don't often work out just how you've planned, just how you need them to. Today they had. Her heart thumped, and her breath wouldn't come, and pretending to update the notes she hadn't kept her shaking fingers scrawled on the telephone pad the same words that hammered in her head.

"Got you, you bastard!"

Three

The phone went in the middle of the night. The first thing Rosie thought of, after regret at being roused from a particularly tasty dream, was Dick Chauncey. If this was another client of The Primrose Path whose life had taken a sudden turn for the worst, he or she was going to get an earful. A week wasn't long enough for Rosie to have forgotten or forgiven.

It was Prufrock. He'd never called her in the night before – he still thought that ten o'clock was a late enough bedtime for anyone, or ten thirty on Saturdays – so she knew something was wrong even before he'd finished apologising.

"Arthur – Arthur, it's all right. What's happened?"

He abandoned the apology, said simply, "It's Shad."

By now Rosie was wide awake. Shad; and not good news. "Where is he? Is he all right?"

"Not really," admitted Prufrock, answering her second question first. "He's in Crewe."

"*Crewe*?" So that was why he was calling. Shad was in Crewe and Prufrock didn't drive. Rosie sighed. "I'll pick you up in fifteen minutes."

"I hate to do this to you," he said. "I know you've a busy day ahead. I'd have made him wait for the first train. But he sounded so odd. He hasn't even any money on him."

Rosie frowned, her brows meeting like amorous caterpillars. "What's he *doing* in Crewe with no money at two in the morning? No, don't answer that. I'll see you in a quarter of an hour, you can give me the full SP then."

It was a fifty-mile drive, though at that time of night they had the outside lane of the M6 to themselves. Rosie drove and Prufrock talked.

"When the phone went, I thought at first it was a nuisance call. He didn't say anything."

He didn't say anything for second after long second. Prufrock was beginning to think it was his own personal pervert, a semi-literate heavy breather who'd misread the phone book and called at intervals in the hope of getting through to Miss Prudence Frock. He snapped waspishly, "Whoever you are, I'm sure it's past your bedtime." Then as the silence stretched, a kind of intuition stirred. "Shad – is that you?"

The sound of his name wrenched a response out of Shad Lucas. "Yes." His naturally low-pitched voice was choked with gravel.

"Where are you? At home?"

"No. A station . . ."

"You're at the *station*?"

"No. I think . . ." There was a pause while he looked around, trying to get his bearings. "I think it's Crewe."

Prufrock stared at the phone in astonishment. It was absurd enough that anyone was standing on Crewe station at two in the morning; it was bizarre that his gardener was; but most peculiar of all was that his gardener wasn't *sure* if he was standing on Crewe station or not. "Have you been drinking?"

Again the pause while the younger man considered. "I don't think so."

"Don't you *know*?"

Shad tried hard to make some sense. "Arthur, I don't know how I got here. Half an hour ago I found myself wandering through some . . . shunting yards or something, and there wasn't a soul in sight, and I didn't know where I was . . ." His voice began to climb with the memory of panic. He forced it down. "Finally I saw some lights, and I found this phone, and there's a sign over there that says 'Crewe', and that's all I know."

Prufrock's mouth opened and closed twice before anything intelligent came out. Finally he said, "All right, Shad; don't upset yourself, we'll sort it out." If he'd had a pound for every time he'd used those same words, injecting calm into chaos and buying himself time to think of an answer, he'd have had a big house up on The Brink instead of a cottage in Foxford Lane. But it always worked. He could sound authoritative, in control of events, when he was as much at sea as everyone else. "Is the Land Rover anywhere about? Did you drive there?"

The sound of pockets being patted. "I don't think so. No keys."

"All right. Have you the money to get home?"

He already knew the answer to that. "I've got two pounds and fifty-seven pence." Which wouldn't get him to Stoke-on-Trent, let alone Skipley.

In earlier times, if one of his charges had called in a similar dilemma Prufrock would have despatched him to the nearest police station and phoned ahead to arrange transport and funds. But Shad wasn't eleven, he was twenty-five and unlikely to receive the same solicitude. Also, he avoided police stations whenever possible. If that was the best Prufrock could suggest he knew Shad would rather hitch, and he didn't sound he was in any state to be doing that.

Prufrock sucked in a deep breath and considered, but there was only one solution. "Stay where you are. I'll call Rosie, we'll come and get you."

"And he's no idea how he got there?" Incredulity sent Rosie's full-bodied contralto soaring operatically.

Prufrock spread small pink hands in a rueful shrug. "Not when I spoke to him. He may have worked it out by now."

"Did he sound drunk?"

"No. He sounded frightened."

Rosie considered. It wasn't just that she owed Prufrock more than a lost night's sleep. She owed Shad, too. He'd had problems enough when they first met but he'd never been shot before. "Arthur, is this about his . . . clairvoyance?"

They never quite knew what to call it, this extra sense of Shad's. 'Clairvoyance' made it sound like an end-of-the-pier attraction. 'ESP' sounded like science fiction but was probably closer to the mark. He had a perception that was additional to the customary quota. He didn't see things, didn't know things, couldn't see the future; but he could feel things that most people can't. Vibrations; memories; the echoes of emotions powerful enough to go on reverberating in the stones of a place long after their causes were gone. Sometimes – not always, it was at best an imperfect perception – he could feel the presence of evil.

Prufrock shook his head, perplexed. He was wearing the deerstalker hat Rosie had bought him in tribute to their last adventure. "I don't know. I don't see how."

"It hasn't happened before, then?"

"Nothing like this. You've seen him do it – he's a bit shell-shocked afterwards – but as far as I know it's never given him amnesia. Is it possible, do you think?"

Rosie shrugged. "Arthur, I couldn't begin to guess what's possible. Shad is the only psychic I've ever met, and there's more in the medical textbooks on the Elephant Man than there is on ESP. I don't know. Since whatever happens must happen within his brain, I suppose it could interfere with other cerebral functions. But it's guesswork. It's not supposed to happen at all, so who knows what the mechanism is?"

"If it is that," said Prufrock slowly, "and if it is the first time it's happened, it could be a worrying development. Perhaps there isn't room in the human brain for everything that's meant to happen there and ESP as well. Perhaps, the more he uses his perception, the more damage he's going to do to himself . . ."

Rosie took her eyes off the road long enough to give him a stern look. "Arthur, stop imagining the worst. I spent twenty years dissecting people's brains: if I don't know what's going on in Shad's, you sure as hell don't. Yes, it could be the start of a neurological problem. It could also be that he got drunk last night, curled up somewhere to sleep it off and . . ."

"Woke up in Crewe?" Prufrock sounded unconvinced.

"Maybe he was sleeping it off on a train," Rosie offered lamely. "Look, I don't know. But it's a long step from one lost night to brain damage, particularly for a twenty-five-year-old male. It happens all the time."

"It never happened to me," said Prufrock stiffly.

Rosie smiled. "No, Arthur, I don't suppose it did."

They might have had trouble meeting. The railway yards at Crewe are enormous. But by the time his lift arrived Shad had found his way out and was waiting at the main station entrance.

Rosie evicted Prufrock from the front seat and Shad fell in wearily beside her. Against the thick dark hair his skin had an abnormal pallor.

"Well, that's one mystery solved," said Rosie, an odd ring to her voice. "We mightn't know what you're doing here, but at least we know why *you* don't know either." She turned on the courtesy light that had gone off when the car door closed. "Not drink, drugs or ESP. You've had a knock on the head." Blood had run from behind his right ear and congealed on his collar. There was more of it on the front of his shirt.

Prufrock switched instantly to mother-hen mode. "Good grief, boy, you look you've been playing Under-Thirteen rugby!" He produced an immaculate handkerchief. "Here, spit."

Shad fended off his well-meant attentions, felt for the damage with cautious fingers. "Ow!"

"Oh yes," opined Rosie, turning his head to the light to afford the injury her professional scrutiny, "somebody's fetched you a right crack there."

It wasn't a considered judgement of the kind she used to put her name to only after extensive and thorough explorations, but it was more than a guess. People who've seen a lot of injuries start to recognise signatures. A broken hyoid bone means manual strangulation; broken knees mean the truck that hit the deceased didn't brake, broken shins that it did. And while people do occasionally walk sideways into head-high protrusions, they don't often sustain concussion and a five-centimetre scalp laceration behind the ear.

From the back Prufrock's voice was shocked. "All right, my lad, hospital for you. We can work out what happened after we get you looked at."

But Shad didn't like hospitals for the same reason he didn't like police stations: they asked too many questions. "I'm all right. I just want to go home."

"It may need stitching!"

"Then Rosie can stitch it. Can't you?" He looked at her with expectancy and just a little desperation.

She smiled. "I expect so." To Prufrock she said, "I think he's all right. Anyway, he may as well be heading home as sitting in A&E waiting for someone to see him. I'll take a proper look when we get back; if I'm not happy with it then I'll take him into Skipley General."

She hoped Shad might nod off for an hour, it would do him more good than trying to work out what had happened. But he showed no signs of sleeping. He bit his thumbnail; then he knuckled his eye; then he rubbed the side of his hand across his forehead. If there'd been room he'd have been pacing up and down. More than ever he looked like a caged bear.

"Why Crewe?" he demanded at last, his voice thin and rough.

"Because it's one of the biggest railway junctions in the country," Rosie answered mildly. "Most everything heading north from Birmingham goes through Crewe."

It didn't help. "So where was I going? Why was I heading north? And why on a train when I've got a perfectly good Land Rover?" This was a slight exaggeration, but he certainly had a Land Rover.

"What do you remember?"

His hands jerked apart. "Nothing! Nothing."

Prufrock interceded. "You edged my lawn on Tuesday morning. Do you remember that?"

"Of course I do!" Then conscience stabbed at him. These people had come fifty miles in the middle of the night to help him out, he had no business snapping at either of them. "Sorry. Yes, I remember. And Mrs Carstairs in the afternoon."

"What about Wednesday?"

His head moved fractionally as he went to turn round then thought better of it. "Isn't today Wednesday?"

"Today's Thursday," Rosie said. "Only just" – it was half-past three now – "but Thursday. Who do you normally see on Wednesdays?"

He normally spent the day at Foxford House up on The Brink. But he didn't remember being there, or doing anything else instead. "I've been out cold for twenty-four hours?"

Rosie shook her head firmly. "I doubt it. Twenty-four hours is a long time to be unconscious. I don't think that injury would have done it, and I don't think you'd be making this much sense if it had. Whatever happened to you was more recent than that, it just took a chunk of memory out with it. It may come back when you're feeling better."

"I've lost my memory?"

"Only a little bit," Rosie said reassuringly. "And perhaps more mislaid than lost."

"Then – *nobody* knows what I was doing in Crewe!"

"Well, somebody does," said Rosie. "Whoever hit you on the head and pushed you off the train."

"And what was I doing on the train in the first place?"

"We'll ask the Thurleys," suggested Prufrock. "If you didn't go to Foxford House yesterday, perhaps you told them why."

"Or maybe you put it in your diary," suggested Rosie. "Check it when we get you home."

Shad had a flat over a shoe shop in Skipley High Street. Access was up fourteen steep steps boxed into a narrow tunnel. It was too narrow for Rosie, who had to go up sideways, and too steep for Prufrock, who had to take a breather halfway. Despite his aching head, Shad managed without much difficulty. All he wanted now was for them to go away and let him go to bed. Perhaps things would make more sense in the morning.

"Look – thanks for coming for me. I'm sorry to drag you out of your beds. I didn't know what else to do."

"You did the right thing," Rosie said, pushing him into a chair under the naked bulb in the kitchen. "Now, look at me. Watch my finger . . ."

A cursory examination was enough to confirm her earlier assessment. She put a couple of stitches in his scalp, her capacious handbag yielding a rudimentary medical kit – including some local anaesthetic that, in the best medical tradition, she didn't leave quite long enough to work. When he yelped she told him not to be so soft.

"You'll live. Paracodol will help with the headache, otherwise it's just a matter of time. Sleep as much as you want to. Arthur, it might be an idea if you stayed here tonight."

Prufrock nodded. "But shouldn't we tell someone?"

"The police? Tell them what? Somebody – we don't know who – hit Shad on the head – we don't know why – on a train going somewhere – and we don't know where. We don't know why he was on the train, and we don't know where or when the attack occurred. It might have been in Crewe, or it might have been miles back and he just stumbled off the train when it stopped. Whoever hit him is long gone. We may just be glad that all it cost him is his wallet, and I don't suppose there was much money in it."

Shad didn't resent her candour. It was obvious to him that a woman who'd worked first as a doctor and now as a newspaper columnist must have more money than a jobbing gardener. Shad made enough for his needs – a modest home, a largely reliable vehicle, serviceable clothes and the occasional visit to his mother – and he made it in a way that was easy for him. He didn't like crowds. Their emotions swamped him.

But it was true that he didn't have much left over at the end of the month. Little enough that he always knew the precise contents of his wallet. He said gruffly, "Twenty pounds and change."

"The change was in your pocket," Rosie said brightly, "you didn't lose that."

"No," agreed Shad. "I spent it phoning Arthur."

"Ah. So, in fact, you're skint." With the same lack of either tact or reticence with which she'd drawn attention to his financial state, now she reached for her handbag again.

"Except for this," said Prufrock. It was the tone of his voice that made them both turn round.

"What is it?" asked Rosie.

"It's a wallet," said Prufrock. "Containing twenty pounds."

Beyond identifying it as his, Shad was too tired to think what it meant. Rosie sent him to bed, promising to get to the bottom of it when they'd all had some rest; but once he'd gone she found that all inclination to go home and sleep herself had vanished.

"Could he have two wallets?"

"Each with twenty pounds in them?" Prufrock arched a white eyebrow in disbelief.

"Then how did it get back here?"

Prufrock shook his head. "I don't think it ever left."

"So now we've got him on a train going God knows where without enough money for a limp lettuce sandwich? Arthur, it makes no sense! Wherever he was going he'd need his wallet. He couldn't have bought a ticket without it."

But plainly Shad Lucas had left his wallet at home the last time he went out.

"Maybe he didn't have a ticket. Maybe he didn't mean to go anywhere – just as far as the paper shop or something."

"He was kidnapped?" Rosie smothered her squawk of disbelief before it woke the subject of their debate. "He was shanghaied, smuggled unconscious aboard a train, and then at Crewe the white slavers changed their minds and slung him out on to the tracks? Arthur, we're looking for a *rational* explanation!"

Nettled by her tone, he scowled. "It makes more sense that whoever mugged him came back here to return his wallet with the contents intact?"

None of it made sense. But Shad had got to Crewe somehow, apparently without the assistance of his wallet.

"And where's the Land Rover?" It wasn't the sort of vehicle you could pass without noticing. Nominally green, one door was painted cream and the other orange. Usually it had a scythe or a lawn mower in the back. Rosie had parked in the High Street: she couldn't have missed it if it had been there. "Are there garages round the back?"

Prufrock shook his head. "The alley isn't wide enough for cars."

Rosie stood up. "I'll have a drive round, see if I can spot it. You stay here and keep an eye on him."

This time both Prufrock's eyebrows soared. "Spot it? It could be anywhere between here and Crewe!"

"I suppose it could. But it's likely to be near the station."

She was back in fifteen minutes. The skewbald Land Rover had been parked – abandoned rather – slewed across the gritty end of Railwayview Street. The driver's door was open and the keys still in the ignition; which was a tribute either to standards of honesty in Skipley, or to the fact that the local car thieves weren't that desperate. Rosie parked the thing properly and locked it, then returned to the flat.

Prufrock had found Shad's work diary. It was lying on the table, closed, and Prufrock was scratching his moustache pensively. "Perhaps we should wait till he's awake. There could be something private in there."

Rosie just clucked and opened it.

There was nothing private. There was nothing helpful. Against Wednesday was the single word: 'Thurleys'.

"So he'd nothing else planned," said Prufrock. "Which suggests that whatever happened to him happened after work."

"That figures," nodded Rosie. "If the Land Rover had lain open behind the station for twenty-four hours somebody would have stolen it, moved it or reported it to the police. So he went out in the evening sometime – to meet someone, to buy a carton of milk, something he didn't need much money for anyway. He was driving behind the station when something surprised him. He got out in a hurry, not even taking the keys, and then . . ." She blew out her cheeks, waiting for inspiration.

"To end up in Crewe he must have got on a train going there," said Prufrock reasonably. "From choice or under compulsion, he boarded a north-bound train. It must have been from choice: why would anyone kidnap him? And why would anyone want to kidnap him in Skipley but change their minds before Crewe?"

"Perhaps he saw something," hazarded Rosie. "Something he shouldn't have. Surprised someone . . . who panicked and hit him."

"And bought him a Rail Rover ticket as a way of saying sorry?"

Prufrock sounded deeply sceptical. "And what can he have seen in Railwayview Street after dark? The lighting up there isn't exactly Blackpool Illuminations."

"When I said he saw something," said Rosie carefully, "I didn't necessarily mean he *saw* something. Maybe he . . ." She hit the language barrier again. "One way or another he knew something was amiss. And he was right. When he went to find out what, someone sandbagged him."

"So how did he get to Crewe?"

"Maybe . . . Maybe the trouble was on board a train. He went to investigate, someone decked him, and while he was unconscious the train pulled out. When he woke up he got off and found himself in Crewe."

It raised as many questions as it answered, but as far as it went it explained the facts they had. If it wasn't the whole truth it was perhaps part of it.

"So what was it?" she wondered softly. "That he saw, that he heard, that he . . . perceived. That made him drive up a dead end round the back of the station, and then pile on the brakes, jump out of the jeep and run straight into trouble. What did he . . . ?"

"Feel," said Shad Lucas with heavy precision, as if it mattered. Rosie and Prufrock looked round in surprise. Neither of them had heard him stir; they thought he was asleep. But the bedroom door was open and he was standing there, holding the jamb for support; barefoot, in moth-eaten jeans and a black singlet, his gypsy-dark face drained of blood and his eyes stretched. His voice was hollow. "It was something I felt."

He looked he'd fall down at any moment. Rosie jumped from her chair, ready to catch him. He looked dreadful: worse than when they collected him, worse than when they got back here.

He looked, she thought, as if he'd remembered something that would have been best forgotten.

She said, quietly but in a tone which demanded a reply, "What did you feel?"

The answer was a long time coming. He looked at her with

his haunted eyes and his lips trembled. His breath was ragged. He shook his head, but the newly salvaged memory remained. His voice cracked when he finally got it out.

"I think," he said, "I felt somebody die."

Four

Detective Superintendent Harry Marsh might have shown them the door but for one thing. Not the big woman's reputation – he had no problems dealing with the Press, by and large he got as much from them as he gave, he never felt intimidated by them. Not the old man's evident anxiety, though it suggested that what sounded like a hoax might not actually be one. And not the story itself, which was vague enough to be unprovable whether there was some truth in it or not.

No, what kept Harry Marsh listening long after he might have made an excuse to get rid of them was that Shad Lucas had a track record as a psychic. The police couldn't conveniently ignore that just because this time he wasn't working for them.

Marsh himself had never called on the young man's peculiar abilities, though he knew police officers who had and who had not regretted doing. Shad Lucas had found bodies buried on uncharted moor that modern technology and old-fashioned dogs had failed to discover. Asked to explain, he said it was a bit like dowsing; asked how he did *that* he was unable to cast any more light.

The first meeting between Skipley's senior detective and the sorcerer's apprentice occurred quite recently, and only one of them remembered it. Shad was in the intensive-care unit at Skipley General Hospital with a gunshot wound to his face. It was his curious talent that got him into that situation too.

So Superintendent Marsh was not fundamentally antagonistic to the idea, as many policemen would have been; as *he* might have been a year ago. He was prepared to keep an open mind, even if it meant wedging something in the credibility gap. But that didn't mean accepting as gospel a story that made no sense just because an apparent psychic was telling it. He supposed even a genuine psychic could be wrong or have reason to lie.

So he made Shad run through his fragmentary account of the night's events again, this time not so much listening as watching him. The blend of reluctance and distress in his eyes. The jerky movements of his hands. The way he answered questions designed to throw him: impatiently, clearly expecting to be disbelieved, but able to pick up any strand of his discrete narrative without having to start at the beginning each time. People who are lying have a problem with that. They don't trust their own memories; they need to keep it neat, organised and logical.

"You don't remember what you were doing behind the station?"

"No."

"It's not on your way anywhere?"

"It's a dead end!" Of course, Marsh knew that.

"So you went there deliberately. Why?"

"I don't remember."

"Guess."

Shad hated talking about his faculty. For years he'd avoided using it at all, even to dowse for water. He found being quizzed on it obscurely humiliating. But he recognised the need and tried to cooperate. "I suppose . . . I felt something wrong."

"Felt?"

Shad gritted his teeth. "Was aware of. Not seeing, not hearing, not smelling, but still . . . aware of. I'm sorry if that doesn't make sense to you. It doesn't make much to me."

Marsh didn't think he was lying, but that didn't make him a reliable witness. He could be imagining any or all of it. No, not quite all. Something had happened to alarm him, and someone had hit him over the head, and somehow he'd ended up in Crewe. It wasn't enough to launch a murder inquiry.

"This person who died. Can you tell me anything about them?"

Shad thought, then shook his head.

"Male or female?"

His eyes opened wide. The wound below the left one had

shrunk to a dark pit in his cheek. "It was a woman!" There was a note of revelation in his voice.

"All right. Young or old?"

He ran blunt fingers distractedly through his thick curls. "I think she was young. She was scared. God, she was scared!"

"What of? Who of?"

"I don't know."

"A man? Men?"

"I don't know!"

"Somebody hit you. Who?"

Shad shook his head.

"All right, when? Before the girl died or after?" But he didn't know that either.

"After," suggested Rosie. "That was what made him stop the Land Rover. He was hit when he went to investigate."

Superintendent Marsh hung on to his patience just barely. "We might make better progress, Ms Holland, if I do the detecting and you stick to advising the lovesick and careworn."

Rosie was harder to offend than that. "You mean I'm wrong?"

Marsh scowled, then laughed. He was a big, square man of about fifty with greying hair and intelligent eyes and a slightly rumpled appearance. Perhaps because he'd been hauled from his bed before six in the morning. "No, of course you're not wrong. You're probably right. But I need solid facts. All speculation and no evidence makes Harry a bad policeman."

Rosie grinned. "Fair enough. Well, if Shad's right and somebody died there's a body somewhere. That solid enough for you? Though I am merely a newspaper columnist and so would not presume to advise a Detective Superintendent, it seems to me that a search of the station area might yield dividends."

Marsh had tried before to dislike Rosie Holland. It hadn't worked and he'd more or less given up. The woman was a nuisance but she was also astute: it made more sense to use her instincts than to squander mental energy trying to keep her at bay. A task comparable, in any event, to keeping out sunshine with chicken wire.

He nodded. "It's worth a try." He picked up the phone and

ordered patrols into the area around the railway yards. "I'll let you know if we find anything. In return, Mr Lucas, you might tell me if you remember anything more."

Shad nodded, cautiously, without moving his head too much. He looked ill. It had been necessary to come here, to report what he'd experienced although he had no expectation of being believed; but now it was done the scant reserves he'd mustered for the task were dissipating like mist after sunrise. He needed to rest. If he didn't lie down soon he'd fall down.

Rosie stood up. "I'll take him home. Call me if anything turns up."

Marsh saw them out. Then he returned to his office and, picking up the phone again, asked for two pieces of information: the routes of all trains that had stopped the previous evening in both Skipley and Crewe, and numbers for CID in the towns which were those trains' ultimate destinations.

If he hadn't done that, the body of Jackie Pickering might not have been discovered for days.

With so much heavy goods going by road these days, the trucks that once linked together in great ponderous snakes along the railway network of Britain now enjoy a leisurely semi-retirement. Cattle wagons and goods wagons, flats and tankers – many rotted away in forgotten sidings all over the country, but others are kept in repair and shuffled round the system whenever the need arises. The short chain of wagons sitting in the sidings at Skipley Station on Wednesday evening were waiting for a train to take them to Holyhead.

That train had arrived, Superintendent Marsh discovered, at eleven-forty and left Skipley, charges in tow, twenty minutes later. It paused in Crewe at one in the morning before continuing its journey west.

If Shad Lucas was on it when it left Skipley, it seemed likely that Jackie Pickering was too. Her dying blood stained the timber floor of the last wagon. Her body was curled in a corner and might have escaped the casual scrutiny of whoever noticed the sliding door standing open by half a metre and went to shut it.

She'd been stabbed. A neat job, said Detective Inspector Lewis in Holyhead: a single wound straight to the heart. She'd have been unconscious in a few seconds, dead soon after.

"A big knife or a little one?" asked Marsh.

Lewis consulted his notebook. "Twenty-two centimetres long, three centimetres at the widest point, with a slight backwards curve, a bone handle and the words 'Made in Sheffield' stamped at the top of the blade."

Marsh stared at the phone. "Your pathologists are a damn sight better than ours."

"The knife was found beside the body," said DI Lewis impassively.

The knife was found in the wagon, beside the dead body of Jackie Pickering, aged twenty-three, a television researcher, originally from Nottingham and recently of Skipley. The door of the wagon was open just wide enough for a man to have climbed out. Shad Lucas left his Land Rover in Skipley sometime on Wednesday evening and re-materialised in Crewe at two o'clock on Thursday morning, an hour after the Holyhead train passed through. It took no exercise of the imagination to suppose that Lucas and the dead girl had travelled in the same wagon.

So, ruminated Marsh, Lucas was drawn to the goods yards – by his own perception or, more mundanely, a scream – and left his vehicle to investigate. He stumbled on the murder and the killer floored him. He left Lucas's body along with the girl's in the wagon where she died and made his escape. He may have known there was an engine due to haul them off to parts unknown, he may not. It was a bonus, not a necessity.

On the grounds that the murder was committed in Skipley, Superintendent Marsh despatched his own Scenes of Crime Officer to Holyhead to supervise the wagon's return. He didn't expect DI Lewis to like him for this, but it made more sense to investigate the crime where it happened. He asked for the knife as well, and for the body of Jackie Pickering to be transferred to Skipley General Hospital.

* * *

The *Skipley Chronicle* came out on Thursdays. It was a busy day for the printers, an oddly quiet one for the editorial staff. It was too late to do anything for this week's paper, too soon to start on the next. The reporters fell into desultory arguments about whether truth is beauty, whether life imitates art, and whether *Coronation Street* was more in need of new characters or new scriptwriters. Only Alex even noticed that Rosie didn't get in until ten.

Alex got in at five to nine on the dot, Monday to Friday. On mornings like this, when she herself arrived either late or hungover, Rosie would glower and call her a teacher's pet. But Alex didn't need to curry favour with anyone: she could have walked out of this office and into any other in Birmingham, and in some of them she could have named her salary. She was a highly skilled, highly efficient, thoroughly experienced secretary whom any chief executive would have killed for. No, she did her job as well as she knew how because that was how she did everything. She took a pride in it.

She favoured Rosie with a look of cool disapproval. "Good night, was it?"

Rosie squinted at her. "No. The first couple of hours weren't bad, but it was downhill from then on." She explained.

Alex's beautiful brown eyes widened as she listened. Instinctively her concern was not for the woman, whom she was unlikely to know, but for the young man whom she did. When Rosie finished she said, "How's Shad now?"

"He'll probably sleep the rest of today. He'll still be sore tomorrow, after that I think he'll be all right. I took them back to Prufrock's when we'd finished with the police. It's better if he's not on his own for twenty-four hours and Arthur'll be more comfortable at home. But I'm not expecting problems. He had a nasty knock but I think he's got away with it."

That wasn't what Alex wanted to hear. "I meant, how *is* he? How does he feel about this?"

"I knew what you meant," admitted Rosie. She shrugged. "The other question was one I could answer. I don't know how he feels. He looks like shit. He felt somebody die – stabbed, murdered. Think how you'd feel if you'd seen it, then multiply that by the difference between seeing something unpleasant and living it. The wonder is that he's not in a padded cell. He's dealing with it, but it costs him the emotional equivalent of blood."

"Have the police found a body?"

"If they haven't yet, they will."

"They'll need to ask him more questions then."

"He may not have any more answers. Even without being hit on the head, there are limits to what he picks up. It must seem pretty arbitrary to an outsider, what he knows and what he doesn't, but there's no point grilling him. He isn't holding back. You can't bully more information out of him – I know, I've tried. It isn't there. Like a badly tuned radio: if you're losing some of the words to crackle, turning the volume up just gives you louder crackles."

"I hope you'll be able to explain that to Detective Superintendent Marsh," said Alex softly.

Rosie nodded. "That'll be the problem, all right. He's a decent enough man, he was listening to what we were saying. I don't think he knew how much credence to give to Shad's account, but that's understandable. A body in the morgue will help with that. But then he'll be under pressure: people will be pushing him for answers and the only place he can get them is Shad. He may need his friends then. If I have to be away from the office will you cover for me?"

"Of course," said Alex without hesitation. "I can keep things ticking over. But maybe you'd better tell Dan? I mean, if all he's able to field for a while is the B team?"

Not for the first time, or even for the first time this week, Rosie reflected on the greatest of the many strokes of luck she'd enjoyed in her life: the friendship of Alex Fisher. Alex organised her, supported her, defused the troubles she got herself into, kept her feet on the ground and, if the need arose, would take over at a moment's notice and leave her free to pursue whatever unicorn had thundered out of the undergrowth. And she did all this without envy or ambition. She didn't want Rosie's job: she lacked the thick skin and bulldog tenacity that let Rosie plough through any amount of hostility if she believed that what she was doing was right. In plain English, Alex was too nice to do what

Rosie did as well as Rosie did it. But Rosie couldn't have done it as well without her.

"Alex, you're nobody's idea of the B team. Ask Dan: he'd much sooner have me off on holiday than you. Without me the place runs smoothly, the only difference is there are fewer complaints. Without you, there are more complaints and the office looks like a bomb site."

Alex smiled. "Don't worry, I can manage. Look after Shad. That's where you're needed most."

Oblivious of the care which went into Alex's toilette every morning, Rosie gave her a hug.

Five

Rosie half-expected a call from Prufrock to say the police were harrying Shad and would she come and lend moral support. But she was a little surprised to hear next from Superintendent Marsh.

He offered to come to the *Chronicle*. But she glanced round ruefully and saw he'd only be able to sit down if he'd hold a stack of cuttings on his knee. She said she'd meet him at the police station.

He had coffee waiting, and some news. "We have the body." His tone was both sombre and matter-of-fact. "Found it in a goods wagon in a siding at Holyhead. Lucas was right: it was a woman. She'd been stabbed through the heart."

Rosie breathed lightly. Knowing what he would find didn't rob the disclosure of its shock value. "I'm sorry," she said. "I can't say I'm surprised, but even when you know what he can do you kind of hope this time he's going to be wrong. Have you told Shad yet?"

Marsh shook his head. "I thought I'd let him catch up on his sleep first. In the meantime, I hoped you could cast light on something rather strange."

Rosie stared. "Me? How can I help? The first I knew of these events was a couple of hours later."

"I appreciate that. All the same, there's a connection between you and the dead woman. It may be only coincidence. I'd like your view on that."

Rosie had gone cold. Someone she knew, someone she'd met; someone she'd advised? Dear God, was that it? She'd given the girl bad advice and she'd died of it? There was a crack in her voice. "Who was she?"

But Jackie Pickering meant nothing to Rosie, however deeply she trawled her memory. "I don't know the name. Have you a photograph?"

"Not yet. And it mightn't help if I had." Marsh considered for a moment, decided to put his cards on the table. "You may never have met. But she knew about you. She worked as a researcher on that programme of Dick Chauncey's. The one where you socked him on camera." He hid a smile. Their business here was no laughing matter, even if there were aspects to it which had given a lot of people a lot of pleasure.

"*You've Been Had*," whispered Rosie, stunned past belief. Whatever she'd been expecting, it wasn't that.

And, like a terrible echo, she remembered having coffee – no, tea – with someone else, and what they'd talked about then. With Prufrock. They'd agreed that an aggrieved Chauncey might try again to humiliate her. They'd agreed that she wasn't particularly vulnerable, but Prufrock had been concerned that next time he'd try to hurt her by hurting someone she cared about.

They'd been worried about Alex. It hadn't occurred to them that, with his history, his unusual facility unsupported by much intellectual understanding, the easiest target of all was Shad.

When she got her voice back Rosie said, "Don't take this the wrong way, Superintendent Marsh. I don't know what happened behind the station last night. And I firmly believe that if Shad remembered he'd have told us.

"But it occurs to me that a researcher for *You've Been Had* might have wanted to meet Shad Lucas. He's an interesting man, well worth making a television programme about. He wouldn't have agreed to that, but she might have strung him along on some other pretext. Maybe that's what he was doing behind the station – he was on his way to meet her. I think you need to see her employers. If they sent her to sweet-talk Shad into doing one of their wretched programmes, they bear a considerable responsibility for what happened to her."

She heard what she was saying too late. Marsh had heard it too: one eyebrow climbed towards his hairline. He looked as if he'd started to interview a casual bystander and been rewarded with a full and frank confession. "And where do you suppose the rest of the responsibility lies, Ms Holland?"

Alex Fisher was an intelligent woman in almost every way, but even after nine months at the *Chronicle* it hadn't struck her that within ten minutes of Rosie going out Matt Gosling always needed a quick word with her.

"Missed her again?" he clucked with entirely phony disappointment, dropping his haunch on to the desk. "I'll wait till she gets back."

"It could be a while," said Alex apologetically. "Detective Superintendent Marsh wanted to see her. Whatever he has to say, I doubt she'll be back before lunch."

That was pretty much the answer he'd been hoping for. He sighed long-sufferingly. "OK. Well, I'll just get my breath back before I tackle the stairs again."

The same blind spot seemed to have hidden from Alex the fact that her proprietor had installed a lift to his office in the attic and always used it except when he came to visit Rosie. Then he needed to muster his strength before tackling the stairs. "Have you time for coffee?"

The glance at his watch was purely for effect. When he didn't have time he made it. "That was a weird business last night." He'd had the gist from Dan Sale who'd had it from Rosie.

Alex nodded, fetched the coffee from the machine in the corridor. They made themselves comfortable in Alex's office. She had her own now that the cramped room in which The Primrose Path was produced had become a suite. The physical impossibility of squeezing in a second filing cabinet – needed because Rosie had filled the first with alcohol and cigarettes – had led Matt to empty the store next door and knock through the wall. Now that Alex had the outer office to herself it seemed much roomier – partly because Alex was built on a different scale to Rosie, but mainly because she put things away when she'd finished with them.

Matt gave the new door an appreciative grin. "If she gets stroppy, we could wall her up in there."

"Of course you could. Along with half your circulation," said Alex loyally.

"You could write The Path."

Alex smiled. "I don't think the Sunday papers would be franchising any advice I could offer."

That might be true, but Matt was biased. For different reasons and in different ways he adored both women, but if he'd only had time to rescue one of them from a burning building his paper's famous Agony Aunt and the profitability she represented would have gone up in smoke. "Don't underestimate yourself. OK, it's Rosie's personality that makes The Path what it is. But without you she'd never make a deadline; and if she did she'd bring the Press Complaints Commission down on our heads."

Alex was realist enough to know that her contribution could be made by any competent PA. That didn't mean she couldn't enjoy the professional respect of a man she admired in return. "It's nice to be appreciated. But I couldn't do Rosie's job if I wanted to."

"But you *do* do it," objected Matt. "I know you do. I can tell which of the replies Rosie wrote and which you did. Hers might be more entertaining but yours are often more help."

"But it's not the helpful ones people buy the *Chronicle* for."

In the part of him that dealt with the accountants Matt knew she was right. But his heart was reluctant to acknowledge the fact. He picked a letter off her desk at random. She'd been dealing with the post when Rosie went out so these were appeals which the counsellor had yet to see.

"I bet," he said, "that whatever the subject of this, your advice would be as sound as Rosie's and a damn sight more sympathetic. If she ends up in Skipley General next time she takes a swing at someone, you'll keep The Primrose Path in print for as long as necessary. Caring may not be as amusing as clever but it lasts longer."

Alex knew that he didn't mean half of it. She knew that Rosie Holland had her proprietor's absolute confidence, that he'd be deeply disappointed if she were to alter her style in the interests of compassion. She appreciated his support but she'd never replace Rosie Holland. Rosie was a one-off.

She glanced at the letter he'd passed her. "You're right; at least about this. It's for the TLC pile." Alex smiled at Matt's expression. Tender loving care wasn't the first thing anyone associated with Rosie. "There are three. I think she got the idea from triage in A&E. Some just need answers to their questions: what are their legal rights, what's the best treatment for a sprain, how do you find a nursing home? Some are personal problems: they don't need answers so much as guidance. Get them to understand what's gone wrong and they can find their own solutions.

"Then there's the TLC pile. We can't help them with either answers or advice. Life's dealt them a bad hand. Sometimes we can suggest some practical help, but they've usually done the rounds already. They've talked to Welfare and the charities, and they still have an intolerable situation to deal with. All we can do is acknowledge that. Reassure them that they're doing as well as anyone could. It's more comfort than you might think. These are lonely people, trapped in a situation from which there is no honourable escape, and sometimes they convince themselves it's their fault. That anyone else would cope better; that they just need to pull themselves together. If we can say to them, Look, just getting through every day in these circumstances is a triumph of the human spirit, they immediately feel more positive.

"They're so relieved some of them burst into tears. They knew it *felt* hard, they'd never been sure it actually *was* that hard. Just telling them, Yes, it really is, and nobody could deal with it any better, lifts a weight off their shoulders. They still have the problem but we've bolstered their self-respect and that's worth something. TLC. It doesn't make the mountain any lower but it makes the climb less soul-destroying."

She hadn't realised how quiet Matt had gone. She looked up from her coffee and found his blue eyes dwelling on her in a kind of wonder, his frank open face mesmerised. For a silly surreal moment she wondered if she'd said something outrageous and hadn't noticed. Her lips formed a question mark. "Matt?"

For a split second he was ready to do it: to heap all his hopes together and throw the dice. She could only say no, and she might not do that. She might not understand. She might ask him to repeat it, her lovely eyes puzzled on his reddening face. That would be deeply embarrassing but at least there'd be no going back; it would be out in the open and they'd have to deal with it. He wouldn't bc working in a vacuum any more, wooing her so subtly she was plainly unaware of it.

On the other hand, she might say yes. Or she might ask solicitously if he'd really thought about this – when he'd thought about nothing else for months! – and then, taken by surprise as she was, consent to giving it some thought herself.

Or she might – and this was what stopped him – give that exquisite blink of reproof that said he'd transgressed and would cause real offence if he continued in the same vein. The look by which a cat marks its disapproval of the sardine in its dish when the family's eating salmon. If she did that, if by word or deed or mere devastating look showed that she had no interest in him, what would be left? He knew he was only going to get one shot at this, which is why he'd been so patient about setting it up.

He wasn't a patient man by nature: all his instincts were to go after what he wanted. As a youth he'd fallen into and out of love affairs with what used to be described as gay abandon until the words acquired a subtext. This was different because of how much it mattered to him. Men always say they'll change for the right woman, and most women have more sense than to believe them. But Matt had actually done it. He'd changed the habit of a lifetime by sublimating short-term desires to long-term aspirations, and he thought, he really thought, he was winning. He thought the moment would come when he could ask Alex Fisher to marry him and she wouldn't respond with that offended cat-like blink and murmur, 'Of course I'm flattered but . . .'

But was it here yet? Was she even aware of his intentions? They'd spent a lot of time together but never on anything resembling a date. Business things, friends things, foursomes with Rosie and Dan Sale, but nothing that said unequivocally, This is getting serious. He suspected it was a transition he had to steer them through before dropping the bombshell of lifetime commitment on her. They had to talk about the future: specifically, whether Alex saw a role for Matt in hers.

He blurted out, "What are you doing tonight?"

She blinked – not offended, just a little surprised. "Nothing, I don't think. Is there something you need me for?"

Matt took his courage in both hands. "Alex, I don't want anything from you. I just want to see you, to be with you. I enjoy your company. I've run out of excuses. There are no more conferences we could go to, and if I rearrange my furniture once more I'll never get the marks out of the carpet. I don't care about the furniture. I don't care that much about the Small Newspaper in the Digital Age. I care about you – about us. I want to talk about us."

He ran out of things to say, dared to look at her. She didn't look horrified, she looked taken aback. "God damn it," he swore disgustedly, "you're not going to say This is so sudden?"

For a moment he couldn't at all read her expression. Had he blown it? He didn't know what else he could have done, how he could have put it better, but suddenly just having coffee with her, going to conferences with her, even shoving his goddamned furniture about, all that a minute ago hadn't seemed nearly enough, was too much to have risked. He didn't want to lose her. If he could only have part of her, it was better than nothing.

Alex bit her lip. "Matt, I've been here for nine months. It took about nine days for the office gossip to get started. I ignored it; I thought you were doing too. I thought that was best."

His heart plummeted. He had, he'd blown it. "You mean, you're not interested."

It would have been easier on him if she'd been a bit more brutal, sent him packing while some scraps of dignity remained to him. Instead she held him in the gentle adamant of her gaze. "Matt, I enjoy working for you. I enjoy your company too. I hope we can go on being friends. But I don't mix business and pleasure. It matters too much when it goes wrong."

He could have left then, but it turned out that he cared too much to take no for an answer. "Who says it'll go wrong?"

Alex smiled. "The law of averages. How many girls have you

dated and not married? At some point, one of you decided it wasn't going to work. There's nothing wrong with that – it's infinitely better than staying with the wrong person – but if you have to work together the next day, and all the days after that, and after one of you has found someone else and the other hasn't, it's going to be a problem. The best way to avoid it is to keep work and private life separate. I'm sorry."

Matt believed that she was sorry. He believed that she valued their friendship. What he didn't believe was that she'd thought this through. Not properly. He couldn't believe she'd throw away what they could have together for a principle.

"Can we at least talk about it?" He heard the whine in his voice and flushed. "I don't mean to embarrass you. But I didn't say this on the spur of the moment. It's been on my mind for most of those nine months. My God, you can have a baby in that time – are you telling me it isn't time enough to hatch a date?"

Alex rewarded him with a laugh. At least his persistence wasn't annoying her. "Matt, please don't take this personally. Ask Rosie – she'll tell you I've always had funny ideas about dating. She counts the number of heads and if it's less than two she'll go out with it. But I'm wary of casual liaisons – it's too easy for people to get hurt. That goes double for casual liaisons with people from work, and by a factor of ten for dating the boss. It's a bad idea, Matt. Take my word for it."

Matt didn't realise she'd finished, was expecting her to say something more. Was still expecting, in spite of all the evidence, that she'd change her mind. But as the silence stretched he began to realise that it wasn't going to happen. The brows knitted over his frank blue eyes like a schoolboy's stymied by calculus. "I don't want you to do anything you're uncomfortable with," he managed at last. "I don't want you to be anyone but who you are. *That's* the person I . . ."

He was too afraid, it wouldn't come. Damn it, spit it out! "Alex, we've known each other for nine months. That's long enough for me. I know what I feel for you: I love you. I understand how you feel about casual relationships, but that isn't a problem because there's nothing casual about this. I can't get round the fact that we work together, but I don't see what happens when we split up as a problem because I don't believe we will. I'll try and prove it if you'll give us a chance."

He watched for signs that she was growing angry with him and saw none. Worse, she went on regarding him with the kindly tolerance due to someone she was fond of but would never love. He exhaled slowly, felt his lungs emptying. "I've made a fool of myself, haven't I?"

Alex shook her head. "Not that. Never that. I mean it, I really am sorry – especially if I've let you think this was an option. But honestly, Matt, it isn't. For both our sakes, you must accept that."

When he was gone she lowered herself carefully into her chair, as if bruised. She thought, Am I being stupid? Should I have done it differently? – seen him a couple of times, then told him it wasn't working? Have I hurt him so much he'll never forgive me?

She drew a shaky breath, aware that she had to get on with the day. She glanced at her watch, was astonished to find it was still only mid morning. There were hours to dispose of yet. She supposed she might as well do some work.

She picked up the letter Matt had taken from the post. It began: 'First, believe me when I say that my lover's happiness is all that matters to me . . .'

Six

Rosie didn't know what to say so she kept it brief. "They've found a body. Superintendent Marsh wants to see Shad again."

Prufrock nodded. "I'll wake him."

There was nothing in his manner or in his astute, pale blue eyes that said he was aware of a subtext. She thought that sooner or later she'd have to confess to her latest attack of foot-in-mouth disease but decided she would only make things worse by doing it now. Besides which, Detective Superintendent Marsh had allowed her to fetch Shad instead of sending a police car for him on the express condition that she didn't discuss his evidence with him.

Marsh didn't think Shad Lucas was a killer. Leaving aside the bump on his head – which just might have been accidental: fleeing the scene he ran into a projection invisible in the dark – his behaviour wasn't that of a man with something to hide. It was he who alerted the police to the possibility of an incident; if he hadn't, possibly no connection would ever have been made between Skipley and a dead girl in a goods wagon in Holyhead. Superintendent Marsh would never have been involved, the scene of the crime would never have been identified and a proper investigation would have been all but impossible. If Lucas *had* killed Jackie Pickering, all he had to do to get away with it was keep his mouth shut.

Instead of which he dragged his friends to Crewe, then told them and then Marsh himself about the possibility of a murder. No killer in his right mind behaved that way.

That was the rub. Arguably, Lucas was not in his right mind;

at least, his worked so differently from other people's that it was hard to judge his actions by the usual yardsticks.

There was also the chance that he had genuinely, because of his head injury, forgotten something that put a whole new slant on events. That if he'd known everything from the start, the last place he'd have gone was a police station. It was that possibility Marsh felt he had to explore.

Marsh met them in the front office, politely but firmly showed Rosie and Prufrock where they could wait while he interviewed Shad. As he expected, Rosie put up a fight.

"As his doctor I ought to be present to monitor his physical condition. As you know, Shad's suffered a head injury. He wanted to come here and sort this out, but you'll have to remember he's not well. I'll just sit in the corner and—"

"Ms Holland," exclaimed Marsh impatiently, "you're not his doctor – you're a newspaper columnist!"

"I *was* a doctor," said Rosie with a pained expression.

"And I used to service my own car, but nobody calls me when there's a vacancy at Silverstone. You're not his solicitor, and he's too old to need an appropriate adult present, so your services will not be required until he's looking for a lift home. And if you don't want to wait, I'll see to that too."

Her bluff called, Rosie subsided grumpily on to a plastic chair. "I'll wait." She glared after him as Marsh ushered Shad down the corridor. "But *as a doctor* I can testify that that lump on his head's the only mark on him right now!"

Prufrock shut his eyes and wished to be almost anywhere but here.

A few hours' sleep had done Shad good. At six o'clock this morning he'd looked haggard, gaunt and frail, the gypsy-dark eyes sunken and underlined by smudges as black as bruising in the pallor of his face. His normally gruff voice had swung unsteadily between the urgent need to tell his story and a plaintive expectation of disbelief. He'd swayed on his feet, and Marsh had had serious doubts about his fitness to be interviewed.

Six hours later he still looked a little battered but much more himself. Both the shock and the anxiety had diminished now that the injuries he'd suffered – the blow to his head and the other one to his emotions – had had some time to heal. Nothing Marsh had in mind would do him any harm now.

He slumped into the chair he was offered with the deliberate carelessness characteristic of his age and sex. It said, You don't scare me. It said, I can walk out of here any time I want. It said, I'll answer your questions, it doesn't bother me, I eat policemen for breakfast.

What it said to Harry Marsh was, I'm out of my depth here, maybe if I act tough nobody'll notice. Marsh had seen it before. He'd seen it in the guilty and the innocent, and in casual witnesses who'd only been asked to describe an exchange between two other people. It didn't mean as much as an untrained observer might have thought.

"Well, you were right," began the Superintendent. "We found her in a siding in Holyhead. The wagon was collected from Skipley about midnight, so whatever happened to her – and to you – happened before that." He waited.

"She was dead?" Shad knew she was; he just needed confirmation.

"Yes."

"How?"

Marsh cocked an eyebrow at him. "Can you tell me? Think about it."

"I *have* thought about it," growled Shad. "I can't remember."

"Then guess." It wasn't as absurd a suggestion as it must have sounded. He was dealing with a man's subconscious: Lucas probably knew how the woman died, even if he didn't know he knew. If they could find a chink and insert a lever the wall would come down and he'd remember what happened.

It sounded ridiculous to Shad; but you could rule out lions, somebody tampering with her parachute, drowning and an explosion loud enough to be heard in Railwayview Street. "A knife?"

"That's right." Marsh invested the words with no particular significance. "She was stabbed. The knife was found beside her. You probably saw it. What was it like? Long, short, broad, thin? A stiletto, a flick knife, a Bowie knife, a kris?"

But Shad couldn't get an image of it. Maybe Marsh was wrong and he never did see it; maybe he'd been hit before he had the chance. "I don't know."

"All right. Then, do you remember handling it?"

"*What*?" The word exploded from Shad in outrage. His eyes were appalled.

Marsh shrugged. "It's not unlikely. If it was lying on the floor; if it was still in her, even. Fingerprints were taken from it: it would be useful to have yours for elimination. Then any others we find will probably belong to the murderer."

It was a reasonable request. Shad knew of no reason not to grant it. "OK."

Marsh nodded. "We'll do that before you leave. You might let me have the shirt you were wearing as well. The blood on it – it may not be yours. Anyway, we know now who she was."

Shad sniffed. "Unless she had a garden I don't expect I knew her."

"No, possibly not. She lived in Skipley, though. She worked for a television programme, as a researcher." He was watching the younger man's face but no flicker of recognition crossed it. "Her name was Jackie Pickering." Still nothing.

He thought for a moment. "Mr Lucas, what's the last thing you do clearly remember? Before being in Crewe, I mean."

Some of Wednesday had crept back into Shad's mind. "I went to Foxford House as usual yesterday morning. Mrs Thurley asked me to clear some of the deadwood out of the shrubbery."

Marsh had spoken to the Thurleys. That was about midday. The housekeeper had given Shad a bit of lunch in the kitchen; after that he'd scythed the paths through the wildflower meadow, and at five o'clock he'd gone home. All that was business as usual. He hadn't seemed in any rush to leave and hadn't mentioned going anywhere else.

"Good. Well, that's something you didn't remember this morning."

But Shad was in no mood for sops of comfort. "But it's not much help, is it?" His eyes smouldered.

Marsh clung to his patience. "It will be if it helps you remember something else. Like, why you left home in the evening. Were you going somewhere? Did you need something from the shop?"

"I wasn't dressed for going out," Shad said in his teeth. "I might have gone to the corner shop like that: if I'd been going anywhere else, or meeting someone, I'd have changed."

"Unless something came up at short notice."

Shad had no answer to that.

Superintendent Marsh thought for a moment. "Your friend Ms Holland. Did you see her on television last week?"

The abrupt change of subject didn't stop Shad remembering the episode with pleasure. "You mean, when she floored the creep?" He grinned. "Worth the licence fee for that alone."

Harry Marsh had felt much the same way, but that wasn't why he'd mentioned it. "That was the programme Jackie Pickering worked for." He left it hanging in the air, watching for Shad's reaction.

Trying to make sense of it, his face toyed with all manner of emotions – concern, doubt, bewilderment, and others that Marsh couldn't put a name to. When his expression settled, what was on top was alarm. "I never met her."

"Are you sure?"

"Yes. Unless you count seeing her after she was dead, which I may have done though I don't remember."

By now Marsh had a photograph of the dead girl. He put it on the table between them. "You may have known her by another name. If she was . . . using . . . you, she may have wanted to keep her real identity secret."

Shad stared at the photograph. "Using me?"

"You're an interesting man, Mr Lucas, you can do things most people can't. You made headline news doing it just this summer. Television feeds on interesting people. The possibility of doing a programme on you was bound to occur to someone. If it occurred to Miss Pickering, she may have approached you on some other pretext – to weigh you up before showing her hand."

Shad looked again at the photograph. She didn't look at all familiar. "I've never seen her before."

"Shad, you have," said Harry Marsh, quietly insistent. "In the wagon, almost certainly. If she doesn't look familiar to you, maybe you're shutting something out. Maybe you were with her last night. Maybe that's why you went out."

"You're saying . . . *I* killed her?" The gruff voice cracked in astonishment.

"No, I'm not," Marsh said levelly. "I'm speculating that you went out yesterday evening in order to meet her. That that's what you were doing behind the sidings. I don't know who stabbed her. Maybe it had already happened when you found her, or maybe somebody jumped the pair of you – floored you and stabbed her. I don't know. But *you* do, if you can get at it.

There's somebody I want you to talk to. A doctor. He specialises in amnesia; he might be able to help."

Shad knew what Marsh was saying. The bottom fell out of his stomach. "A psychiatrist?"

"Yes. You won't have to go to the hospital: he'll see you at his house if you'd rather."

"You've already talked to him?"

The superintendent nodded. "I need you to remember what happened. You need that, too."

Shad sucked in an unsteady breath. "What if I refuse?"

Marsh watched him. "You have that right. But people might wonder why you'd want to exercise it."

"I don't want anybody messing round in my head!"

"I understand that. But there's a killer out there, and the only one who can help us find him is you. If he kills again you'll never forgive yourself." Which was true, if a bit below the belt. "Why don't you talk to Doctor Cunningham, see if you can find a way of doing this that doesn't worry you?"

He wrote on a piece of paper. "This is his home number: give him a call. He knows what it's all about. If he doesn't think he can help he'll say so. If you don't want to work with him, we'll try to find another way. But it's important we make progress quickly. I have a dead girl in the morgue, if I'm going to make an arrest I have to find out what happened. I need your cooperation, Shad. Whether or not you knew her, you're the only one who can help Jackie Pickering now."

Seven

Alex was trying to concentrate on the job in hand, which was composing a reply to Fran Barclay on the subject of her relationship with Jamie. Instead she kept finding her thoughts drifting to her own relationship with Matt Gosling.

Would he accept her wishes in this? Or would the office become a battlefield as she fought first his advances, then his resentment?

On the other hand, if he really had felt like this for nine months and done nothing until now, maybe in his heart he knew it wasn't a good idea. But what if he wouldn't take no for an answer? In a world of chancers and bullies Matt Gosling was the closest thing she knew to an officer and a gentleman; but still, where basic feelings are involved no one's responses are entirely predictable. She couldn't work in an atmosphere that persisted longer than a week or two while he got the disappointment out of his system.

She turned her attention once more to the letter Matt had selected from the post.

First, believe me when I say that my lover's happiness is all that matters to me. For that I would sacrifice my own. If I was sure that his long-term fulfilment depended on my departure, I might sob all the way to the bus station but I'd go. He's that important to me.

The problem is, I'm important to him too. But so is his job, and I'm the biggest obstacle to success in it. I really don't know why. I'm perfectly presentable, and even if I wasn't I never show my face at his office. But Skipley is a small town in many ways: everybody knows everyone else, and unfortunately the people on whom Jamie's advancement depends are stuck back in the 1950s. It would be different if we were able to marry; it would be all right if he lived alone; but while we live together I'm an albatross around his neck. It isn't fair, it isn't right, you'd think there'd be a law against it, but the plain fact is that I'm stopping him from doing as well in his career as his talents, application and sheer hard work warrant. No one will ever say this is why, but it is.

So what do I do? He says Sod them, and I think that right now he means it. But what of the future? At thirty-four he's too young to be stuck in a dead-end job, too old to start afresh somewhere else. I'm terrified the time will come when he'll regret what our relationship has cost him. That he'll resent me. I'd rather go now, while we still mean something to one another, than wait for that to happen.

I don't know what I'm expecting from you: this is our dilemma, only we can resolve it. But I'm so worried, I felt the need to tell someone, if only to crystalise how I feel myself. If it was something I could talk to my mum about I wouldn't have bothered you. And I know what Jamie wants: I'm just not sure it's what he needs. I know what I *want, but I'm not sure it's what Jamie needs. If I fell under a bus tomorrow – and I'm talking hypothetically, I really don't see suicide as an option – he'd be devastated, but I think maybe his life would go forward then in a way that it can't while we're together.*

Heaven knows why, but I feel better just for putting pen to paper. If you've any useful suggestions I'd be glad to hear them; otherwise feel free to consign this to the round file. At some point I'll decide what I have to do and then I'll do it. Wish me well. Keep writing The Primrose Path, it keeps me sane!

Her initial assessment had been right, thought Alex: TLC. When Rosie read this she'd lose her temper, demand to know where Jamie worked and march round to confront his bosses who thought that (a) their employee's domestic arrangements were any of their business; and (b) even if they were, a partner as loving as Fran could be anything but an asset to him. Of course she'd probably make things worse, but she'd think she was sticking up for the star-crossed lovers.

Alex agreed with Fran: there probably wasn't much to be done except decide how to live with the situation. There was employment legislation protecting people from prejudice, but Jamie's employers could always find some other reason for not promoting him. Racial and sexual discrimination were amenable for prosecution because it was usually possible to make a direct comparison. But a man in middle management who might have gone further but then again might not? Even if the whole building knew it, how could you prove that his superiors' disapproval of his partner was the reason?

Alex turned to her keyboard and slowly began to write. There was no easy answer to this: she had to be sure that any contribution of hers would make Fran feel better even if the problem remained. The words began scrolling up on the screen:

You're right: it isn't fair, there should be a law against it, and if Jamie decided to leave he could try to claim constructive dismissal. He might succeed, or his employers might offer compensation to avoid going to court; but either way it could be a Pyrrhic victory. Jamie could end up with a few thousand pounds in his pocket but no job and a reputation for being difficult to employ. If that's the course he decides on he would be wise to seek alternative employment first. It would reduce the compensation payable, but a few thousand pounds is no substitute for a regular wage.

As to what you should do, I think what you must *do is talk to Jamie about this. I suspect he'll be appalled that you're considering ending your relationship. I suspect he'd rather sweep the streets and come home to you than be Managing Director and go home to an empty house. But even if I'm wrong, it's his decision. When he's got over the shock he'll be deeply touched that you care so much about his happiness. But if someone has to choose which of two prizes will make him most happy for longest, it has to be him.*

Personally, I have no doubt which he'll go for. But if I'm wrong I'll pass on the names of all the men I know will write in offering to give up their jobs, their Porsches and all they have for a girl like you.

Alex printed her reply and put it in an envelope. If a return address was enclosed they always sent a personal reply in advance of publication. It was not only courteous, it was a chance to catch NGIs – non-genuine inquiries. If the recipient of a letter phoned up to say, 'What the hell are you talking about?' and it turned out to be a hoax perpetrated by an acquaintance with a third-form sense of humour, there was still time to change the page before the *Chronicle* was printed.

Alex went back to the in-tray to see what else awaited her attention. There was plenty; but as she toyed with the keyboard it wasn't a reply to a query that started to appear.

Dear Primrose,

I have the privilege of working for one of the nicest men in the world. He's kind, courteous and funny: the sort of man any woman would give her eye-teeth for. Except me.

Even that isn't entirely true. I've enjoyed his friendship for nine months. But it seems friendship isn't enough for him any longer. We're both free; you couldn't find two people who get on better; the only obstacle is what everybody I know considers a stupid prejudice of mine.

I don't want to be the boss's girlfriend. Everything I have today I've earned: I don't want people to think anything different tomorrow. I'd much sooner stick with the thoroughly rewarding relationship we've had until now. But I'm not sure we can have it any more. Half of me is angry at him for spoiling it, the other half is angry at me for being obstinate. There doesn't seem to be any room to compromise . . .

* * *

The fact that Shad didn't want to discuss his problem with Rosie didn't stop Rosie discussing it with him.

It was late afternoon before they left the police station and the roads were beginning to fill up with people sneaking home early. Rosie drove in fits and starts, racing for the traffic lights then piling on the brakes with an obscenity when they changed. Shad could have walked home in five minutes; being driven by Rosie took about twenty and involved going the scenic route so they could drop off Prufrock. It also involved getting her opinion.

"I know how you feel about sharing this with people," she said, squeezing the big estate into a bicycle-sized space and glaring at the driver behind her. "I know it was hard talking to Marsh about it; it may be harder still talking to a shrink. I know you're afraid of losing control: of being passed round the experts like a prize specimen, peered at and poked to see what makes you react. I know that worries you. I understand why.

"But Shad, we're talking about finding a man who killed a young woman. We don't know who, and we don't know why. He may just have had the urge to kill and picked someone at random. If that's how it was, it'll happen again. Marsh has to find him first, but he has nothing to go on. The Forensics Laboratory will do their best, but forensics is better at proving a suspicion than at finding a guilty party. For that you need a witness, and the only witness we know of is you."

"I know that," growled Shad. "That's why—"

"I know, you don't think you can tell him anything more. And maybe you're right. But unless you work with the shrink you can't be sure. You could hold the key to a murder. If you won't even look for it, the killer will go free."

"I know," Shad said again. "So—"

"Jesus, Shad," exclaimed Rosie, "I *know* what I'm asking! I'm asking you to sweat blood. I'm asking you to do something I couldn't do myself. All right, that's an imposition. But it's also a privilege, all right? – to be able to do something for your fellow citizens that the man in the street couldn't. I know it costs you. But there are rewards too. You can maybe get justice for that poor girl when nobody else can."

"Rosie, I know," said Shad in exasperation. "I don't need talking into it: I'll give it a try. If I ever get home I'll give this Doctor Cunningham a call."

Still blithely believing she'd persuaded him to do the right thing, Rosie took Shad home to Skipley High Street. Then she headed home herself. It was five o'clock by then, too late to go back to the *Chronicle*. By this time on a Thursday even Alex would have called it a day.

But as she climbed out of the car she dropped her handbag, shattering one lens of the reading glasses whose protective case she had long ago mislaid. She kept another pair in the office: she sighed, got back in the car and went to fetch them.

Which is how she came to find the letter which Alex had left in the absolute certainty that she'd have plenty of time to dispose of it before Rosie could see it.

Alex had a small flat in a quietly prestigious block overlooking the Brickfields park. It was characteristic of the two women that, when they first came to Skipley, Rosie had been quite sure she'd be a resounding success and had bought the Old Vicarage while Alex had hedged her bets and rented instead. She might buy something if the *Chronicle* job still looked permanent in a year's time.

Alex was washing her hair, answered the door with her head turbaned in towelling. "Rosie! Come in. I wasn't expecting . . ." But as soon as she saw the older woman's expression she knew what had happened. "You've been to the office."

Rosie nodded. Her broad face, usually so animated, was sombre, her eyes compassionate. "You probably don't want to talk about it . . ."

Relieved, Alex turned away, squeezing water out of her long brown hair. "No, not really. I don't know why I wrote it, let alone why I left it there. I fully intended to tear it up first thing tomorrow."

Rosie continued without drawing breath, without acknowledging that Alex had spoken. ". . . But I think we should. Mostly because you're my friend and I care if something's making you unhappy. Partly because Matt's my friend and I care that something's making *him* unhappy. And also because there's one solution to this which is in my hands, but if that's the way, we're going we have to talk about it – with Matt as well. I won't spring it on him as a done deal."

A sense of humour was not one of Alex's strongest assets. But she had a sudden vision of how Rosie could help and gave a peal of delighted, slightly unsteady laughter. "Rosie, that's wonderful! I hope the two of you will be very happy."

Rosie laughed too, more Quasimodo than the bells. "Somehow I don't think Matt would consider it a fair exchange. That wasn't what I had in mind."

"Then . . . ?"

"As a last resort," said Rosie, "we could do the same job on another paper."

Alex spun on her, clearly horrified. "You can't do that to them! Matt could lose his paper. Dan and the rest of them could lose their jobs."

Rosie hid her satisfaction and shrugged. "I said it was a last resort – if you two really can't work together any more. Matt owns the *Chronicle*, we can't sack him. But we can leave."

A fine spray spattered the pastel furnishings as Alex shook her head. "No. Rosie, we're not joined at the hip. If I have to leave the *Chronicle* I will, but I won't be responsible for robbing Matt of his best chance to make a go of it. We both know that the paper's finances are about as sound as a chocolate teapot. Without you, without The Primrose Path, it may not survive. Matt's put everything he has into it. I won't see him broken just because he's fallen for the wrong woman."

"You don't want to punish him then."

Alex's eyebrows rocketed. "Of course not. Rosie, Matt hasn't done anything wrong. I won't have you wrecking his dream out of some misguided notion of loyalty."

Rosie had helped herself to the larger part of the sofa; after a moment, hugging the damp towel, Alex sat down beside her.

"Tell me again," murmured Rosie, with a flash of the insight that had made her a household name in Skipley and beyond, "how Matt's feelings are entirely unrequited. How you've no more interest in him than the result of the Swedish general election."

"I never said that!" retorted Alex. "I never said I didn't care what happened to him. He's been a good friend to me, to both of us; which is why I didn't want this to happen. I'd give anything to be back where we were last week – friends, two people who could rely on one another – and not have to worry about one another's feelings!"

"Because that's you all over, isn't it?" said Rosie ironically. "Only ever thinking of yourself, never giving a damn for anyone else. I can see how having a man say he's in love with you would really cramp your style."

Alex stared at her, too troubled to be amused, too sensible not to see that there was a funny side. "You think I'm mad, don't you?"

Rosie smiled and shook her head. "Not mad. I think you take life too seriously. I think you worry too much about things that might happen when they probably won't and wouldn't be so terrible if they did. So what if you and Matt broke up? You're two intelligent adults and that's how you'd deal with it. People fall in and out of love all the time; it only seems a big deal to them and then only for a little while.

"I wish you'd trust yourself more – because that's the problem, isn't it? Not that you don't trust Matt to behave like a gentleman, but that you're not sure you'd behave like a lady. You're like Shad – you're afraid of losing control. But hell, girl, it's not like your A-levels, there isn't a passing grade. You make it up as you go along. You make your mistakes and either you learn from them or you make them again. But the things you regret are never what you did wrong, they're what you were too afraid to do at all."

Alex said, doubtfully, "We have to have standards."

Rosie hooted with mirth. "Alex, you're a one-off, you really are. You want to describe this standard of yours that Matt Gosling doesn't measure up to?"

But Alex wasn't going to be mocked into submission. "You're trying to make me sound like some prim little virgin fresh from school, and I'm not."

"Which?" asked Rosie innocently.

"Either," Alex said firmly. "I know what works for me, and until now not dating colleagues has worked fine. The only question is whether it might be sensible to make the occasional exception. If I thought that, I'd make one for Matt. I'd take the risks – and, if need be, I'd take the consequences."

"Then what's stopping you?"

"I don't want anyone to get hurt! Not me and not him."

Rosie didn't know whether to hug her or slap her. "Alex, look at you! You're miserable. And whatever Matt's doing right now, I bet he's miserable too. How can you make that worse?

"I'm not trying to talk you into anything. It's none of my business whether you get together with Matt, with someone else or no one at all. I want you to be happy – I don't give a damn how. If these principles of yours were making you happy, I'd say OK – weird, but good luck to you. But they're not. I don't know if you and Matt can make a go of things, but there's only one way to find out."

"What if we end up hating each other?"

"Why should you hate each other? You're two nice people, that's not going to change. If it works out, great. And if it doesn't, you'll still be two nice people who once had something going and now don't. You'll take a week's holiday, and when you get back Matt'll take a week's holiday, and when *he* gets back you'll both be ready to move on. And I won't need to hold painful little heart-to-hearts with both of you in quiet corners where the other one won't hear."

"*Both* of us?" Alex's scrubbed face shone with indignation. "You mean you've talked to Matt about me?"

"Of course I have," said Rosie cheerfully. "The man hired his own personal Agony Aunt – where else would he go for advice? Damn it, Alex, if it wasn't for me he'd have jumped you months ago. I told him to be patient. And he has been – more patient than I ever imagined. He's behaved impeccably. Now, for heaven's sake put the poor guy out of his misery!"

She picked up the phone. "Call him. Ask him for dinner."

Alex took the handset, stared at it as if it had grown tentacles. "But – what . . . ?"

Typically, Rosie assumed she was wondering what to feed him. "I'm not sure you can beat steak and chips," she said ingenuously. "Listen, I'll leave you to it. But chicken out and you really could be looking for another job. And you wouldn't want the reference I'd write you!"

Her rejection seemed so final the last time they spoke that for a moment Matt genuinely didn't understand what Alex was saying. There was no way she could make it clearer so she said it again.

"I said, I may have been wrong. We ought to talk. If you've no other plans this evening, would you come for dinner? About eight."

As a matter of fact Matt had made plans. He was planning to go to his mother's for a country weekend and a bit of spoiling. He was feeling unloved, and the best antidote he knew was being fussed over by the celebrated Fane sisters. Now mostly in their sixties – his mother was the youngest – they were still the vibrant heart of Buckinghamshire society with their improbable millinery, their unsuitable liaisons and their happy habit of marrying into money.

All six of them lived within a ten-mile radius, and a visit by Matt or any of his cousins was excuse enough to gather the clan for the sort of party that would get people with neighbours arrested. Last time he was at his Aunt Isobel's he opened the scullery door, looking for something to get trifle off his dinner jacket, and found his Aunt Emerald humping the wine waiter. It was impossible to stay depressed in company like that.

He already had a bag packed. If Alex had called ten minutes later he'd have been on his way. But the thing about families, even entertaining families, is that they're always there. It never for a moment occurred to Matt to put her off, to ask if they could make it another night.

"No," he said swiftly, "no plans. I'll be there at eight. Can I bring some wine?"

"That would be nice."

It occurred to Alex, after she'd put the phone down and was trying to steady her shaking hands by clasping them together, that she should have been more specific. She didn't want him to misunderstand. When she'd said they ought to talk that was exactly – and all – that she meant. If he came here expecting more . . .

But she should have trusted him. He turned up at five past eight with a bottle of good white burgundy. No red roses, no champagne.

Eight

Self-restraint was not the attribute most widely associated with Rosie Holland. But by an almost superhuman effort she managed not to phone Alex that night but to contain her curiosity until they next met in the office and she could ask without making a big deal of it.

Nobody in the *Chronicle* building, where work started from eight o'clock onwards, could remember Rosie ever being in before ten on a Friday. After being asked to hold the fort, Alex wasn't sure she'd be in at all. But when she opened her door at five to nine, Rosie sprang at her like a fourteen-stone jack-in-the-box.

"Well?"

It wasn't like Alex to be deliberately obtuse but on this occasion she considered it warranted. "Perfectly, thank you," she said sweetly, hanging up her jacket. She kept a padded hanger at the office for this purpose. Rosie had a nail behind her door.

"I mean," exploded Rosie, and stopped when she realised that Alex knew exactly what she meant. She sniffed. "All right, so it's a big secret. See if I care."

"You mean, if I don't tell you you'll go and ask Matt."

"I meant nothing of the sort," Rosie lied loftily. "I just assumed that, since you got me involved in the first place, you'd want to tell me how things worked out."

Alex relented. "We had dinner. At first it felt strange – just us, and not business. But it was nice. We talked about the situation. We decided that as long as we behaved like adults we'd be able to handle it. We decided to try it and see how things went."

"*And . . .* ?"

Alex looked down her perfect nose at the older woman. "You mean, *And* did we end up in bed? No. We talked until about one o'clock this morning and then he went home. There's a concert in Birmingham tomorrow evening, he's trying to get tickets. We're going out. We're going to see if we can make this work. All right?"

Rosie was delighted. They'd made more progress than she'd expected. She wouldn't have been surprised to learn that Alex had never made the phone call. But she pretended to be disappointed. "I thought you said you were going to behave like adults."

"Being adult makes it legal for every date to end in bed," Alex said calmly. "It doesn't make it compulsory."

Rosie grinned and threw a plump arm around her. "Anyway, best of luck."

She reached round her own door for her handbag and car keys. "If anybody's looking for me, I'll be at the Palmyra Café for the next hour. I haven't had my breakfast yet."

By merest coincidence Rosie found herself driving back to the *Chronicle* along the High Street just as Shad's door opened. He crossed to the Land Rover and climbed inside.

He wasn't dressed for turning compost. As far as Rosie knew he only had one shirt with no grass stains on it and one pair of trousers without knee patches, and he was wearing them. He looked positively respectable.

He looked like a man visiting the doctor.

Rosie nodded to herself, satisfied. She hadn't known Shad Lucas very long but he was growing in her estimation. This thing in his head – she knew it troubled him, frightened him sometimes, that sometimes he'd give anything to be as insensitive to other people's feelings as everyone else.

Dowsing was different: he enjoyed that, got a kick out of tuning in to the energy of hidden waters surging along deep underground. But this business of feeling other people's pain: there wasn't much of an up-side to it. She knew that he'd have chosen not to be blessed. For years he'd kept it entombed at the bottom of his mind, had disinterred it only because she needed him to. That gave her an obligation to help. She wanted him to get professional guidance. Shad, she knew, really wanted to put it back in the cellar and hope time and cobwebs would cover it up. Two things stopped him: wondering if he had any right to squander something this rare; and the fear that if he didn't use it, one day something would happen that he could have prevented.

But there was a strength to him, besides the physical strength of his muscular young body, and a raw courage that made him face his demons head on. Rosie had never really doubted that he would do as Superintendent Marsh asked and work with the psychiatrist to chisel away at his amnesia. She hoped they would succeed quickly, before it cost him too much. Before scar tissue became the only kind of healing possible.

It was Friday morning so, in the normal way of things, Shad would have been at Prufrock's. The gardens around the cottage in Foxford Lane weren't extensive enough or – the topiary hedge notwithstanding – ornate enough to require the services of a jobbing gardener twice a week. But Prufrock had reached an age when things he would once have taken in his stride were beginning to pose a problem. Shad could turn his hand to a bit of house maintenance as well as pruning the roses, and rarely had much difficulty filling the time.

Because Prufrock was an early riser he usually started there soon after eight. His appointment with Doctor Cunningham meant he couldn't keep to that. Prufrock wasn't sure whether to expect him at all; but he delayed making his morning coffee on the off chance, and at eleven-thirty the growl of the Land Rover in the lane was his reward.

Shad had come straight from the doctor's house without taking the time to change. He had his jeans, boots and a tee-shirt in a plastic bag bearing a garden-centre logo.

"Sit down before you start," said Prufrock, pouring the coffee. "Tell me how it went."

A curious relationship had developed between these two. Not purely business; not an ersatz father/son thing, for though the old man had raised a thousand boys he had never been a father, and the younger man had never known one; and certainly nothing improper – Arthur Prufrock could honestly say he'd never in his entire career felt an unwise stirring for any of the gilded youths of his acquaintance. Which just left friendship.

With more than forty years between them they weren't obvious candidates for that either. Neither of them had ever gone to sleep on New Year's morning sucking a champagne cork and hoping to meet the other. But then friendship is not a poor substitute for love. Less authoritarian, more enduring, it worships at other altars and demands fewer sacrifices. Shad might have daydreamed about Kim Basinger, and Prufrock about Geraldine McEwan, but it's possible that a few good friends were closer to what each of them needed.

Shad's heavy brows gathered as he planted his elbows on the kitchen table. "OK, I think. The guy was trying to help – it wasn't, like, the third degree." Under his good shirt the broad shoulders shrugged. "But I don't know if we achieved very much. If Marsh is expecting a PhotoFit of the murderer after this morning, he's going to be disappointed."

"It may take longer than that," agreed Prufrock. "Are you seeing Doctor Cunningham again?"

"Tomorrow," nodded Shad. "He thinks we should keep at it. Is it OK if I skip Tuesday? I'll have to make up the time I'm losing."

"Of course. It's a matter of priorities, and my hedge is an also-ran beside Superintendent Marsh's business."

Shad looked at him slyly over his mug. "Could cut it a lot quicker if it was simpler."

Prufrock scowled. "I don't care what you say, I like my peacocks. They're distinctive. You're not lopping them off."

"Distinctive," echoed Shad, sinking into the comfort of the old argument like a familiar armchair. "Is that another way of saying Eyesore?"

With a murder investigation underway Detective Superintendent Marsh couldn't afford to take the weekend off. Because it was Saturday he had an extra hour in bed, and he wasn't wearing a tie as he drove to the pleasant house in Brindley Road where Jackie Pickering's producer lived and where Dick Chauncey had got his memorable come-uppance. As he drove he thought.

He saw three broad areas of possibility: that the girl's death was linked to her work; that it was linked to her private life; or that she was the random victim of someone she'd never met before Wednesday. As her producer, Marta Frank should know what Pickering had been working on in the weeks prior to her death, and whether any of it might have put her in danger.

Ms Frank was a small, dark woman in her late thirties with shrew-sharp eyes and an air of intellectual pragmatism. A career woman; a woman who measured herself, and those around her, in terms of success or failure. A woman, Harry Marsh speculated, who might value ends enough to turn a blind eye to means. A younger woman, looking for advancement from Marta Frank, might feel driven to take risks that would seem unwise in the cold clear light of day.

He wished he'd put a tie on.

Ms Frank showed him into the breakfast room. "If you haven't eaten, I hope you'll join me. If you have, at least have a coffee."

He had eaten, but it was a couple of hours ago now. He helped himself to toast and jam as they talked.

"How long was Miss Pickering with you?"

"Fifteen months." If the news that one of her staff had been murdered had come as a shock – Marsh hadn't told her himself, Detective Sergeant Burton had interviewed her in the course of establishing the girl's movements – Ms Frank seemed to have got over it. She was cool, professional, helpful, and almost totally uninvolved – which took some doing when what they were talking about was the possibility that her employee had died doing her job. "She came straight from university. Media studies. She got a good degree."

"She came as a researcher?"

Ms Frank gave him a tight smile. "She came as a gopher. The streets are paved with people with good degrees in media studies; it's enough to get you an interview. Everybody starts at the bottom. But Jackie got the hang of things pretty quickly. She got the first assistant researcher's post that came up, and did it well enough to be made up to researcher in the last round of promotions. She had a good career ahead of her."

"She worked exclusively for you – for the Dick Chauncey programme?"

Ms Frank's smile grew tighter. "Well, for *You've Been Had* anyway. It's only the Dick Chauncey programme as long as we pay him to front it."

Marsh raised an eyebrow. "It sounds as if there's some doubt about that."

She gave a minimalist shrug. "There's always some doubt about it. It's a matter for contractual negotiation. Anchormen get the idea they *are* the show and that they can hold you to ransom. But the truth is, anyone who can read an Autocue can do the job. What matters is the ideas. A good researcher contributes more to the show than the front man."

"Had there been some friction? Between Chauncey and Miss Pickering, for instance?"

"There's always friction," said Ms Frank, "between everyone and everyone else. TV production runs on coffee and angst. I wasn't aware of any particular friction between Dick and Jackie. I doubt he'd condescend to acknowledge her existence." She blinked. "You're not thinking – Dick and Jackie? Good grief, man, not in this life. Front men don't go for researchers, they go for weather girls. Researchers look for a basic minimum of intelligence: they go for cameramen."

Marsh was finding this insight into the real-politik of programme-making fascinating. It was too soon to know if any of it would be helpful. "Any particular cameraman?"

Ms Frank shook her head. "If she had a boyfriend, it was no one from work. Maybe there was no one. She was an attractive girl, bright and good-looking, but she always struck me as a bit of a loner. A lot of girls – and it's the girls more than the men – want to get their careers on line before they start thinking about personal commitment."

"Could she still have been seeing someone from university? Which university anyway?"

"Nottingham. I suppose it's possible, but she never brought anyone to the office bashes. Unless you count Debbie."

"Debbie?"

"A friend from the media course. I don't remember her other name. Jackie wanted me to give her a job, said she needed to get her life on track. I don't know why, she looked perfectly normal to me. Jackie brought her to the Christmas party and on the summer outing; mostly as a form of subtle blackmail, I think." She seemed amused rather than resentful.

"And did you give her the job?"

Ms Frank shook her head again. "There were always better candidates. A nice enough girl, but she hadn't Jackie's personality or self-confidence. And sometimes those are the only things that get you through the day in this job."

Marsh nodded, still just absorbing information. "So Jackie was good at her job. What's the routine? Did she take her assignments from you?"

"For the most part. A good researcher will also originate ideas but the choice of a subject is mine. We discuss how we'll tackle it, work out a plan of campaign, then somebody tells Dick. Next time we talk about it he thinks it was his idea."

"So Jackie wouldn't have been harassing – sorry, researching – anybody without your knowledge?"

She flicked a cool smile at his slip of the tongue. "Unlikely. You can't rule it out completely – for a researcher to make producer she has to initiate enough good ideas to make an impression, so she could have been sounding somebody out, trying to decide if they'd make a good show or not. But long before she got pushy enough to annoy somebody, I'd have to know. And I don't think the target she was currently researching is very promising murderer material."

"No? You might be surprised. In the right circumstances almost anybody can commit murder."

"A seventy-six-year-old grandmother with forty-four foster children to her credit?"

"Ah. Maybe not."

*　*　*

Doctor Andrew Cunningham and Shad Lucas didn't stop for the weekend either. They met again on Saturday morning, and on Sunday morning.

On Sunday afternoon Superintendent Marsh walked up to Doctor Cunningham's house on The Brink. They'd been neighbours since the psychiatrist took a post at the prestigious Fellowes Hall Clinic the previous year. The Cunninghams lived on top of the wooded escarpment, the Marshes further down the slope. They shared the same local: The Bear in Foxford. During rush hour they shared the same traffic jams.

Marsh wasn't sure how much cooperation he could expect in the current circumstances. But he got a cordial welcome.

"Come on through, Harry. I'm doing a bit of paperwork in the study. Let's open a bottle of June's elderflower wine."

Psychiatrists come in two colour schemes: rubicund and grey. Cunningham was one of the latter. He wore grey suits for work; today he wore a grey cashmere cardigan and flannels. Even his hair had gone prematurely grey. It was cut ruthlessly short, as if to emphasise the general spareness of the man.

Marsh had a study in the space under his stairs. Cunningham's was a deep room running from the front of his house to the back, lined with books at one end and with prints at the other. There was no couch. Presumably there was another room for consultations, smaller and more intimate, where he saw Shad Lucas.

Over the elderflower wine Marsh framed a cautious approach. "I'll try to avoid giving you any kind of professional dilemma, Andrew. Lucas agreed to see you in the hope that you could jog his memory as to what happened on Wednesday night. He told me he was willing for us to discuss any progress you made. I'm hoping he told you the same thing."

To his relief, Cunningham nodded. "That's the situation as I understand it. Confidentiality isn't an issue – unless at some later date he wants to make it one. But I don't expect he will. If something comes back that he'd rather you didn't know, he just won't tell me. He may stop coming altogether."

"But for now we can talk about your sessions with him?"

"Certainly. It's what he wants. He sees it as taking some of the pressure off him."

"He feels to be under pressure then."

"Of course he does – he's the only person you know of who was at the scene of a murder! It hit him hard. You know about his history, I suppose."

Marsh nodded. "He located the graves of a number of children hidden in the Clee Hills. Forensic examination of the bodies provided the evidence on which the killer was convicted."

"And he was how old at this point?"

Marsh knew damn well that he knew. "He was seventeen. Andrew, don't twist my heartstrings over this, it wasn't my idea. It wasn't even my force. I know it was tough on him. It was still the right decision. Free, the man would have gone on to abduct, abuse and murder God knows how many other children."

Cunningham conceded a half-apologetic smile. "I don't mean to criticise. I just want you to understand that what happened on Wednesday didn't occur in isolation in Shad Lucas's mind. It linked up with those events eight years ago and forged an iron conviction that the world's a deadly place. For everyone, but more for him. He feels other people's pain as well as his own."

Harry Marsh regarded the psychiatrist dubiously. "You believe that? He's not just . . . imaginative? You're convinced he is genuinely psychic?"

"I don't *know*," said Cunningham precisely, "any more than I've been told. I'm no better equipped to judge his story than you are. But the fact remains, he found those children after conventional methods involving dogs, technical support and massive quantities of manpower had failed. Since someone else was convicted I presume there's no question that Lucas put them there, which leaves two options. Either he was in league with the killer, or something extraordinary goes on inside his head. Until I have some reason to think otherwise I'm inclined to accept his description of what it is. Just because I've no experience of it doesn't mean it can't exist."

"You haven't come across it before?"

"No. There is a body of writing on psychic subjects, but I'm not sure anyone claims to understand it. Mostly you fall back on the Sherlock Holmes method: if you've ruled out natural phenomena, trickery and misinterpretation, whatever remains must be the truth. Even if it's telepathy; even if it's clairvoyance. Even if it's a gardener dowsing for dead babies."

Harry Marsh sipped his wine. "The amnesia has something to do with that?"

Cunningham shrugged. "I can't cut open his head to see what's happening inside, I have to guess. But yes, I think so. It was a bad time for him. He was very young, not well educated, without much family support. His conscience made him do it but it hurt. If he'd broken down at the time he'd have been looked after and the issues could have been dealt with. Instead he hauled himself together and got on with his life.

"But unresolved feelings don't go away, they just fester. Eight years later, after he thought he was safe, the hags reached out of the darkness for him again. The safety was an illusion. He's never going to be safe anywhere, not as long as he has that . . . faculty in his head. I think the amnesia may be him trying to seal it up where it can't do him any more harm."

"Can you get through it?"

"*I* can't," said Cunningham firmly. "Shad probably could, if he wanted to."

"But he doesn't?"

"He's afraid. He wants to help. At a conscious level he wants to know what happened as much as you do. At a subconscious level he's afraid of letting the genie out of the bottle when he doesn't know if he can squeeze it back in."

"Can you help him?"

Andrew Cunningham smiled. "That's my job – helping people to understand what's going on in their own minds. I can't force him to remember, and I wouldn't if I could. But I can make it easier for him. I can reassure him, I can show him how to proceed. But, in the end, it comes down to him being prepared to confront that genie."

"Are you seeing him again tomorrow?"

"Every day, for as long as it takes."

Marsh chewed on his lip. "Andrew, there isn't time for this to expand into an intellectual exercise. He isn't coming here for the good of his soul; he's coming because he may hold the key to a murder inquiry. I need answers. I need them soon."

"I understand that, Harry," said Cunningham patiently. "But you have to understand that I too have professional commitments. *Everyone* who comes to me does it for the good of his soul. I won't sacrifice Shad's needs to yours, worthy as they may be. He wants to help you, I want to help you, but not at any cost. You can't build your case on the wreckage of another human being."

Marsh stiffened. "Then I'll simply remind you that the longer this goes on, the greater the likelihood that Jackie Pickering's murderer will escape detection and, if he has a mind to, will kill again. I don't mean to hold that over you, Andrew. It's just, if we have to weigh one thing against another, that's a hefty piece of kit."

Cunningham considered. "I suppose I could speed things up a bit."

Nine

First thing on Monday morning Dan Sale wanted to see Rosie. Rosie came in keen to hear the latest from Alex, but Alex was on the phone so she went to quiz Matt instead. But on the way up to his office she met him on the way down. "Did you get Dan's message? He wants to see us both, soonest." So she had to put her personal curiosity on hold until they'd found out what was bothering the editor.

Essentially, Sale was concerned about what always and only ever concerned him: his newspaper. He was worried there could be aspects to the Pickering affair that might reflect on the *Skipley Chronicle*.

Rosie frowned. "Run that by me again, slowly."

Sale breathed heavily, radiating patience under strain. "Pickering was a researcher for Dick Chauncey's programme. Chauncey wanted revenge for you humiliating him. When Pickering was found, the only person known to have been in the immediate vicinity was a friend of yours. Rosie, are we absolutely sure this is a coincidence?"

Her mind staggered as if he'd cannoned into it. She was scarcely able to believe he was suggesting what it sounded like. It took her a moment to find a voice. "You're saying . . . *Shad* killed Jackie Pickering?"

"Of course I'm not," Sale retorted roughly. "I don't know. All I know is how it looks. I suppose what I'm after is your assurance that he didn't – and now I come to say that out loud," he went on, his voice softening ruefully, "of course you can't give me any such thing. You don't know what happened behind the station. Lucas himself doesn't know. Then, using your experience of him and your best judgement, do you think there's a serious danger that he may have done?"

"Of course not!" Rosie exclaimed indignantly. "Dan, Shad's not a thug! He's got something going on in his head that most of us haven't got, and sometimes it scares him and sometimes it makes him difficult, but there's no earthly reason it should make him a murderer! He isn't violent. I'd trust Shad Lucas with my life."

"I'd trust him with *your* life," agreed Sale. "But it's not your life we're talking about: it's that of a young woman who may have tried to use him in a particularly underhand and hurtful way. To get at you, or because he'd be a good catch for a freak show. She was young, pretty, intelligent and a lot more worldly than him. If she befriended him – hell, let's use the right word: if she seduced him – and then he found out she wasn't even after his body so much as to make a quick buck out of him, are you still sure he couldn't become violent? Just for a moment – just long enough to stab her?"

Rosie didn't think so, but Sale was right – she couldn't be sure. She argued a different premise. "But Jackie Pickering wasn't killed in the heat of the moment. Her murderer wasn't an angry man striking out at someone who'd abused his trust. He arranged for her to be at the railway yards late in the evening – either he thought up a pretext to take her there or one to meet her there – and he went armed with a knife. Not a penknife, such as anyone might carry, but the perfect shape and length of knife to kill Jackie Pickering in the way that she was killed. It couldn't have been more premeditated. That wasn't Shad. I feel absolutely confident of that."

Sale was nodding slowly. "All right. Good. Because I don't mind telling you, Rosie, if you're wrong about him it could be bad news for the *Chronicle*. He's your protégé – if it turns out he's unstable enough to—"

"He is *not* my protégé!" Rosie shot back fast. "He's a friend. He does my garden. Four months ago he helped me solve the mystery of the missing bird-watcher for The Primrose Path, and he got hurt doing it. That puts me in his debt, but it doesn't make him my protégé."

"Rosie, it does. In the public mind, that's exactly what it makes him. And the public mind is what'll come down on you like a ton of bricks if it turns out you've misjudged him and there's a girl dead because of it. It may not be reasonable, it may not be fair, but fickle is the public's middle name and they can turn against you as quickly as they took to you. You've been a huge success in this town, Rosie. People like you being a bit outrageous. But only so far. If you're implicated in what's happened, however innocently, they'll turn on you as they turned on Dick Chauncey."

Along with the indignation he'd provoked Rosie felt a crawl of unease along her spine. "Dan . . . are you making this some kind of a warning? Putting me on notice?"

Sale's brow wrinkled unhappily. "Hell, Rosie, I don't mean it to sound like that. Yes, it's a warning, because I think maybe I can see a danger looming that you can't. Put it down to experience: I've been in this business a long time, I've seen people scale extraordinary heights and I've seen them brought down. It's that sort of a business. I don't want the *Chronicle* to suffer, but I also don't want you to get hurt. Putting you on notice? – of course not. But what kind of a friend would let you walk into a danger you weren't aware of without trying to warn you?"

Her hand shot out with impulsive warmth and clasped his on top of his desk. He looked startled but not displeased. Dan Sale had been divorced for some ten years: it may have been longer than that since a woman last held his hand.

"I'm sorry," Rosie said honestly. "That was unfair and uncalled for. I *know* you've only our best interests at heart. If I say stupid things sometimes it's because I'm trying to find my way in a field I'm still not familiar with. That means I need your guidance even when I don't recognise the fact. Perhaps particularly when I don't recognise the fact. Maybe as time goes on I'll be less of a trial to you."

Her quick grin as quickly faded. "But Dan, I don't know what I can do about Shad that'll make you rest any easier. As things stand, the police consider him a potential witness and he's doing everything he can to help with their inquiries. He's working with a psychiatrist to try and find the missing hours. It may be they won't succeed; or if they do, they won't find anything useful – he was floored before he saw a face. But he's doing his best to behave like a responsible citizen, even though someone tinkering around in his mind is what scares him most."

"Maybe he's scared of what they'll find."

Rosie frowned and shrugged. "What can I tell you? – I don't believe it. And if Shad thought there was any danger of that, you wouldn't get him within shouting distance of a shrink. I can't give you any guarantees, but all the evidence is that what happened is what looks to have happened: he stumbled across a murder and the killer decked him and made his escape. That's what Shad thinks, it's what Detective Superintendent Marsh thinks, and it's what I think too."

"And if you're wrong?" Sale's voice was flat, uncompromising. People never thought of him as a particularly tough man until they'd had to negotiate with him.

Rosie blinked. "I suppose there's an outside chance that we're wrong. I personally would be devastated – but I still don't see how the paper would be damaged. Whatever happened on Wednesday, the fact remains that four months ago Shad Lucas risked his life to help me help one of our correspondents. We owe him for that. Of course I wouldn't help him escape the consequences of a crime, but I wouldn't disown him either. If he'd got himself into that much trouble he'd need his friends more than ever."

Rosie was puzzled by the tone of the conversation. She seemed to be being accused of something, as if knowing someone who'd found a body showed lack of judgement. But high on her hate list were fair-weather friends. She could no more have tiptoed away from Shad Lucas and his troubles than she could have danced the Dying Swan at Covent Garden. She thought it important that her editor and her proprietor understood that.

"I still don't believe it, but imagine the worst – that Shad killed Jackie Pickering and that's the trauma his mind can't face. If you're telling me that the *Chronicle* would need me to cut him adrift, Dan, then I have to tell you we'd have a problem. He'd need me – not to get him off but to get him through. If the precise combination of circumstances arose that led to him killing someone, and just what he is and can do became the subject of official scrutiny, your precious public would be baying for his blood. The only thing standing between him and the mob would be one or two friends.

"Abandoning him then would be a betrayal of everything The Primrose Path stands for. You can't want me only to help people whose situations aren't too serious! I don't mind dealing with the trivia but I'm not going to limit myself to it. I'm not going to help only those who can count on public sympathy – the attractive, the educated, the well mannered. I won't condone a crime, but even criminals have rights that need protection. I'll try not to embarrass the *Chronicle*, Dan, but I won't throw Shad to the wolves rather than risk it."

Matt Gosling saw a juncture approaching at which the two people who mattered most to his dream of a successful newspaper were going to dig themselves into trenches it would be hard to leave. Professionally, he was sure Sale was right; on a human level he could see that Rosie was. To him it didn't matter which of them had the better case, only that some compromise be found. If it wasn't, he'd be in the invidious position of having to back his editor against his star columnist or vice versa, and the *Chronicle* would lose one of them.

"Hey, guys, come on," he pleaded, "we can deal with this. We're all reasonable people and they're both reasonable positions – what we have to do is reconcile them. You're not telling me we can't find a compromise?"

Sale sniffed. "Matt, I'm not telling you anything more than you pay me to: what sells papers, and what gets papers into trouble. If Shad Lucas killed Jackie Pickering, and he did it because she was using him to get at Rosie, we are in deep shit. Our one shot at damage limitation would be for her to dissociate herself. Lucas helped her once, it was months ago, she pays him to mow her lawn – she's no more responsible for his actions than the man who services her car. If she attempts to stand by him there'll be such a backlash against the *Chronicle* that we may all be queuing at the Labour Exchange by the end of the month." It was a measure of Dan Sale's professional success that Job Centres were called Labour Exchanges the last time he was in one.

Rosie hadn't had much need for them either, wouldn't actually need another job if she lost this one. So it was easy to make a grand gesture. "Dan, if you need my resignation before I'm seen helping someone who's done his best to help me, who was probably trying to help someone this time, and who's scared shitless by what's happened to him, then so be it. Alex'll run the page for you, good luck to you and no hard feelings. I'd be sorry to leave that way, but I'd sooner go than put the boot into a boy who, to the best of my knowledge, has never harmed or tried to harm anyone."

"I'm not suggesting that!" snapped Sale, incensed. "I'm saying you need to protect yourself by putting some distance between you."

"Oh, so rather than put the boot in myself I should hold the coats of those who're doing it for me? Yeah, Dan, that makes all the difference. Me and Shad'll both feel a lot better about that."

She'd nailed her colours to the mast: she wasn't going to drop them. Matt tried appealing to Sale. "Dan, isn't there room for us to condemn the crime without abandoning the man? Newspapers do sometimes take up the case of people who've committed crimes. Women who kill abusive partners, people driven to violence by circumstances beyond their control. The public can understand if they're helped to."

Dan Sale's wrinkles were twitching with the effort to contain his ire. He was the editor of this newspaper: he was responsible for everything that went into it. He worked with his proprietor because, on the whole, it was good for the *Chronicle*, but he wasn't used to having to justify either his motives or his decisions. He was due Matt Gosling's support as of right. At the end of the day a proprietor has only two honourable options: to back his editor or to fire him. He made allowances for Matt, partly because he hadn't been in the business long and partly because he tried so hard to do it well. That tolerance didn't extend to letting him think he had any sanction in this other than the final one.

"Yes, it happens. Sometimes: in very precise circumstances, two of which are indispensable. The crime has to be committed by a weaker party against a stronger; and the criminal's got to be photogenic. We couldn't find anything to say in defence of a fit man who killed a girl. Even if there were mitigating circumstances, I can't see a way of telling the story that wouldn't make readers identify with the pretty, bright young television researcher and against the freak who stabbed her."

Rosie felt that like a knife under her own ribs. She actually gasped. For a split second she glimpsed the world through Shad's eyes and it was a hostile place. A place where decent, honest, liberal professional people thought of him as not fully human. A freak. People he'd never harmed, who had no reason to think he might, were afraid of him. What he had – they called it a gift but really it was a curse. It separated him from everyone around him. If he used it, even if it was to help them, they resented him. If he didn't, it squatted in the bottom of his mind like a toad in a well, growing in the dark.

Of course he was afraid! She'd thought it was the perception he feared; she'd told him to get it out in the daylight, to map it and use it and learn to control it. But it wasn't the toad that frightened him, it was this: that people like Dan Sale, who knew him, who knew what he'd done and what he hadn't, could sum him up with such devastating succinctness. His identity was in their hands. If they said he was a freak then he was one.

Rosie lurched to her feet, spilling her chair unheeded. Her broad face was flushed with fury. "My God, Dan – that's it? You can define another human being in one word? Twenty-five years living and growing, loving and losing, laughing and crying and struggling to make a place for himself, and you can distil that down to one hard word. There's something about him – just one thing – that's different to how you are, and that entitles you to call him a freak.

"So what makes you such a perfect template? Being a white middle-class male? Congratulations, Dan, it was a smart move picking your genes like that. No getting stuck with a sub-standard set. Wish I'd thought of it: I'd have had thin ones. Jonah" – Jonah McLeod, the *Chronicle*'s chief photographer – "would have had tall ones: save him taking a stepladder to markings. Shad could have had five senses like everyone else, the Town Clerk could have avoided that wall eye, and as for people who deliberately pick genes with an extra chromosome on them – well, you can't call that normal, can you? Freaks, the lot of them! Only a matter of time before they all murder someone."

Dan Sale had been subjected to a lot of abuse in his time, every journalist has. But not much of it had come from colleagues, and none had accused him of prejudice. He hardly knew how to respond. He thought it was monstrously unfair. But even when they were arguing he respected Rosie Holland's opinion, and it was enough to stop him dismissing it as febrile nonsense. He'd never seen himself as a bigot. But had he become one? Had other people seen him that way all along?

Rosie saw his hesitation as weakness and went in for the kill. "In fact, it's hard to see why we need a problem page at all. If everyone's problems are basically their own fault, maybe we're just encouraging them by trying to help. Tell you what – in future we'll just print a photo of you and the caption: 'It is your patriotic duty to be exactly like this'. Only grow a little toothbrush moustache first."

She was out of the office and stamping down the corridor before either man found the presence of mind to shut his mouth.

Alex was on her way back from the coffee machine when she met Rosie emerging from the offices of The Primrose Path with a cardboard box under her arm. She stared until her eyes began to water, then she blinked. "Where are you going?"

"Home," said Rosie shortly.

"But . . ." It was Monday morning, still too early for lunch, even in Rosie's book. "We have things to do . . ."

"No," Rosie corrected her savagely, "*you* have things to do. Specifically, you have a page to produce. I have two bits of advice for you. Don't take risks; and anything that goes wrong in the next six months, blame me."

Alex had no idea what she meant but not for a moment did she think Rosie was joking. "Tell me what's happened."

But Rosie shook her head. "Don't get involved, Alex. I have to, I've no choice, but you don't. Do what they need you to do, what Matt wants. At least think long and hard before you decide not to. There's a good job here for somebody: the right person can have a lot of fun and do a lot of good. I just don't think that person's me any more."

She went to shoulder past before Alex could see that some of the glitter in her eyes was not anger but tears. But Alex stood her ground firmly, a greyhound defying a pitbull terrier.

"Rosie, I can see you're upset. I don't know why, I don't know who said what, but I'm absolutely sure that nobody wants you to leave. Not Matt, not Dan, and not you. Put that box down while I get another coffee and we talk about this."

Protesting weakly, Rosie nevertheless allowed herself to be backed into the office. She put the box on Alex's desk, where she could sweep it up again with more speed and dignity than if she put it on the floor, and lowered herself into Alex's chair. She looked like a buffalo ready to stampede at a moment's notice.

"Now, don't you move," said Alex, her gaze like nails. "If you get out of that chair before I come back I will never speak to you again."

She meant to be away no more than a minute. A stranger to the word Urgency, Rosie never did anything in under a minute. But as she wrestled with the geriatric coffee machine, the lift door opened and Matt, warm-cheeked and flustered, spilled out. "Alex! Is she still here?"

Alex gestured back along the corridor. "She's in my office. Matt, what's happened?"

He shouldn't have told her. At least, he shouldn't have told her then. There were more pressing needs that had brought him here at as close to a run as his prosthetic foot could manage. But he couldn't brush her off while he dealt with the immediate crisis. He told her what had passed between Rosie and Dan Sale in the editor's office.

Alex listened in open-mouthed horror. "She called him a Nazi?"

"She did. But not till Dan called Shad a freak."

Alex put both hands to her face. "Oh my God. No wonder she's ready to leave!"

"She is? Alex, I have to talk to her. Things have gone quite far enough, the fences between them are going to take some mending as it is. If she storms out of the building, I don't think she'll ever come back."

"What will you say?"

Matt gave a harassed shrug. "Beats me. But something. They have to get talking again. Through me, if that's the only way they can. I won't let everything they've achieved end in meltdown!"

Alex nodded. "All right. We'll talk to them. We'll talk to them both. When they've calmed down they'll start seeing sense, trade apologies and work out what's to be done about all of this." She set off along the corridor at a brisk walk.

But they'd wasted too much time already. Alex's door was open and the office was empty. Rosie and her cardboard box had gone.

Ten

She didn't go home, she went to Prufrock's. She knew she'd behaved badly, needed someone to confess to.

The piebald Land Rover was parked in Foxford Lane.

Her first instinct was to come back later. She wasn't sure why, but she didn't particularly want to see Shad right now. It wasn't that she blamed him for any of this. It was more embarrassment that kept her sitting in her car outside the little red-brick house. She was ashamed of what had been said about him. He'd never know about it because she wasn't going to tell him and she couldn't imagine anyone else doing. But she knew if she saw him now she'd be unable to look him in the eye. Better to avoid him until she had her own emotions under control.

But her best intentions went for nothing when the front door – it really did have roses round it – opened and Prufrock peered out. She felt she'd been caught reading under the covers after lights out. "Rosie? I thought I heard your car. Don't just sit there, come inside."

Any excuse she made now would sound impossibly phony. She sighed and did as he said.

"We're in here." Prufrock led the way through to the little kitchen with its Welsh dresser precisely stacked with Albert roses china. Shad was hunched on a bentwood chair, his elbows on the table. From the way he looked up, Rosie thought he was about as glad to see her as she was to see him.

"Shad," she said levelly. The gardener grunted a reply.

He wasn't dressed for work; he was dressed as he had been the morning she saw him setting off to see his psychiatrist. "How are you getting on with Doctor Cunningham?"

His eyes flicked her face as if she'd suggested something faintly improper. "'Right." If he'd clipped the word any shorter he'd have been left with just the vowel.

Sometimes Arthur Prufrock seemed totally oblivious to other people's feelings. Rosie had puzzled over this, thinking it an odd failing in a man whose career had consisted of nurturing sensitive young souls towards manhood. Then she'd realised it wasn't a blind spot but a deliberate policy. He ignored their silent pleas to be left alone when he knew that what they really needed was to talk.

So he took no notice of the set of Shad's shoulders and his monosyllabic responses and acted as though the three of them were here for a jolly chinwag. "Shad was telling me all about it," he said cheerily. "It sounds fascinating. Tell Rosie about the hypnotism, Shad."

Almost against her wishes, curiosity stirred in Rosie's breast. "Hypnotism?"

Shad shook his head, the thick curls in his eyes. "Not really."

"Near enough," said Prufrock encouragingly. "Go on, tell her." But he didn't.

With a jolt of surprise Rosie realised that he didn't want to talk to her for exactly the same reason she didn't want to talk to him. He was embarrassed. Had they been talking about her? But Prufrock's brow was clear; besides which it wasn't his style. If he'd had anything critical to say he'd have said it to her face. So someone else had said something to Shad on the subject of Rosie Holland.

"Andrew Cunningham," she said musingly. "Should I know that name? Have we met, I wonder?" Not that she worried overmuch about telling untruths, but she was pleased with how she'd managed to give a false impression without actually lying.

"Shouldn't think so," said Shad rapidly, which was all the confirmation Rosie needed. There was no reason he should know one way or another, and no need for him to venture an opinion, unless Cunningham had raised the issue first.

Rosie raised an eyebrow. "It's not that unlikely. We're both members of the medical fraternity."

Shad actually squirmed. "He's not from around here."

"Neither am I." Then she started feeling a little guilty. So Doctor Cunningham had commented on their friendship. It wasn't a secret, nor was Shad responsible for whatever he'd said. He'd probably been looking for a way to get the taciturn young man talking, began with the story that had made the national Press four months earlier. Nothing wrong with that. Maybe he'd made a joke about the *Skipley Chronicle*'s Agony Aunt which, with characteristic gravity, Shad hadn't recognised as such. "Maybe I'm mistaken. Where is he from?"

Shad didn't answer. Prufrock did. "North Midlands, Shad was saying. Terribly well thought-of, apparently. One of *the* top men at recovering lost memories."

"Well, that's what we want all right," nodded Rosie; though it occurred to her to wonder who had acquainted Shad with these complimentary assessments. Perhaps Marsh had. It hardly seemed likely that the great man himself would stoop to impressing a gypsy gardener. "So what's this about hypnosis?"

This subject pleased Shad no better than the last. His broad shoulders gave an awkward shrug. "It isn't hypnosis. He just . . . talks. He turns the light down and tells me to relax, and then we talk."

"About what happened?"

"I don't *remember* what happened," he said for the hundredth time. "Why is it so hard for everyone to believe that? Don't you think I could have made up a better story if I wanted to? I don't remember going to the sidings, and I don't remember what happened there. All right? I'm not pretending, I'm not covering up, I just don't remember."

"Then what do you talk about?" asked Rosie mildly.

"Different stuff." His dark eyes dropped, his manner defensive.

Like me, for instance, thought Rosie. She didn't mind being the butt of a joke – she'd made enough in her time, many in extremely dubious taste, to recognise laughter as the uniquely human divinity – but she couldn't think what they'd said to leave Shad feeling so guilty. Or why a psychiatrist tasked with something this important should be wasting time poking fun at someone who wasn't involved. "What – the power of the yen in the Tiger Economies?"

He didn't know what she was talking about. His expression triggered a pang of remorse in her. She knew it bothered him when people talked over his head like that and she still couldn't break the habit. The problem was that he was intelligent but not well informed; as distinct from many of her acquaintances who were well informed but not terribly intelligent. This sort of thing passed as light banter around the coffee machine at the *Chronicle*, but Shad spent his working day around vegetables and had never learnt the art of repartee. Because he couldn't keep up he felt stupid and never wondered if there was any point to it.

Rosie sighed, pulled out another of the kitchen chairs and sat down. "Sorry, Shad. I've had a bad day."

Prufrock glanced at the clock with a raised eyebrow. "Already?"

She shrugged. "How long does it take to get sacked?"

She hadn't meant to announce it quite so bluntly. But it was a relief to have it out in the open, not to be waiting for a suitable moment.

If she'd been looking to create an effect she could hardly have bettered the way the little room went suddenly still. Prufrock sat down abruptly and Shad sat up.

"Rosie – what have you *done*?" Prufrock managed at last.

She blew out her cheeks. She might tell him what she and Dan Sale had argued about, but not now, not with Shad sitting there. "I compared my editor to Adolf Hitler. I suppose it could be considered a constructive resignation."

"Well, for heaven's sake," said Prufrock, "go back and apologise! Before he tells everyone what happened and can't change his mind."

"I *will* apologise," Rosie promised. "I shouldn't have said that, it wasn't fair and I'll tell him so. I have no problems about apologising to him: he's a good and decent man, and I'm sorry I lost my temper. But it won't alter the fact that we were arguing over something so fundamental that I can't work for him any more. He won't do things my way; I won't do them his."

"There's no room for compromise?"

She shook her head. "It's an either/or situation. There is no middle way."

Prufrock was nodding slowly, the kind of mesmeric nodding engaged in by parcel-shelf German Shepherds. "That can happen. Sometimes there is no room for accommodation. I still think you should talk to him – explain that – when you're calmer and not as ready to throw insults at one another."

Of course he was right. "I will."

"Soon."

"Arthur, I will. Tonight, after work. I'll catch him after everyone else has left. We might have come to a parting of the ways but it doesn't have to be this acrimonious."

Shad levered himself up from the table and stood for a moment, looking as if he didn't know what to do with his hands. They were large and strong with dark hairs on their backs, and for once they were clean. He shoved them out of sight in his pockets. "I'd better get off. I've a couple of calls to make."

Prufrock saw him out. "I'll see you on Friday, if you have the time." He gave the impish smile that surprised people who thought him a dry old stick. "There'll be plenty of time to tidy up the topiary then."

Shad grinned. That was the sort of joke he understood.

Rosie was waiting when Prufrock returned to the kitchen. "Isn't he coming tomorrow?"

"He can't. Another appointment with his psychiatrist."

Rosie frowned. "How often does he go?"

"Every morning," said Prufrock. "For an hour from ten o'clock. Except sometimes it runs over, which is why he's getting behind with his work."

"To say one of them's only interested in something the other's forgotten," said Rosie, "they're doing an awful lot of talking."

"That's how it seemed to me," confessed Prufrock. "But I've never had any dealings with psychiatry, I don't know how long it takes."

"Well, it's not like lancing a boil," admitted Rosie. "It does take time. I'm just surprised they're still spending so many hours on it if they're making no progress. I'd have thought it was time to go back to Marsh and say, you know, something may surface eventually but don't hold your breath."

"Apparently he thinks they'll succeed," said Prufrock. "He told Shad it's there to be found if they can just find the right key."

"I admire his confidence," said Rosie. "Miracles performed instantly, the impossible takes a little longer?"

Prufrock nodded. "Seven days at the outside."

"*What*?"

"That's what he told Shad. At least," Prufrock amended honestly, "that's what Shad thinks he said. That they can expect a breakthrough inside a week if they keep at it."

Pathologists and psychiatrists almost never cross one another's paths. The patients of the one are too far gone to be of interest to the other. Pathologists know surgeons – usually nervous ones – and psychiatrists know physicians, and some physicians admit to knowing a surgeon or two, but that's about as far as interdisciplinary relations go. The only contact between the mortuary and the shrinks is the lady with the tea trolley.

The inevitable consequence is that psychiatrists and pathologists don't understand one another's science and doubt one another's usefulness. Rosie had never in her life referred a patient for psychiatry; equally, no one in analysis ever felt better for a trip to the morgue. So Rosie didn't need to know anything against Doctor Andrew Cunningham to have reservations about his procedures. She was predisposed at an almost genetic level to think that psychiatry was as helpful for traumatic amnesia as decapitation.

Her brow furrowed. "You can whip somebody's leg off in a minute and a half if you have to, but mostly psychiatry takes longer than that."

"I don't suppose there's usually this sort of urgency," said Prufrock reasonably. "Mr Marsh needs results. Doctor Cunningham has to find a way into Shad's mind, and sooner rather than later. I imagine that's why he needs to see him so often. An appointment once a week might achieve as much, but it would take too long to do it."

Rosie sniffed. "I just hope Marsh is pursuing his inquiries by other means as well. Whoever killed that poor girl is safer with every day that passes, and I'm not convinced Shad can help however hard he tries. If he didn't see anything and doesn't know anything, it doesn't matter how deep they delve, they won't find an answer."

"I suppose," said Prufrock slowly, "they have to find whatever's there. Until they have, they won't know if they're missing something. Can hypnosis help?"

Rosie shrugged. "That depends who you ask. A lot of reputable practitioners swear by it; people who undergo it mostly find it a positive experience. On the other hand, there are those who claim there's no such thing – that it's an illusion shared by the practitioner and the patient and you get the same results by telling the patient to pretend he's been hypnotised. I suppose, if you get results you're entitled to call it a success."

Prufrock was struggling with this. "You mean . . . if he's suppressing what happened, as long as he believes that hypnotism will release it he's able to let it go?"

"Something like that. Hell, Arthur, don't look at me like that – it's a long time since I had to consider the mental state of my patients!"

"But doesn't that suggest he has something to hide?"

"It suggests that maybe there's something he doesn't want to deal with. It can be something he feels bad about without being in any way to blame."

"For example . . . ?"

To Rosie it was obvious. "For example, apart from her murderer Shad was the only living soul who knew that girl was in trouble. He knew, he was there, and still he couldn't save her. That would make anyone feel bad. But most of us would know we weren't responsible. Shad thinks with his emotions. Maybe what happened is that when he woke up beside the girl, and she was dead, the guilt of letting it happen swamped him, and the only way he could get through was to batten it down under hatches.

"Where a psychiatrist can maybe help is by persuading him that it's all right to lift the hatches again. That her death is the responsibility of the man who killed her, not someone who tried to save her and failed. That it's natural to feel he could have done more, but hindsight is a wonderful thing and what matters is that he tried to help. If Cunningham can convince him of that, if it really is a psychological barrier then maybe he'll let himself remember."

"Then I hope it's soon," said Prufrock quietly. "I don't very much like what it's doing to him."

Rosie frowned. She hadn't noticed much of a difference. Of course, she'd been preoccupied too. "In what way?"

Prufrock considered. "It's all he can think of. What Doctor Cunningham said, what Doctor Cunningham wants him to work on, what Doctor Cunningham had for his breakfast near as damn it." He wasn't a man who swore: for him this was strong language. "As if the man was his guru. Shad's not like that. He's not easily impressed by people. The last time he talked about someone like this, as if they knew the whereabouts of the Holy Grail . . ." He stopped abruptly. The pink cheeks blushed furiously red.

"What? Arthur?"

It was too late to wish he hadn't started. Honesty was the only policy now. Under the little white moustache he gave a wry smile. "I'm sorry, I shouldn't have said that. He'd be deeply embarrassed if he knew. But he's a big fan of yours, Rosie. If you ever need a getaway driver for a bank robbery, Shad's your man. He'd never run off at the sound of sirens and leave you standing on the pavement with a sack marked Swag."

Rosie grinned at the picture he conjured up. There were things she could imagine doing time for but bank robbery wasn't one. Deeper than the amusement, she was surprised and touched that she'd had the same sort of effect on Shad Lucas that he'd had on her. The first day they met she'd recognised him as an extraordinary individual, as difficult, delicate and rewarding to nurture as some of his flowers. She knew what she'd gained from knowing him – not least, a part of the success she'd made of The Primrose Path. Well, up until now. She'd bullied him, used him, finally got him hurt. It was more than she'd hoped for that he reckoned to have got something out of knowing her too.

"Actually," she said, "I'd always seen you in that role."

Prufrock shook his head firmly. "I don't drive. I'll have to be the look-out man."

Rosie kept her word. At six fifteen, when she knew Dan Sale would be the last man left in the *Chronicle* building, she let herself in and moved quietly through the empty corridors. She was in no hurry. This had to be done, but she wasn't looking forward to it.

As she approached his office she heard the printer attached to his computer terminal chattering inside. Rosie drew a deep breath and tapped at his door.

"Come in," said Sale. Though he had thought himself alone in the building, he didn't sound surprised.

Instead of marching in breezily as always, Rosie opened the door just wide enough to stick her head through. Her voice was subdued; small, even. "You're sure?"

The editor came slowly to his feet like a stick insect unfolding behind the desk. A spread hand repeated the invitation. "Rosie," he said patiently, "will you stop acting like a convent girl who's been caught reading *Stud* and come in here and talk to me properly."

Meekly she took the chair he indicated. It was the large, strong one he'd bought after she came to work here. "I am sorry, Dan. I said all sorts of things I shouldn't have – and not just because you're my boss but because they aren't true. You aren't any of the things I called you, and I'm sorry if I hurt you. I'm sorry, too, if I've let you down."

Dan Sale smiled. People who'd known him for years had never seen him smile. They thought it was because he hadn't a sense of humour. But it's impossible to survive in journalism without one. It was more that Sale had the perfect face – long, lugubrious, the wrinkles deeply entrenched – for his sort of humour, which was wry and satirical rather than gut-busting. He didn't smile much because he'd learned to keep a straight face.

This wasn't one of those occasions. His smile was warm and

understanding, two facets he kept hidden from young reporters. But Rosie wasn't one of his young reporters.

"A newspaper," he said, "is more like a family than most businesses. Right and wrong, wise and unwise, fair and unfair aren't always clear, and there's room for honest people to disagree. Sometimes it goes a bit further than polite disagreement – though I don't remember the last time anyone called me Hitler!"

Rosie squirmed with embarrassment.

"All I'm saying is, it's nothing to worry about. I mightn't have been called that before, but in nearly forty years in this business I've been called worse. One of the things I'm paid for is having a thick skin. So don't worry about my feelings, Rosie. Some of it I had coming: I shouldn't have called Shad a freak, of course it upset you, you were entitled to be angry. No, I wasn't hurt – well, only momentarily. And I've never felt you have, or were likely to, let me down.

"There's only one thing you have to worry about – and I'm worrying about it too – and that's how we're going to proceed. Because we still have the dilemma we had first thing this morning: if Shad comes out of this badly, the *Chronicle* does too."

Rosie nodded. "Not if I resign."

Impatience flickered across Sale's face. "Rosie, the last thing I want is your resignation! And the second-last thing I want is for you to do something you're uncomfortable with, and I suppose that includes leaving him to cope alone with whatever mess he's got himself into. If he has. Maybe he hasn't, maybe it'll all work out all right. Damn it, maybe he'll identify the killer and make heroes of us all! But I feel we should be prepared in case that isn't how it happens."

From this perspective it was hard to remember how they'd let a discussion of the options deteriorate into a slanging match. Rosie nodded slowly. "If the worst comes to the worst, would it get the *Chronicle* off the hook if you fired me then? As publicly as necessary?"

He thought about it. "Probably. But I don't want a sacrifice. You're worth more to the paper writing your page than hung out to dry to appease the mob. I think we have to brazen it out. Keep emphasising that we've done nothing wrong, that you stood by a friend at a time when there was no evidence against him, that when that changed – if that changes – you behaved honourably in a difficult situation."

In every way that mattered he'd come round to her point of view. Which was ironic, really, because the more she thought about it the more she thought he was right first time. "I appreciate that, Dan. And like I said before, I don't think I have much choice as to what I do now. But you have to protect the paper. If this blows up in our faces, I'll go. Alex will run the page. With any luck people won't see her as involved, so when I go they'll want her to succeed."

"Rosie, you haven't listened to a word I've said!"

"I have, Dan. And I really do appreciate it. But I'm not going to put thirty people's jobs and Matt Gosling's investment at risk. If we find out that Shad killed that girl, you can have my resignation or you can fire me, but one way or the other I'll go."

Sale didn't say anything because he hoped, even in that extremity, he'd be able to persuade her not to.

After a moment Rosie spoke again. "Dan, tell me if it would be a mistake. But I think maybe I ought to go over to PVF and talk to them. If – and God forbid – Shad stabbed that girl, the most likely reason is that she was pursuing him for their poxy programme. If I ask her face to face, I think maybe Marta Frank would tell me. If she was – well, at least we'd know the worst. If she wasn't, then it was someone else and we could start breathing again."

Sale too would be glad to know, one way or the other. And one way or the other, he thought it could take some of the heat out of the situation if the *Chronicle* and PVF were seen to be on speaking terms again. "All right. With one proviso."

"Which is?"

"However much she annoys you, you don't deck her too."

Eleven

PVF was a very small television company: the receptionist had to ask someone in a back office to watch the desk while she showed the visitor upstairs. If it hadn't been Rosie Holland she might simply have given her directions, but she was uneasy about giving Rosie free rein in this place.

You've Been Had wasn't the only show they made but it was the only one with much of a following. As its producer, Marta Frank was entitled to a decent office on the second floor and her initial in the company logo. The others were Peters and Vaughn, but the partnership was known throughout the industry as Puff TV, which was unfortunate, but better than not being known at all.

Frank was waiting at her door, showed Rosie warily inside. She didn't know what to expect of this meeting, only that it was better to get it over than to avoid it.

All the way over Rosie had been rehearsing what to say, and how to say it without getting thrown out. In the event it wasn't a problem. Whatever else Marta Frank was, she was a professional – she wanted to know why Rosie had come. If she decided to throw her out after that, she'd get someone bigger to do it.

Rosie kept her voice low and stuck rigidly to the point. "I suggest that, as far as we can, we put past differences behind us and concentrate on the present situation. The murder of Jackie Pickering makes everything that's gone before vanishingly trivial. I don't know if it's anything to do with me or you; I think we'd both feel a lot better if we could establish that it wasn't."

It was a promising start. Frank dipped her head in fractional acknowledgement. It was Rosie's turn again.

"All right. I don't know how much the police told you about how Jackie was found. Did they tell you who found her?"

This time Marta Frank shook her head fractionally.

"Shad Lucas."

Rosie left his name hanging in the air. If it meant nothing to Frank, their business was largely complete: Pickering wasn't hunting Shad and it was merest coincidence that he stumbled on to her murder. In that case both women could down a stiff whisky in celebration and get on with their lives.

Marta Frank's narrow eyebrows rocketed up her alabaster brow, and Rosie's heart plummeted. Her voice was leaden. "I see the name means something to you."

"Of course it does! I read about him in your newspaper. I didn't know he found Jackie." A pause while she thought about that. Rosie saw a shock wave travel through her eyes as the implications struck. "You mean . . . he didn't *just* find her?"

"I don't mean anything of the kind," said Rosie roughly. "I don't know what happened. *He* doesn't know what happened. He can't remember. But the same thing occurred to me that's just occurred to you – that if he went to the station to meet Jackie it was because of what occurred between you and me. If she lured him there to have a shot at him for your programme and he panicked and lost control, then you and I are not blameless in her death."

Frank's voice was thin with shock. "Ms Holland, what exactly do you want me to say?"

"I want you to say that I'm imagining this. That it never occurred to you to get back at me by hounding a vulnerable young man who has the misfortune to be a friend of mine. That Jackie may well have annoyed someone on your hit list, but it wasn't Shad and therefore it wasn't because I hit Dick Chauncey. That's what I *want* you to say. What I *expect* you to tell me is the truth, however unpalatable it may be."

She didn't get a reply for so long she was beginning to think she wouldn't get one. It wouldn't be difficult to draw an inference from that. Rosie was beginning to fear the worst.

Then Frank drew a slow breath. "All right. Cards on the table? We considered it. I knew we wouldn't get under your guard again;

I thought that turning our attentions to a friend of yours might be just as rewarding. Shad Lucas was an obvious choice because of who he is, what he does. What he's done for you. If you use the services of a psychic you have to expect raised eyebrows. From our point of view, it was a win/win situation. If he's genuinely clairvoyant it would make an amazing programme; and if he isn't it would be screamingly funny, not least because of how it would rebound on you.

"So yes, I thought about doing a programme on him; and I knew he wouldn't cooperate so it would involve subterfuge. But the more I thought about it, the more uneasy I became. I decided we weren't justified in exposing him to ridicule primarily in order to embarrass you."

"That was generous," murmured Rosie.

Frank twitched a brief grin. "Not really. If it went off half-cocked, we'd have got the backlash. What we do, it's only funny if nobody gets hurt. You weren't hurt by what we did: annoyed maybe, but not hurt. Most of our subjects aren't even annoyed. When they've got over the surprise they enjoy the joke. It's their fifteen minutes of fame. I don't want to see anyone damaged."

"And you knew you could damage Shad."

"So I decided not to do it. He's a very private young man, isn't he? I don't know if that's from choice or necessity or just how it's worked out, but I was afraid he'd be unable to cope with either the fame if he acquitted himself well or the ridicule if he didn't. I have no idea if he's a real psychic, or even if there is such a thing, but the more I learned about him the surer I was that he's not entirely normal. After that I didn't see how we could use him. It would be like making fun of the mentally handicapped – too easy for it to be amusing."

Rosie hadn't expected her to have scruples, even these rather pragmatic ones. "I'm glad you recognise that people are entitled to their privacy."

Marta Frank bridled. "The pity is that you didn't reach the same conclusion three months ago. Shad Lucas lived here in total obscurity for six or seven years until you came along. You used him. You hurt him two different ways: you got him shot and you made him famous. Now everyone in Skipley knows it's not just water he can find, it's missing persons and dead bodies. That's a lot of fame for someone whose only ambition for eight years was to keep his head down."

That hurt; and it hurt because it was true. Rosie's voice actually trembled. "You think I don't know that? That's why I'm here. Because I'm scared shitless that I started a sequence of events that led to a killing. I don't think, in his right mind, he'd harm anyone, however much they threatened him. But I can't quite dismiss the possibility that someone threatening him with that – notoriety, exposure, the full glare of publicity he wouldn't begin to know how to handle – would drive him momentarily crazy. That that's what he daren't remember: a moment's madness in which he struck out at something that terrified him and Jackie ended up dead. That's what I need from you, Ms Frank: your word that, whatever they were both doing that evening, they hadn't gone to the station to meet one another."

Occasionally Frank did cruel things but she wasn't a cruel woman. She could have prolonged this for her own satisfaction, but she didn't. Her voice warmed a little. "Rosie, I understand how you feel. I feel the same way: if you're implicated, so am I. So I'll tell you everything I know. We looked at the possibility of doing a programme on Shad Lucas, and we dismissed it. I can't swear that Jackie wasn't there to see him, but she wasn't there to see him for me."

The relief was almost enough to make Rosie cry. She cleared her throat instead. "Um . . . OK. Fine. Then what *was* she working on?"

"For me? Nothing that could have got her into any trouble."

"Could she have been working for someone else as well? Doing research for another programme? – something hard-hitting enough to pitch her against someone with more to lose than his dignity?"

Frank considered. "She wasn't working on any other programmes for us. She just might have been working on her apprentice piece."

"Apprentice piece?"

"Researcher isn't the best job in television. It's hard work, long hours, it can get unpleasant and it doesn't get the recognition it deserves. Mostly you only get noticed when you've cocked up. But it's a good way to get started. It puts you where the action is, and if you're good enough at some point you get the chance to show what you can do. An ambitious researcher is always looking for the story that everyone else missed. You get a good one and you may not be a researcher much longer."

"So Jackie could have been looking for her ticket to a better job?"

"I'm sure she was. No one ever accused Jackie of lacking ambition. But if she found it, I don't know what it was."

Rosie thought about it; and as she thought she felt the sense of relief that none of this was her fault begin to grow thin and dissipate like morning mist burning off. "There's one possibility – that Jackie thought she could land Shad after you'd given up on him. She knew you wanted another crack at me; she knew you quite fancied Shad until the difficulties became obvious. If she thought she could land him safely, that could have been her apprentice piece.

"She was a bright girl, I gather, and Shad isn't much of a ladies' man. He hasn't a lot of friends: if she took the time to cultivate him he'd have flowered for her. But if he thought she liked him too, and then it turned out she was only using him to get at me . . ." Rosie shook her head unhappily, the brown curls dancing. "If she was complaining he'd slapped her face, that I could believe. But a knife? Whatever she did to him, I don't believe he stabbed her."

"Somebody did."

"Then it was somebody else." She wasn't sure if she genuinely believed that or was trying to convince herself. "So maybe her story was on someone else too. Would she have told anyone in the office?"

Frank doubted it. "I think she'd keep it to herself. This was her bid for the top, she'd be scared of someone muscling in."

"What about notes? Did she keep any?"

"The police looked when they came here on Thursday. They took her diary, her notebooks and her computer. But I don't think they found anything. I wouldn't expect them to."

"The other researchers – might they know anything?"

"Again, nothing the police found helpful. But you're welcome to talk to them." She led the way down the corridor to the large room shared by the junior staff. Four of the desks were occupied; another was empty and unnaturally tidy.

Marta Frank didn't need to tell them who Rosie Holland was but she did anyway. She asked them to help if they could.

They were young, around Jackie's age, keen and bright, and they filled in the gaps for themselves. Frank wanted this sorted quickly and the blame lodged if possible on someone unconnected with *You've Been Had.*

"I'll leave you to it." The producer smiled. "Just in case there's something the GC know that senior management isn't supposed to."

"GC?" asked Rosie when she'd left the room.

"Gophers Club," said one of the researchers. "It defines our status in the organisation so aptly that no one even thinks of it as a joke any more."

Rosie sympathised. "Which is why, I suppose, researchers want to become producers."

"That and the money."

"And the best way is by pulling off a coup."

"It's about the only way, at least around here." That note of sourness in the girl's voice reflected the frustration which had driven her colleague to hunt a dangerous quarry.

"Would a psychic gardener have been a suitable candidate?"

"Ms Holland," said a young man in a bow tie, "if Jackie'd said she could get Shad Lucas *we'd* have killed her, and scrambled over the body to get there first."

Someone said, "Tom!" disapprovingly, but no one contradicted him.

"Did she ever mention what she was working on for this apprentice piece of hers?"

"Not to us. I wouldn't expect her to: television is a dog-eat-dog world. Maybe to a personal friend?"

"Who were her friends?"

A chorus of shrugs went round the room. "There was Debbie," suggested Tom.

"Debbie?"

"Debbie Burgess. They did their degree together. I don't know where she lives but they talked by phone at least once a week. Jackie tried to get her a job here, but Marta didn't think she was tough enough. There was a bit of a history, I think."

"A history?"

"I think so," said Tom. "I'm only going off what I overheard, but yes, there was something. I could never quite make out if it was a mental illness, trouble with the law or what. For obvious reasons Jackie kept her voice down when they were talking about it."

Rosie nodded, just absorbing information. She went and stood by Jackie's desk, hoping for inspiration. "How did she seem? In the last week or two, say."

"All right," said one of the girls.

But Tom knew better. He seemed to have taken rather an interest in Jackie Pickering. "I thought she was preoccupied."

"Really? In what way?" But he wasn't able to be specific. Rosie tried putting words in his mouth. "As if, maybe, there'd been developments in something she'd been working on?"

He nodded. "That could have been it."

"But she didn't talk about it, and she didn't keep notes."

"'Fraid not."

Defeated, Rosie's gaze dropped to the desk. At length she said, "Chicken fried rice, spring rolls, lychees."

They stared at her as if she was mad. The boy in the bow tie ventured, "Pardon?"

"Chicken fried rice, spring rolls, lychees. It's what it says on the phone pad."

They thought it was pretty obvious why. "It's what she ordered for lunch."

"When?"

One of the girls knew. "Wednesday. I had some of her lychees. It was the last day she was here." She sniffed.

"So she'd have phoned the order in . . . when – about midday?"

"Nearer eleven thirty. *Why*?"

"Because it isn't the last thing she wrote on this pad. Over the top, and therefore after eleven thirty, she scribbled, 'Got you, you bastard!'"

Nobody knew what it meant, but clearly the police had missed it when they cleared her desk. Rosie found an envelope and manoeuvred the pad into it with a pencil. "I'll take it round to Superintendent Marsh. Just in case it's significant."

Marsh was in his office when she arrived so she took it up and explained how she'd come by it. He listened patiently, giving little away. She couldn't tell if he thought it meant anything or not.

But he was glad she'd brought it to him. It occurred to him she might have served her own cause better by concealing it. He felt moved to offer something in return.

"Forensics have come back on the samples we sent them. The fingerprints on the knife were Lucas's – all of them. And the blood on the front of his shirt was Jackie Pickering's."

Neither was unexpected. Shad had tried to help her and she'd bled on him. The absence of any other prints on the blade could suggest merely that the killer had been more careful than the man who discovered the body.

"None of this proves Shad killed her, you know," Marsh said gently.

"I know," said Rosie. "I just wish I could find something that proved he didn't. Or that someone else had a reason to."

Warning bells rang in Harry Marsh's head. "Ms Holland, that's my job, not yours. Don't get involved. You'll only get in my way and if by any chance you were successful you'd put yourself in danger. Leave it alone. I'll get to the truth."

"I suppose so."

He'd had more ringing endorsements. "Suppose?"

She forced a smile. "I mean, of course you will. I'll let you get on with it."

But from the way she reversed out of his office, Detective Superintendent Marsh was almost certain she had her fingers crossed behind her back.

Twelve

"I need to talk to Debbie Burgess," Rosie said thoughtfully. "If anybody knows what Jackie was working on, she does."

"Where does she live?" asked Prufrock.

"I don't know. She went to university in Nottingham but that doesn't mean she lived there."

"The university admissions office would have a home address for her. Though they mightn't give it to you."

"I'll ask them nicely." She meant, I'll lie.

She didn't ask for the admissions office, she asked for one of the media studies lecturers.

"It's Rosie Holland here, at the *Skipley Chronicle*." Prufrock nodded approvingly: the truth so far. "I've done something stupid and I'm hoping you can help. We had a graduate of yours looking for a position here. We want to offer her the job but I've lost her address. Debbie Burgess. You don't know where she lives?"

There was a pause as the man at the other end thought. "They were a local family. West Bridgford, I think; yes, Dootheboys Avenue. I don't know if they're still there."

"I don't suppose you know her father's name?" The initial would make the phone number easier to find.

There was a pause, not long but still slightly longer than it took either to say no or to give it. "Roy. I'm not likely to forget that, am I?"

"I suppose not," said Rosie, though she had no idea what he was talking about. "Roy Burgess?"

"Well, I don't expect it made the same impression in Birmingham that it did here."

"No," agreed Rosie. "What didn't?"

"That business with Debbie and her father. Oh God," he groaned then, "maybe I shouldn't be telling you. If she wanted you to know she'd have told you herself."

"Oh, she did," lied Rosie gamely. "About her father. I thought you meant . . . something else." She was making this up as she went along, hoping the man would keep talking long enough to start making sense.

"I suppose there's no point being coy about it after you've been in court. You should know that nobody here considered Debbie to blame."

Rosie shook her head vigorously. "Here, either."

"Good. Whatever actually happened, she was the victim."

"Undoubtedly."

"I'm glad she's finally got a job. I had a lot of time for Debbie, I always thought she'd make a good reporter. It was a great pity all that came up in the middle of her studies."

"Yes, indeed."

"Give her my regards. Tell her to drop in sometime."

"I will," nodded Rosie.

"Will you?" asked Prufrock when, with a sigh of relief, she put the phone down.

"And have to repeat that pack of lies? Of course not." She told him what had passed between them. "Now – what do you suppose it was all about?"

"A court case," reflected Prufrock. "Something involving Debbie Burgess and her father. And nobody at the university thought Debbie was to blame."

"I wonder who they blamed instead."

When Prufrock looked at her he could almost see the cogs and wheels spinning behind her eyes, the machinery of intellect in full production. "Rosie? What are you thinking?"

"So far as anybody knows, Debbie Burgess was Jackie Pickering's closest friend. They did the same course at university, afterwards Jackie tried to get her a job. But something happened to Debbie during those three years that the people at PVF called a mental illness, that her lecturer said resulted in a court case, that involved her father and that people didn't think was her fault. So maybe they thought it was his."

"Perhaps they did. How does that help?"

"Maybe it doesn't," admitted Rosie. "Unless Jackie blamed him too. Let's face it, doing research for a programme like *You've Been Had* gave her the opportunity to settle an old score if she had a mind to. Maybe, whatever he did or didn't do, Jackie blamed him for Debbie's illness and saw a chance to pay him back. Maybe Roy Burgess is the bastard on the phone pad."

Prufrock stared at her askance. "It's a shot in the dark," he said diplomatically.

"Of course it is. I don't care whether he's the bastard or not, as long as Shad isn't. The only reason anyone has to suspect Shad, apart from him finding the body, is that Jackie just might have been researching him, on the sly, for that accursed programme. Well, she just might have been researching Roy Burgess as well. It's neither more nor less likely."

"There's no reason to suppose he was even in Skipley."

"Until someone asks, there's no reason to suppose he wasn't."

Prufrock frowned. He knew Rosie quite well enough now to know that insouciance on her part was always an act. "*You* can't ask him anything," he said pointedly. "If you want to know, tell Mr Marsh about it – he'll make inquiries."

"I'll think about it," promised Rosie, which reassured him hardly at all.

"Got you, you bastard!"

Harry Marsh was still pondering that over lunch – a sandwich at his desk. There was something about it that bothered him, that wasn't right. It was too . . . personal. She wasn't referring to someone she was researching but to a quarry she'd been stalking. Someone who'd given her trouble, who'd given her the slip a time or two before finally succumbing.

Why should she feel that way about Shad Lucas? There was no evidence they'd even met. But perhaps that wasn't it. Perhaps that note of triumph came not from any baggage with him but from her situation at work. Marta Frank had considered fishing for Lucas, dismissed him as too difficult to land safely. If Jackie had seen a way, baited her hook and, at last, over the phone, persuaded him to bite, then 'Got you, you bastard!' was an understandable reaction.

But if Jackie had phoned him on Wednesday, hours before the blow to his head, why didn't Lucas remember? Well, because head injuries are like that – you forget the wife and kids but recognise the cat. There's no logic to it. He still didn't remember much that happened on Wednesday. Marsh knew he'd been at the Thurleys' until five because they said so.

So if she had spoken to him, it had to have been after five fifteen. He couldn't have been home before that. She'd called him, asked for a meeting – on God knows what pretext – and one of them had nominated the station later that evening. Why? If Shad was willing to see her, why not at home? If Jackie was worried about going to his flat, why go to the railway yards after dark?

But wait. Jackie left the office at five on the night she died; DS Burton had established that when he was mapping out her movements. If she'd called Shad later than that it had been from somewhere else – so what was the note doing on her desk?

So it *wasn't* Shad she called but someone else. Someone who had a reason to kill her? Someone she had reason to consider a bastard. But the same question applied: why agree to meet someone like that in such risky circumstances?

Maybe she hadn't. Maybe she'd met her killer somewhere that seemed safe; only one way or another he'd got the better of her and taken her to the sidings. That suggested the same kind of premeditation as the knife. He may not have gone to the meeting determined on killing her, but he was ready to if the need and the occasion arose.

'Got you, you bastard!' She *knew* something about him. Had they had dealings before? Certainly she knew something to his discredit. But she had to meet him. She needed something only he could give her.

Money? Was she blackmailing him? If the victim had been someone else, that was a line Marsh would have pursued. But

Jackie Pickering had a different agenda: she had her whole career to get on track. A good story would have been worth more to her than a suitcase full of unmarked notes.

A good story about whom? Marsh scowled into his mug. How long is a piece of string? How many angels can dance on the head of a pin? The question was meaningless. If Shad Lucas didn't kill Jackie Pickering, whoever did had been clever enough – or lucky enough – that his connection to her had not yet emerged. That was mainly her fault: in her wariness to keep her big story secret she'd been her killer's best ally. But something had led her to him, and it could lead the police to him too. There was a trail somewhere, if Marsh could pick it up.

The phone went.

"It's Andrew Cunningham, Harry."

Lengthy concentration had let cobwebs gather in Marsh's eyes. He blinked them clear. "Andrew, yes." Then, because he could think of only one reason for Cunningham to call him, his voice dropped an octave and he said it again with a quite different inflection. "Yes?"

"I think you should come round here."

The hairs on the back of Harry Marsh's neck stood up. "Is Shad Lucas with you?"

"Yes."

"Has he remembered something?"

"I think you should come round."

The piebald Land Rover was parked on the raked gravel in front of Cunningham's house. If he'd been their gardener the Cunninghams would have made Shad park it out of sight round the back. The idea that a patient might turn up in such a thing had clearly never occurred to them.

Dr Cunningham met Detective Superintendent Marsh and Detective Sergeant Burton at the door before they could ring the bell. "Come inside. Thanks for coming so quickly."

"It is a murder investigation," Marsh reminded him, a shade stiffly. "There aren't many things that take priority."

Cunningham nodded, without comment. "Two things I should

make clear. I called you because Shad asked me to. And I can't vouch for the truth of what he says. If you want my opinion, it's that he believes the story he's about to tell you. But there's nothing I can test or measure to prove it, no litmus paper I can stick on his tongue that'll turn black if he's telling fibs or remembering wrong. I'm not suggesting that is the case, just reminding you that psychiatrists get lied to quite as much as policemen. We too develop an instinct for spotting it, but we too can be wrong. I want you to be aware of that before you start interviewing him."

"All right, Andrew," said Marsh flatly, "I'll try to remember that sometimes people tell porkies. Can I see him now?"

There remained a faint ambivalence in Cunningham's expression. But he led the policemen through the office where he and Marsh had drunk elderflower wine to a small room off it. A study or den perhaps, it had been built without windows and was presently lit by a low-powered, reddish bulb in the desk lamp. The walls were lined with books, there was a leather armchair behind a table and another in the corner of the room which was currently occupied.

Shad Lucas didn't get up when Marsh went in. He remained sitting in the deep shadows, his face, half-hidden, cradled in one hand, his elbow on the arm of his chair.

"Shad," said Marsh, by way of acknowledgement. A fractional nod was all the reply he got.

He tried again. "Doctor Cunningham tells me you've made some progress at remembering what happened. On Wednesday night." As if they might have been talking about something else.

There was a long pause. Then Shad's voice came out of the shadows, low and breathy like something that had been lost. "I remember what happened to her. I saw what happened."

Doctor Cunningham had returned to his chair behind the table. There was a set of library steps of the sort that convert to a stool; Marsh moved them a little closer to Shad and quietly sat down. "Tell me about it."

He began where he'd begun before. "She was so scared. It wasn't what she expected. She thought she was in control of the situation. She'd worked through every move in her head, everything she would say, everything he could say or do. She thought she'd covered all the bases. She thought she had him in a corner, that he'd no choice left now but to do as she wanted. She thought she'd won.

"But it was a trap. She wasn't hunting him any longer, he was hunting her. He knew what she could do to him, what she meant to do, that she'd destroy him. He couldn't *survive* what she meant to do to him. He'd do anything to avoid it: anything. If he could have talked some sense into her . . . He didn't want to kill her. But mostly he wanted to be safe."

He was hardly making sense at all. He was talking about things he had no way of knowing – at least, things no eyewitness could have known. They were into that fuzzy area again, where Shad Lucas could be at once more helpful and less credible than the average witness. But Marsh was reluctant to stop and quiz him for fear he'd lose his way entirely. Also, he wasn't sure yet what he was hearing: a memory that had been lost, a memory that had been suppressed, an honest confusion of truths, half-truths and fantasy, or a downright lie. It seemed better to let him talk and go back to clarify the details later.

"They met on the station because she thought it was safe. There were plenty of people around, even at that time. She wasn't sure how he'd react when she told him what she had on him: shout, call her names, slap her face, just turn and walk away. She knew what she had to say would rock his world. But she thought she'd have the advantage of surprise, hadn't realised he already knew. He knew who she'd been talking to and the questions she'd been asking. He wasn't there to give her an interview: he was there to buy her silence, one way or another.

"She told him what she'd found out and what she was going to do with it. She had the whole damn programme mapped out – who'd come on and talk about him, what they'd say. She was pleased with herself; despite all the difficulties, she'd achieved what she'd set out to. She didn't think there was anything he could do now to stop her.

"But while they were talking, arguing rather, they were walking, and she was too wound up to take much notice of where. By the time she realised they'd gone beyond the end of the platform and were walking beside the tracks there was no one close enough to see she was in trouble. He grabbed her arm and dragged her deeper into the dark. When they came to the last wagon on the track, he threw her inside."

The silence stretched so long then that Marsh began to think he'd finished. But he hadn't, he was just looking for the courage to continue.

"She still thought she could talk her way out. Even then she couldn't believe he meant to harm her. In spite of what she'd done, what she knew, what she'd tried to do to him. She thought he might threaten her. She thought that if she went along, pretended she was too scared to go any further with it, he'd let her go and she could get her own back later. When she saw . . . when she saw . . ."

His voice had fallen to a whisper, grown so thin that any pressure on him now would have ripped great holes in it.

Harry Marsh hunched forward, peering at the young man's face, ashy-pale in the shadows, the sunken eyes burning as if in the grip of fever. Marsh thought fleetingly, Is this what it's like, being him? Is this what his gift means to him? The privilege of feeling other people's fear as if it were his own, other people's pain? How can he live like that? How can he stay sane?

Is he, in fact, sane?

He said softly, "What did she see, Shad?"

Shad sucked an unsteady breath through his teeth. "The knife. He had a knife. When she saw that, she knew she wasn't going to talk her way out of anything. The fear . . . It was like a tidal wave. I couldn't breathe for it.

"For a moment she froze. I thought, *Move*, oh Christ Jesus, move! – if you don't move you're going to *die* here! And after a second she did. She threw herself at him, tried to force her way past him; thought if she could catch him off balance, if she could just make the doorway, she might lose him in the dark. But he was ready for her. He moved the same time she did, brought the knife up between them. She ran herself on to it.

"It wasn't so much pain then as the shock. Her eyes were like saucers; her lips moved but there were no words, just a little spit. Then she was falling. The fear, the terrible fear, swelled out once, and then her thoughts began drawing inwards. Like water going down a plughole, spiralling tighter and tighter, and the darkness crowding in. The last of her consciousness faded and she was gone."

Marsh went on staring at him, amazed and aghast, long after the words had dried up. He had no idea how he was going to make a case of this, but perhaps that wasn't necessary. Perhaps, when he knew who was responsible, he could bring his case another way. He found his own voice, and was not surprised at the gravel in it. "You felt her die. You saw her die? You saw who killed her. Describe him, Shad. The man with the knife. Who is he? Where do I find him?"

In the dark of his corner, his eyes still shaded by his hand, Shad blinked. He looked puzzled, like a man roused from a trance. "What? I . . . I'm sorry, I'm not making it very clear. I didn't see anyone."

Marsh was confused utterly. It was as if he'd been reading this and turned over two pages at once. He stared at Shad, at Doctor Cunningham behind his desk, at Sergeant Burton who replied with a little puzzled shrug of his own. "But you said . . . You said you saw what happened."

Shad nodded slowly. He rubbed the side of his hand across his brow. "Yes. Oh yes. Of course I saw what happened. I was there – right there. There was no one else. My prints on the knife, her blood on my shirt – the explanation's obvious. So bloody obvious I never thought . . ."

He straightened in the chair, levered himself up on his strong arms and stood, still in the shadows, swaying slightly. "Call off the manhunt, Superintendent, you have your killer. I swear to you, I didn't know before today. But I know now. It was me."

Thirteen

Prufrock was cleaning his parlour when he heard the familiar engine and, looking out, saw the car he'd waved goodbye to only a couple of hours before pulling up once more at his gate. He went to the front door, was about to call a greeting and ask what she'd forgotten, then he saw the expression on her face and forgot everything else.

"Come inside. Tell me what's happened."

"It's Shad."

Almost nothing else would have brought her here looking like that. Grey wasn't a colour you associated with Rosie Holland.

Prufrock steeled himself. He closed the door and followed her into the parlour. Mostly they chatted in the kitchen, but that was because it was the only place Shad could join them without cleaning up first. But Shad wasn't here.

She didn't sit down. She stood in the middle of the little chintzy room, unsure how to start.

"Spit it out," Prufrock recommended softly.

So she did. "He says it was him. He says he remembers what happened, and what happened is that he killed Jackie Pickering."

The silence in the room was more than an absence of sound: it was a vacuum, a state in which sound was inconceivable. Neither of them would have been surprised if the clock had stopped ticking or a bird paused in flight outside the window.

Finally Prufrock found a voice of a kind, cracked and run up high, a plaint. "What have they *done* to him?"

Rosie breathed unsteadily into prayer-folded hands. She shook her head. "It isn't like that. Nobody beat a confession out of him.

You know he's been working with Doctor Cunningham to get back what he'd forgotten? Well, he succeeded, and this is what he found. This is what was lurking at the bottom of the black lagoon."

Prufrock stared at her in astonishment. "Rosie! Don't tell me you *believe* this nonsense?"

Her mouth opened and shut a couple of times before anything came out. In the short time she'd had this information – Marsh had called her because he didn't want to be responsible for an elderly ex-schoolmaster's heart attack – she'd agonised over how it had happened and why it had happened, but it hadn't occurred to her to wonder if it *had* happened. She wondered now. It seemed incredible that Shad could have got it wrong – imagined it, remembered wrong, lied . . . But it made no more credible a truth. Prufrock was right: there was room for doubt.

But she'd been too long answering. Anger, and hurt which was worse, flared in the pale blue eyes, clear and sharp as ice on periwinkles. "You do! Rosie, he's your friend. You know him, you know what he's like. He's not . . . smart. He can't make witty conversation to save his life. He's as out of place in the vodka and Volvo belt as you and I would be in the front line of the Bolshoi Ballet, if you want someone to make up the numbers for a glittering social occasion you'd be better asking Dolly the sheep.

"But if you need someone to stand by you when it matters, when all the witty, clever, sophisticated people you know have found urgent business elsewhere, when standing by you is going to take stamina and courage and the only reason anybody'd do it is the obligation which true friends owe to one another, then you could count on Shad Lucas as you could count on very few others. He's as honest as people come. You know that, Rosie. How can you think he might have killed a girl?"

Rosie was feeling pretty rotten, but not rotten enough to take that lying down. One unplucked eyebrow lifted querulously. "You mean, apart from the fact that he says so?"

"Says so!" snorted Prufrock. "You know the state he's in. Something horrendous happened to him, and six days ago he'd no idea what it was. Yesterday he thought he'd witnessed a murder; now he thinks he committed one. But why should we trust his memory now when it's been playing silly beggars for a week? There is such a thing as false memory, you know, where people remember something that never happened."

"I know that," snapped Rosie. "But it's not like he remembers meeting Elvis on the steps of Buckingham Palace. What he says he remembers is perfectly feasible. We know he was at the scene of the murder. He handled the knife, and he was close enough to the victim to get her blood on him. There's no proof that anyone else was present. In those circumstances, if he says he stabbed her we have to listen to him."

"It's a memory dredged up a week late out of an injured brain," retorted Prufrock. "If he found her dying, of course he'd try to help. He held her; perhaps he pulled the knife out, thinking that without it he could stem the bleeding. I know it's not good medical practice, but he isn't a doctor, he was just someone trying to deal with a grim situation he'd been catapulted into. Neither his fingerprints nor her blood make him a killer. We don't have to believe it just because he does."

They were shouting at one another because they didn't know where their anger should be directed. They had reacted to the shock in characteristically different ways: Rosie by trying to understand it, Prufrock by refusing to accept it. This was a reflection of their professional experience. When people confessed outrageous acts to Rosie, they were telling the truth and looking to her for some insight. But his own career had taught Prufrock the value of scepticism. He believed only that which made sense. This didn't, and he trusted his own judgement better than Shad's memory. He'd known Shad Lucas for two years – well enough to have seen him through triumph and disaster, well enough to have seen him in love, in pain and in tears – and he didn't believe he was capable of murder.

"All right," said Rosie, a tremor in her voice, "all right." She sat down. After a moment Prufrock did too. "So we aren't convinced. I don't think Marsh is either."

"What did he say?"

The superintendent had said that a confession obtained that

way had to be treated with great caution; that he'd require clear corroboration before he'd prefer charges; that there were problems with the timing; that Doctor Cunningham was continuing to work with Shad in the hope of uncovering details that would put the matter beyond doubt. Details that only the killer could know; or else some elaboration of the story that proved it a fantasy.

"Then, what?" asked Prufrock, puzzled. "He's sending him home?"

"Not exactly."

Fellowes Hall had been Doctor Cunningham's idea. Shad was afraid that whatever madness had driven him to kill and then hide the fact even from himself could recur. And indeed, if he'd done what he thought he'd done, reacted to a pushy TV researcher with lethal violence, then behind bars was the only place for him.

But Marsh didn't just want a man in jail, he wanted the right man in jail, and he didn't think he had the full picture yet. He wanted to understand what had happened, and with all that Shad had remembered he hadn't be able to explain why Jackie Pickering had to die. Until he could, Marsh wasn't prepared to rely on his recollections. He didn't consider the confession of a man who'd been suffering from amnesia a good foundation for a murder charge. There were also practical considerations. With strict limits to how long he could hold a suspect for questioning, he was reluctant to start the clock ticking until he could count on getting the answers he needed.

Cunningham proposed, as a compromise, admitting Shad to the addiction clinic where he was the senior consultant.

"Addiction clinic?" exclaimed Prufrock, his voice soaring. "They think he's made a habit of this?"

The point about an addiction clinic, Rosie explained, was that people arrived voluntarily, but most of them would leave within a day or two if there weren't systems in place to encourage them to stay. Fellowes Hall wasn't secure in the way that Broadmoor was secure, but the whole ethos was designed to keep damaged, irrational, often hysterical, sometimes violent people where they could be helped. It was an environment in which he could continue working with Shad until the doubts were resolved.

Prufrock mulled it over. "I suppose it makes a sort of sense," he conceded quietly. "Can we see him?"

"We can go now."

"It's that damned shrink's fault," Prufrock said thickly. For him, this was strong language. "I never did trust psychiatrists."

They were in the car now, heading east into the Warwickshire countryside. Rosie gave an awkward shrug. "You're not being fair. All he did was help Shad to look behind the wall he'd erected in his mind. You can't blame Cunningham for what they found there. He's doing his best. If you're right and Shad's mistaken about how it happened, Cunningham will find out."

Even in her own ears it lacked the ring of conviction. Prufrock noticed too.

"*If* I'm right?" he echoed quietly. "You mean, you think I could be wrong?"

She shook her head unhappily. "Arthur, I don't know what to think. It's true that everything people think they remember didn't necessarily happen. So yes, there's reason to hope we can clear things up and get him home before word of this gets about. But you should be ready for two possibilities. If matters drag on long enough for Shad's involvement to become public knowledge, there'll be a reaction beyond anything you'd get if Jackie Pickering had been killed by a mugger or a jealous lover. People who consider themselves at the forefront of modern, scientific, twenty-first-century thinking will start chanting slogans that haven't been heard since the Inquisition. We're all liberal thinkers until we feel threatened by something we don't understand; then we're mediaeval villagers again, nailing horse shoes to the door and hanging garlic from the rafters for fear of the powers of the dark."

She was talking about a witch-hunt. And that wasn't the worst thing she'd thought of. "And the second possibility?"

Rosie risked taking her eyes off the road for a moment to cast him a sidelong look. "That he did what he says he did."

Prufrock refused to meet her gaze, stared haughtily out of the window. "No."

"Arthur, you don't know. Believe in him, by all means. Give him the benefit of every doubt. But don't close your mind to the possibility that it happened just as he remembers. She targeted him – to expose him, to ridicule him – she cornered him, he panicked and lashed out. It's possible. Don't count absolutely on some mistake coming to light."

"It *isn't* possible," insisted Prufrock. "Whatever she did, however she upset him, he wouldn't react like that. Not with a knife. I know him better than that."

"Better than he knows himself?"

"Much better," said Prufrock dismissively. "He's always been afraid of what he could do. It's a great pity his uncle died when he did: Shad needed guidance from someone with the same sort of sensitivity. But Jacob died and Shad was left to cope alone, struggling with a faculty he only half understood. It's no wonder that by the time I knew him, even by the time you knew him, he'd come to think of his gift as something dangerous and outside his control. He was always afraid that it would jump the rails one day and . . ." He broke off abruptly, staring straight ahead once more.

She finished the sentence for him. "And something like this would happen. Arthur, that doesn't make it either more or less likely to be true. But it's no use closing our eyes to the possibility. If we're really his friends, we have to face the truth, or how do we help him to?"

They drove the rest of the way in silence.

She was expecting a Jacobean mansion, all grand vistas and inferior plumbing. But too many winters under too few slates had reduced the original Fellowes Hall to a dereliction beyond repair and it had been levelled to make way for the clinic: a range of low, streamlined buildings in conker-coloured concrete with smoky-brown windows. The name was etched discreetly on a copper plate by the gate; no explanation of its function was offered.

Doctor Cunningham met them at the door. After days of hearing his name in every conversation, it came as a little shock to both of them that they'd never seen him before. He was a tall man, slender in a steely kind of way. He moved deliberately but gave the impression he could move rather faster if he had to; which in his job was probably just as well. He spoke with an odd mixture of softness and precision.

He showed them to his office. "I'm glad you came. Shad could do with cheering up."

"I dare say he could," said Rosie. "Is there anything he needs?"

"Ask him," suggested Cunningham, "but I don't think so. He brought some things from home. What he needs most is to get this matter settled, and we're working on that. Even if there's no happy ending, he can start coming to terms with it once he knows the worst."

"You think there's some doubt then," said Prufrock, more hopefully than he probably intended.

Doctor Cunningham smiled sombrely. "We don't know the full story yet. If everything Shad says is true, there may still be mitigating circumstances. He may have forgotten something which will alter the entire picture. I don't want to encourage false hopes but it's a possibility we can't yet discount. I'll go on working with him until I'm sure there's nothing more to be recovered."

"And your honest feeling about what he's saying?" Rosie watched closely for his reaction.

Cunningham's gaze flicked reproachfully at her. "I'm neither his judge nor his jury: his culpability is something for others to decide. If you're asking whether I have any reason to disbelieve what he's telling me, then no, I haven't. But Shad thinking it's true doesn't necessarily make it so – particularly after a head injury and a week's amnesia. He could believe it absolutely and still be wrong."

"Detective Superintendent Marsh said you've done a lot of work with amnesiacs. Had a lot of success."

"That was kind of him. Yes, recovered memory has been a speciality of mine."

Rosie frowned. "Funny place to pursue it – a drying-out clinic."

Cunningham gave her a tight-lipped smile. “Some people are genetically predisposed to addiction. But there’s usually a trigger factor somewhere in their past. Getting them to confront it is a necessary step in controlling their addiction.”

It made as much sense to her as anything else in the realm of psychiatry. Rosie stood up. “Can we see him now?”

“Of course.” Cunningham walked them down the corridor. There were no padlocks, but there were doors he needed a swipe card to open. “One thing: routine is important in our work here. We find it helpful to restrict visits once patients have settled in. I don’t mean I want him in isolation, but perhaps you could let me know when you’re coming again.”

He’d stopped at a door, tapped and opened it. “You have some visitors, Shad.”

One thing was clear: Fellowes Hall treated the better class of addict. Expense had not been a limiting factor in furnishing the place – Shad’s room was more comfortable than his flat over the shoe shop. The television was bigger, the furniture newer, the decorations fresher, and parked in a corner beside the slimline radiator was a trouser press. Rosie wasn’t sure Shad owned an iron, let alone a trouser press. Of course, there were people who thought the same about her.

Shad was lying on his back on the bed, one arm across his eyes. He didn’t move; his voice was muffled by his sleeve. “I don’t want any v—”

“Too late,” said Rosie briskly, shouldering her way into the room, “we’re here now. Thank you, Doctor Cunningham, we’ll let you know when we’re leaving.” Certainly she didn’t put him bodily outside, but somehow he found himself standing in the corridor with the door closed.

Prufrock could think of nothing to say. The pale sharp eyes that had instilled respect in generations of schoolboys filmed over. “Oh, Shad.”

If they’d thought they were doing him a favour by rushing over here they were mistaken. He was appalled to see them, the last thing he wanted to do was talk to them. He was ashamed and afraid, and he didn’t want Prufrock’s fussy paternalism or Rosie’s celebrated smart-with-a-heart trying to make it better.

In a very real sense he was grieving: not for the girl but for his own lost self. Until today he'd believed himself one kind of man, and now it turned out he was another. Discovering what he was capable of was shocking beyond words. He wanted to crawl into a hole somewhere and pull the sods on top of him. Quite literally, he wished he was dead.

Only a fraction of this showed in his face. He'd spent a lot of time as he grew up learning to keep his emotions out of sight, precisely because of their innate power. They frightened him, he knew better than to put them on public display. He raised enough eyebrows as he passed: an intense young man with the faintly dangerous looks of his gypsy forebears; a strange man plainly listening to the beat of a different drum. He didn't need to give the impression of being unstable as well. He learned to filter. He did it so automatically now that most people who met him thought him curt and detached. He was doing it now. He didn't want anyone, even friends, to know how deep the pain went.

And still he looked as if his soul was in shreds. Desolate, tormented, riven to the core. He was a gardener, sturdy and fit, muscles hardened in physical toil, but right now he looked so frail Rosie's heart swelled and cracked within her.

She said gruffly, "You look like shit. I imagine you feel the same way."

Filtered or not, kindness would have broken him. Unvarnished honesty he could just about cope with. He nodded jerkily. He sat up and braced his back against the wall as if anticipating assault.

Rosie wasn't good at small talk either. Only one thing interested her: she came straight to the point. "How sure are you? About what you told the police?"

His eyes thought she was mad. "I *remember*."

Prufrock shook his head. "It doesn't make any sense, Shad. Perhaps you're remembering wrong."

A sound that was half a laugh and half a moan burst from him. "Jesus, Arthur! Don't you think, if there was half a chance . . . ?" His head rocked back in despair. "There isn't. I remember what happened. What I did."

"In that case," Rosie said levelly, "tell us why."

His eyes fell. "She worked for that" – a suitable adjective eluded him – "TV programme. They were going to . . . do me." He said it as if he meant rape. "She set me up. She was really friendly, I liked her – and then she sprang this on me. I told her to drop it, I wanted nothing to do with it. She said the programme was going out anyway, I might as well have my say. She said I was going to make her famous. That we were both going to be famous, only she'd enjoy it more."

"And you killed her."

His chin sank on his chest. "Yes."

"With a knife you just happened to have taken to the railway station."

"Yes."

"Where was it?"

After a moment he looked up. "What?"

"This knife. It had a blade long enough to reach up under her ribs into her heart. It would have poked a hole in your pocket. So how did you carry it?"

"In my hand, I suppose."

"And nobody noticed? You met her on the platform, surrounded by other passengers, and nobody noticed you had a knife in your hand?"

"I suppose."

"Where did you first meet her?"

"What?"

"Come on, Shad," Rosie said sharply, "you say you've got your memory back. So where did you first meet Jackie Pickering? She approached you, she was really friendly – so where did you first meet?"

"I . . . I . . ." But he didn't remember. "I don't know."

"Why did you go to the station?"

"To meet her."

"Why there?"

He shook his head. "I don't remember."

"How did you get hurt?"

"Hurt?"

"Shad, you had a head injury! We assumed that whoever killed the girl hit you and left you in the wagon. If you killed the girl, how did you hurt your head and why were you still on the train when it got to Crewe?"

"I must have walked into something, knocked myself out."

"In an empty goods wagon? What do you suppose happened? You stabbed her, you held her while she died, then you put her down and head-butted the wall?" Rosie sniffed sourly. "I'm not surprised Marsh won't arrest you on the strength of this. Arthur's right, it makes no sense. Maybe you killed that girl and maybe you didn't, but it's no use telling me you remember what happened when you can't answer basic questions about it."

"I'm not lying!" he shouted, resentment and misery surging in a pastiche of anger. He hated having to keep saying it. He'd thought that confessing to Marsh would be the worst part. But he'd expected that to be the end, that justice would then take its course. He hadn't expected to be disbelieved, to have to keep insisting on his guilt. "Why should I? Why would that make more sense? I may not remember everything, but I remember what I did. I killed her. I stabbed her, and she died. She threatened me and I killed her. Is that basic enough for you?"

"Truthfully?" asked Rosie. "No. You're giving us edited highlights when what we need is the whole movie. Not only what but why and how. The details you can't recall: they're not the icing on the cake, they're what the cake's made of. A snapshot may not be a lie but it proves nothing. Without a context you don't know what any single image represents. The Birth of Venus? – or a memorial to a naked pearl fisher who took an incautious step into a giant clam? The Death of Marat? – or a man falling asleep after adding bath salts to his grocery list? Liberty Leading the People? – or Will somebody grab Aunty Joan before she whips off more than her vest?"

Despite the gravity of the situation Prufrock, who had the education to appreciate her artistic allusions, could not resist a little smile. Shad stared at her without comprehension. He was talking about murder. She was wittering on about a bunch of people he didn't know.

He'd never committed a crime before. All he knew was what he'd learnt from TV. The scene with the prisoner's friends was meant to end either with them turning their backs on him or, more humiliatingly, in gushing pity. All right, so Rosie Holland was never going to gush; and he hadn't thought either of them would react to the crisis by pretending not to know him, though he'd have understood if they had. What he couldn't understand was what good they thought blank denial would do. If there'd been any doubt he'd have valued their support. But there wasn't. He knew what he'd done, he remembered doing it, felt oddly diminished by their search for another explanation. He didn't want to wriggle out of the consequences through a gap in the evidence. Sticking stubbornly to the truth about her death was all he could do for Jackie Pickering to set against the monstrous wrong he had done her; and it wasn't much.

"Please," he struggled, "I know you mean well" – the deadliest words in the language – "but you're making it worse. I don't know how I let things go so far, but I did; and the girl's dead and I can't bring her back. I can't make it right. All I can do is tell the truth."

"Shad," said Rosie softly, "have you thought what prison's going to mean to you?"

Of course he had. Fear crossed his face like a moon shadow. "It's *meant* to be hard."

"Not as hard as it'll be for you. Please, give us a chance to help. I know you think you're to blame for this, but it's just possible that you're wrong. Help us to find out."

But he shook his head, mute with despair. It was as if she'd asked his help in proving the earth was flat. He knew better.

Prufrock stood up. All they were doing was grinding salt in his wounds. He was still too stunned to consider the matter objectively. "All right. Perhaps we should go now, leave you in peace. We'll come back in a day or two. In the meantime, give some thought to what Rosie says. Until we know the full story we can't be sure we understand any part of it."

Shad was too exhausted to argue any more. He just nodded. "OK."

In the doorway Rosie turned back – to wish him well, to tell him to look after himself, not to worry too much – pathetic little clichés that would serve only to underscore the helplessness of his situation. But she never got it out. Instead she saw what he'd managed to keep to himself until then.

Thinking himself alone, he'd relaxed just enough to let the horror surge back. All around him, separated by mere masonry, were people living their worst nightmares: racked bodies craving drink and drugs, hag-ridden spirits riding on the air, taking any escape they could find. It was like an explosion in a distress factory. A natural psychic too sensitive to ignore the onslaught, too unschooled to defend himself against it, he couldn't keep it at bay. Pain ripped through his eyes and twisted up his face as if the torch of a flame-thrower had swept across his body. It hurt that much. It would go on hurting.

Prufrock hadn't seen, and Rosie saw no need to add to his grief by telling him. She swept out of the room and down the corridor and didn't speak again until they were back at the car.

Then she said, with granite determination, "We have got to get him out of there."

Fourteen

Marsh was sympathetic but not much help. "It's not me keeping him there. He could leave today."

"He thinks he killed someone. He won't leave until you convince him otherwise."

The detective breathed heavily. "That isn't actually my job. I want to find out what happened, certainly. That may clear Lucas or it may not. Either way it may take some time."

"Time that Shad's going through hell!"

"I can't do much about that, Ms Holland," said Harry Marsh tersely.

"Then we'll have to."

"Don't get in my way," he warned her.

"Hard to see how we can," she retorted, heading for his door, "when we'll be out there trying to discover who killed Jackie Pickering, and you'll be sitting on your hands in here."

Prufrock waited till she'd calmed down before asking carefully, "When we'll be doing what?"

Rosie threw up a hand in despair. "I have no idea why I said that. Mainly to annoy him, I think." She glanced at her friend, a faint glitter in her eye. "All the same, there might be something we can do."

Prufrock smiled. "That's what I hoped you meant."

"I'm not proposing to turn private detective. Only, our job is easier than Marsh's. He has to find out who killed the girl. We only have to show that Shad didn't."

"And how do we do that?"

Neither the ex-schoolmaster nor the ex-pathologist had ever conducted a criminal investigation. But Rosie had never let inexperience stand in her way. "I can think of two people who may be able to cast some light: Jackie Pickering, and her best friend Debbie Burgess."

"Except that one's dead, and our only way to the other is through the father who is the best suspect we have except for Shad."

Rosie didn't see a problem. "Dead witnesses are much more reliable than live ones. They don't lie, they don't exaggerate, they don't shy away from the consequences. You might not always understand what they're saying, you might sometimes take them up wrong, but it's always the truth. As to Burgess, we were always going to have to talk to him sooner or later. Now we have to do it sooner."

"No," insisted Prufrock, "we don't. Detective Superintendent Marsh does. Talk to *him*, tell him what you suspect."

"I will," promised Rosie; "just as soon as I know what it is I'm telling him. What this court case was; what he might have done that Jackie still hated him for this long after. Why she thought him a bastard."

"Marsh can do all that."

"But will he? He hasn't the same incentive we have. I'm not going to do anything stupid, Arthur, I just want to get the ball rolling."

"You'll phone Burgess?" Prufrock couldn't see how even Rosie could get into too much trouble over the phone. He had momentarily forgotten that Jackie Pickering had.

"I want to know about this court case first. Where do I find out?"

She really should have known. "The local paper. They'll have it in their back issues."

"Right. Arthur, can I leave that to you? Will you call them – it'll have to be tomorrow now, the office is probably shut – see what you can find out? And I'll go round to the hospital pathology department, see what the autopsy report says. It may give us useful information about both of them, Jackie and her killer."

Prufrock nodded, still without much enthusiasm. "And then

we pass it over to Mr Marsh. Seriously, Rosie, I think this is his province."

"Oh, so do I," agreed Rosie acrimoniously. "But his priorities are different. He wants to solve the crime; I only want to get Shad home. I'm hoping we can do that faster. Once we've persuaded him he's not responsible for this, the police can take as long as they need to catch whoever is. But I want him out of there, Arthur. Before it destroys him."

Jackie Pickering's death was as suspicious as they come so the autopsy had been carried out as a special. Doctor Sharma performed it as soon as the body was returned from Holyhead, on the Thursday afternoon when he should have been at his youngest son's birthday party. In a career waymarked by the dead, many of them taken before their time, he would always remember Jackie Pickering with particular fondness.

Rosie had never met him, though she was aware of his reputation as he was probably aware of hers. Pathologists always know one another, at least by repute. Some of them hardly know anyone else.

Two years ago Rosie could have walked down the discreet steps behind Skipley General Hospital that led to the basement mortuary, introduced herself to Yussuf Sharma and immediately been welcomed as a kindred spirit. He'd have known about her contribution to solving the Jacuzzi Murders in Bristol; she'd have complimented him on identifying the cause of death in the bizarre case of the Telford Toad-Licker; and they'd have been giggling like old friends within minutes.

She wondered what kind of a welcome she could count on as the *Chronicle*'s Agony Aunt. Working for a newspaper opened many doors, and didn't stop a conversation in its tracks the same way, but just this once it would have been nice to be able to drop the name of a hospital.

Sharma was a big man of about forty, square and solid, with the pronounced nasal twang of the Birmingham native. Birmingham is one of the great melting pots of Europe: it's no coincidence that so many people with nothing going for them but talent have made their fortunes in the Second City. Sharma himself was a second-generation Brummie; and as a local man he knew both who Rosie was and who she used to be. When she appeared in his basement domain soon after he did on Wednesday morning he welcomed her gravely and asked how he could help.

When she told him, his dark eyes like melted chocolate opened wide and then shut in a mute demonstration of good nature taken advantage of. "I'm sorry . . ." he began.

Rosie shook her head crisply. "Don't be sorry, you obviously haven't understood. I'm not here to obstruct justice but to assist it. Call Detective Superintendent Marsh if you like, he'll have no problems about you talking to me."

"Even so . . ." But Doctor Sharma got no further with his second sentence than with his first.

"OK," said Rosie, "let's cut the crap here. Shad Lucas, who's the prime suspect for this crime, is a friend of mine. He thinks he did it; neither Marsh nor I are convinced. But if he is charged he'll have the right to nominate an independent Forensic Medical Examiner to carry out a second post mortem. I am both qualified and experienced, so we both know who he'll ask for if that situation arises.

"What I'm suggesting is that we spare the deceased's family the trauma of a second autopsy if at all possible. Talk to me. Let's get our heads together and see if we can sort out what the poor girl's trying to tell us."

"Actually," murmured Dr Sharma, "I've already done that."

Rosie let out the gust of laughter that was her secret weapon. Most people found it impossible to be angry with someone who laughed like that. "Of course you have. I'm sorry, I didn't mean to suggest otherwise. But we're both working in the same cause so it makes sense to pool our knowledge. For instance, I know things about the accused person that you don't. Could this murder have been committed in the way it was by someone with achondroplasia?"

Sharma stared at her in astonishment. "The suspect is a dwarf? Nobody told me! That alters . . ."

She'd let him finish a couple of sentences now. If they knew one another long enough, some day she'd let him finish a paragraph. She shook her head. "No, he isn't. That's my point: you didn't know, and I did. We can help one another. All it needs is a little professional courtesy."

The pathologist could have fended her off a while longer but not for ever. She was right: an accused person has certain rights. If he didn't want her unpicking his stitches he might as well cooperate now. "What do you want to know?"

She wanted to know if he'd found anything that ruled out Shad Lucas as the killer. She wasn't expecting anything conclusive, would have settled for something that merely cast doubt on his newly recovered memory. Even that proved elusive.

Rosie could tell from his report that Sharma had done a thorough job. There was no point pressing for another autopsy on the grounds that he might have missed something. Anything the body of Jackie Pickering could tell them was already in his notes.

After they'd been over the physical findings they reviewed the blood work. Still there was nothing to cast fresh light on the events behind Skipley station.

"I'm wasting your time, aren't I?" Rosie admitted at last. "I'm sorry. I hoped – I don't know – there'd be something to say she'd been killed by a six-foot-three, left-handed Presbyterian with a rare skin complaint. Stupid, isn't it? You'd think I'd have done enough of these to know that's not how it works. But it's different when someone you care about is involved. You think the answers have to be there somewhere."

"It's a common mistake," nodded Sharma. "Confusing pathology with alchemy. Policemen make it all the time."

Rosie managed a rueful grin. "They certainly did in my time. I believe I may have told them as much, now and again."

There wasn't very much left to say. She'd pinned a fair bit of hope on this visit, had thought the biggest problem would be getting the man to talk to her, was disappointed that even with his help she'd been unable to advance her case. She thanked him and headed for the door. Sharma showed her out.

"I hope things work out for your friend. At least, if he didn't do it I do."

"That's my problem too," acknowledged Rosie feelingly. "I want him not to have done it. But if he did do it, I don't know what the hell I want."

"What does he do for a living?"

"He's a gardener. Why?"

"I don't know." She looked at him; he was wondering whether to say something. Her gaze decided him. "Look, it was only something that occurred to me – it probably doesn't mean much. A gardener? Well, maybe; he'll be used to using tools, I suppose, even knives. Though I'd have thought . . ."

Rosie stopped and made him face her. "Doctor Sharma, what are you wittering about?"

He collected his thoughts. "The wound. There was only one – well, you saw the report. It was very clean. He didn't have to hack at her. He inserted the point of a long blade under her ribs and directed it up into her heart. Now, that could have been luck. In the same way that an infinite number of monkeys playing with an infinite number of typewriters will eventually write *Hamlet*, sheer luck will occasionally let the clumsiest assailant produce a surgical murder. But I wondered if the man who did this had some specialist knowledge."

He gave an embarrassed smile. "I said as much to my porter; we have a little bet riding on it. I thought it would be a butcher: they're used to handling knives, they're familiar with anatomy and accustomed to killing efficiently. But Lenny reads a lot of paperbacks: he plumped for a professional assassin. Neither of us considered a gardener. Well, you can't be right all the time."

"No," agreed Rosie, deep in thought. "You don't have to be right all the time. Just when it matters."

Prufrock had no luck with the local paper: back issues older than twelve months were bound and filed at the central library. So he phoned the library.

The librarian consulted an index and turned up the right issue first time. She faxed a copy of the report to the *Chronicle* where Rosie collected it. It referred to a case in the Crown Court in March 1997. The defendant was Roy Burgess and the charge was incest.

"Dear heaven," whispered Prufrock, white-faced. "She was raped by her own father."

"Actually," said Rosie, who'd kept reading, "no, she wasn't. At least, the jury didn't think so."

"You mean . . . she just *said* she was?! That's almost worse. What kind of people do that?"

"Sick ones," said Rosie. "And mad ones, and bad ones. The other possibility, of course, is that she wasn't lying. That the jury was wrong."

"And that's what Jackie was doing? Trying to get justice for her friend?"

Rosie blew a silent whistle. "It's possible, isn't it? It would certainly have made a humdinger of a show. If she could pull it off, correct a miscarriage of justice in front of a TV audience, she wouldn't be stuck as a researcher much longer."

"So she went after Roy Burgess," ruminated Prufrock. "She found evidence that wasn't available to the jury, that would have changed their whole view of the case. Another victim, perhaps; some other vulnerable young girl he'd had contact with?"

Rosie picked up the thread. "Only he got wind of what she was doing. She may even have told him, invited him to come clean before she exposed him on television. He'd just about lived down the trial, he was damned if he was going to have the whole thing raked up again. A man who'd abuse his own daughter – he wouldn't find it hard to kill someone else's."

"What does he do for a living?"

Rosie scanned the report. The answer was disappointing. "He's a motor mechanic." Then her voice dropped half an octave. "But he used to be in the SAS. Arthur, you were in the forces. Tell me if that means what I think it means."

"Oh yes," he said, with hollow conviction. "They're trained to kill, all right. I mean, every soldier is – it's the only reason for having an army – but the SAS are specialists. They'll kill anyone with anything, but knives are the weapon of choice. Easily concealed, easily explained, silent, fast and untraceable. Jackie Pickering could certainly have been murdered by an ex-member of the Special Air Service."

All at once it was coming together, almost quicker than they could deal with it.

"Why the station?" mused Rosie. "Well, because he lives in Nottingham and she lived in Skipley. She wouldn't give him her address, thought she was safe meeting him off the train. He came by rail because it was safer – there was no chance of a security camera picking up his car numberplate, proving he was in town."

"Why did she meet him? Why take that risk?"

"She wanted a confession. For the programme, and for her own satisfaction. I bet she had a tape recorder on her. It wasn't found, but only because he got there first. If she could wind up her programme with a confession she had it all. Producer? – they'd have made her a partner for that. She wanted two things, and she wanted them desperately enough to get careless. She wanted justice for her friend, and she wanted advancement for herself. She gambled on getting both at once, and she lost."

"Then why does Shad think *he* killed her?"

Rosie had no idea. But even before she was paid to have all the answers she hated admitting to ignorance. "Well, because he's a psychic and . . ." No, that didn't seem to work. "Perhaps he's . . ." She knew she wasn't fooling him, gave up before she dug herself in deeper. "Arthur, I don't know. When we know exactly what happened perhaps we'll understand that too."

"So – *now* we talk to Superintendent Marsh?"

"No. Now we go and see Roy Burgess."

"What!"

"I'm not accusing a man of murder without ever setting eyes on him. What if he's crippled with arthritis? What if he lost an arm on active service? We don't even have to talk with him, but we do have to see him – just to make sure I'm not making a complete idiot of myself."

"Rosie, he could be – if this is Shad's way out he *has* to be – a murderer! You can't just walk up to him and count his limbs. You need a cover story for when he asks what you want."

"All right," agreed Rosie, "then I'll tell him . . . I'll say . . ." She thought a moment longer. "Then *you'll* tell him you want your car serviced. You're a sweet little old gentleman: he'll never suspect you of subterfuge."

"He might. When he asks me what's wrong with it and I can't remember which is the brake pedal and which is the . . . you know, the go-faster one. I can't drive, Rosie! I've never driven, and I've never owned a car."

"Oh, don't be so defeatist! He'll never notice."

Fifteen

Before they left for Nottingham, Rosie rang Fellowes Hall. She was still looking for proof, but from believing that Shad had probably done what he thought he'd done, she'd come to think it was most unlikely. There was the wound that didn't look it had been inflicted by a gardener. There was the court case in which Jackie's best friend had been branded a liar and the man who may have raped her set free. There was the researcher's desire to make a name for herself with the story no one else knew about, that she was bringing to some kind of a climax the day she died. Someone may have had a good reason to kill her, and someone may have known how to do it; and Shad didn't fit the bill on either score. Rosie wanted him to know that.

But Shad and Doctor Cunningham were mutually engaged, so she left a message with the receptionist. "Tell him he didn't do it and we're going to prove it."

Shad Lucas drifted on a blood-red tide, almost detached from reality, too far from shore for any cries of his to be heard or heeded. The ghosts of memories, not all his own, washed in and out, little snapshots of experience he couldn't connect with. He understood very little of what was happening to him. A voice came through the red mist – not from the shore but from above: the voice of God – reassuring, telling him everything was all right, but he didn't understand that either. He had no sense of time or direction, only the vague awareness that if he could get his wits together he'd be very much afraid. But something was stopping him. Not the voice – which was saying words he ought to know but which remained stubbornly meaningless – but the tide. Something in the blood-red tide was coming between him and what was. He didn't know how he'd got here. He didn't know if he'd ever be able to leave.

The voice said, "It's all right, Shad. You're safe. Let go. I know you're disorientated: that's just the drugs. Let go of the present and drift back. You're warm, you're comfortable, you're quite safe. Drift back until you come to the railway yards again. There – do you see them? There's not much light but you can see the moon glinting on the rails. Are you there?

"Good. You're not alone. There's someone with you. Do you see her? That's right – Jackie's walking beside you. You're talking together. Arguing? Is she angry?"

The merest whisper of breath escaped him. "Afraid."

"Before that, Shad," said the voice of God. "Before she was afraid. Wasn't she angry? Weren't you both angry?"

"We were?" It wasn't like being there. It was like seeing an image begin to coalesce in a tray of photographic developer. He was looking at nothing, and then the words made the picture appear. "We were."

"Why were you angry?"

"She used me."

"Why was she angry?"

"She . . ." The fractional shake of his head set the whole of the blood-red tide rocking. "I don't know."

"Yes, you do," God insisted gently. "She was using you. You didn't want to be used like that, you tried to stop her. She was angry because you wouldn't cooperate. Isn't that right?"

"Yes."

"So you argued and you walked. Why didn't you just leave her there?"

"She had enough . . ."

"Ah. She already had enough on you to make her programme. You had to stop her."

"Yes."

"But she wouldn't give it up. It was her key to a better career and you were the price of it. When did you realise she wouldn't change her mind?"

A long pause while the red tide rocked. "At the wagons? No, nearly. I held her arm and kept her walking. She started to shout: I put my hand over her mouth. She struggled but she wasn't strong enough. I pushed her into the last wagon and got in after her."

"Where did the knife come from?"

"Under my shirt. Taped to my side, out of sight." He was so tired.

God nodded. "I see. You thought you might need it?"

"She used me," he said again. "She was going to . . . going to . . ." He drew a breath. "People don't understand. They're afraid. They think I'm something . . . other. A freak. I get that from their heads. Freak. Look at the freak. Don't go near the freak. That freak'd better not come near me.

"What she was going to do – she'd have crucified me. I couldn't . . . All those scared, angry people. In my head. After my hide."

"You were afraid."

"Yes."

"You thought that if she exposed you, people wouldn't understand. Would be scared of you, want to hurt you."

"Yes."

"A witch-hunt."

A barely audible whisper. "Yes."

"It was self-defence. You thought you had to kill her to protect yourself."

"I . . . killed her."

"Did you, Shad? With the knife you had taped to your side? Because if you hadn't she'd have crucified you? Is that what happened?"

"Yes." Tears welled under his shut lids and ran back into his hair, and by that way trickled down into the blood-red tide. So he came to understand the nature of the sea he was adrift upon. Blood and tears; and he thought there was no way back.

Alex enjoyed holding the fort. The office was very quiet: of course, on a Wednesday everyone involved in producing the *Chronicle* was at full stretch. Once Dan Sale stuck his head in with a query and left satisfied with the answer; otherwise she saw no one. But she felt more content than she had for some time – and not just since Matt had dropped his bombshell. She no longer had any doubts about the wisdom of what they were doing. It couldn't feel this right and be wrong.

She'd rather hoped he might come down from his eyrie in the roof and join her for a sandwich at lunchtime. But he didn't and, on reflection, she appreciated his tact. It had been Alex who'd worried how the new developments would affect their professional relationship. She was pleased Matt wasn't going to embarrass her with his attentions; at least not yet.

In fact, she was having lunch when the phone rang. It was the front desk. "Someone to see you, Alex. Apparently you wrote to a Fran Barclay, in reply to a letter?"

"Oh yes." Her mind scanned swiftly over what she'd written but she couldn't think what the problem was. Maybe the girl only wanted to thank her for her advice. "I'll be right down."

She extracted the original letter and the copy of her reply from the file and headed for the lift, refreshing her memory as she went. The girl who loved her man enough to leave him if that was what his career demanded – that was the one.

Sylvia Stone, who manned the front desk and the switchboard, took in small ads and orders for photographs, and advised people who came in to complain about something but weren't sure who they needed to shout at, was engaged with one of Skipley's undertakers when Alex got out of the lift and she didn't like to interrupt. The Funeral Homes sent in lists of death notices early in the week, with the option to update just prior to publication. If someone else died, that is: names were almost never deleted.

She glanced around the small office, with its front door on to the street and its back door into the works where once the great presses had thundered, now full of computers and sloping glass tables where the pages were made up. There were two people waiting for Sylvia but neither of them looked like her correspondent: one was an elderly lady, the other a young man. Alex waited patiently until the undertaker took himself off.

"What happened to . . . ?"

Sylvia nodded over her shoulder and Alex turned round, puzzled that she'd managed to miss someone in the tiny office.

She hadn't. The young man smiled at her. He was tall and fair, with a fair moustache and warm eyes. "Miss Fisher? I wanted to thank you for your letter. I also wanted to clarify something."

Alex returned the smile. "You must be Jamie."

The man crinkled his nose in a rueful sniff. "Well, that's what I wanted to explain. I didn't make myself very clear, and I was afraid it might affect what you would have written. The last thing I want to do when you've been so kind is embarrass you, so I thought I'd better just . . . well . . . introduce myself. Jamie's my partner: I'm Fran."

"I want to get my car serviced," said Prufrock, trying to assess the mechanic's bodily fitness without looking at him.

"Sure," said Roy Burgess. "This one?" He nodded at Rosie's Volvo parked beside the kerb.

"Er, no," said Prufrock. (He thought Burgess might dive under it there and then and start unscrewing things.)

"So what is it?"

"Um – a green one."

Rosie passed a hand across her eyes. She should have known better. The old man could dissemble persuasively on any number of subjects, but fell apart at the thought of the internal combustion engine. And, indeed, much simpler forms of technology. Rosie had always suspected that the real reason a man with a cottage garden needed a gardener was that he couldn't master the strimmer.

She couldn't leave him to stew. She got out of the car. "I'm sorry, Mr Burgess, I think he's missed his medication again. Jump back in the car, Arthur, there's a good chap."

Prufrock didn't mind being slandered if it got him out of an embarrassing situation. He did as he was bade.

Burgess watched him go in some confusion. "Doesn't he have a car?"

"Doesn't even drive, poor chap."

"Then . . . why did you bring him to a garage?"

Roy Burgess had all the physical appurtenances necessary to have taken the life of Jackie Pickering. He was a man of about Rosie's age, not big but sturdy and compact. He had close-cropped hair, veering from sandy to grey, and straight grey eyes, and he spoke with the hint of a Derbyshire burr.

A murderer? It's not the sort of thing you normally wonder about people you've just met. Rosie was having to fight her way past the usual conventions to try to get a glimpse of who this man was behind them. Half a minute wasn't enough. She needed to keep him talking long enough to reconcile what she saw before her with what she needed him to have done.

She glanced around. They'd tracked Burgess Motors to an alley behind Arkwright Street, a couple of miles from his home. As a main road into Nottingham Arkwright Street was permanently busy, but The Vennel was the sort of back alley where dark deeds could be done with impunity. Apart from the three of them there was no one in sight; none of the buildings round about boasted an occupied window. It wasn't a good place to start annoying an ex-SAS man who was already suspected of murder.

"Sorry," she said. "I didn't realise it was a garage." She began backing towards the car.

"I suppose it's the name," he said, watching her go. "A bit ambivalent, that. Sometime I'll get the sign repainted so it says 'Burgess Motors: A Garage'."

Rosie gave a weak smile, got back in the car and drove away.

Sixteen

"It's short for Francis," said the young man with the fair moustache. "My father's Frank, he always expected his son would be just like him. I think the fact that I wasn't going to be probably surfaced fairly early. I don't remember anyone ever calling me Frank Junior."

Alex was serving him coffee in her office. She needed a minute to think about this and how, and even if, it affected what she'd written.

She came to the conclusion that it didn't. "As I see it, there are two ways we can handle this. We can leave it as it stands. It's honest, it's accurate, and the answer applies equally whether we're talking of a mixed-sex relationship or a same-sex one." Her eyes flicked up at him. "I'm sorry, do you prefer the term Gay? It just sounds so frivolous – flappers and feather boas and Bright Young Things."

Fran shook his head, hazel eyes sparkling. "I know what you mean. It makes you think bells must be involved somewhere. If you want the truth, when it's just us we still call ourselves Queers."

Alex beamed, liking him. "The other option is for you to reword your letter, making clear the nature of the relationship, and for me to do the same with the answer. The substance of both would remain the same, but you might feel it would properly acknowledge a specific problem facing" – she hesitated but couldn't quite bring herself to say it – "same-sex partnerships. It really is up to you. Do you want to talk to Jamie? I realise people at his work know about you, but perhaps he'd rather not remind them. As long as I know by Monday I can make any changes necessary."

"I'll talk to him tonight. I think, if he's agreeable, I'd quite like to have it out in the open."

Alex blinked. She wasn't a woman who saw sexual innuendo everywhere. If Rosie had been here she'd have roared and said it again, and made sure everyone else got the joke as well. But it was one of those conversations that was always going to be fraught with possibilities. She cleared her throat. "We don't use names, for obvious reasons; but people who're close enough to you to be part of the problem can often work it out. Check that Jamie's ready for that. If he is, I'll do the rest."

By slow degrees the red tide ebbed. Shad found himself back in his room, on his bed, his clothes and the sheet under him drenched with sweat. His head sang and he couldn't focus his eyes. His tongue was thick in his mouth. "Well?"

Doctor Cunningham finished sponging his face. Then he straightened up with a sad smile. "More detail, the same story."

Shad bit back a sob. "Then it's true. It's what happened. We're not finding anything else because there's nothing else to find."

Cunningham rocked a hand. "That's too sweeping. It may be I'm not asking the right questions, or asking them the right way. Or using the right drugs."

"There are others?" He tried to keep from his voice his terror at going that route again.

"Yes, but I don't know if there are any better ones. You have to understand, there are risks. I can't justify doing something that might damage you."

"Christ Jesus!" swore Shad, the breath rattling in his throat, "does it *matter*? If I did it, I'm a murderer. If I just think I did, I'm a madman. Either way I have nothing to lose."

"You have the same as everybody else," Cunningham retorted sharply: "the rest of your life. Maybe it won't be what you hoped, but it's the only one you've got and I'm not going to risk it on a quest to which there may be no happy ending. I'm not going to resort to unapproved methods in the hope of finding something – another answer, a better answer, one that will let you sleep nights – which may not exist."

Only the two men's breathing punctuated the silence. In here the walls didn't have ears, they had acoustic padding.

Finally Shad said, "What methods?"

"Not one of our better performances," said Prufrock judiciously. "Where now?"

They crossed the Trent into the pleasant suburb of West Bridgford and hunted up its main arterial for the turning that was Dootheboys Avenue. The Burgess house was a square brick dwelling built into rising ground with a rockery for a front garden. A Japanese fastback crouched in the sloping drive.

"Must be the wife's car," said Rosie, parking on the other side of the road. She'd been afraid they'd find the house empty. Now the prospect of a difficult conversation loomed.

"Are you sure we're wise approaching her?"

"I don't know about wise," shrugged Rosie. "I think it's what we have to do next. What I have to do, anyway. You'd better stay in the car this time: we don't want to look like a delegation. Toot the horn if you see Burgess coming." She tapped the centre of the wheel. "That's the horn."

Only having something useful to do kept him from going with her, uncomfortable as the meeting was likely to be. Though it was mid afternoon and Roy Burgess was unlikely to be home for a couple of hours, he saw the advantage of an early warning system. "Be careful."

"Count on it," said Rosie fervently.

The woman who answered the door was small, dark-haired and probably in her mid forties. "Yes? Can I help you?"

Crossing the river Rosie had decided on a mixture of truth and wilful deceit falling just short of lies. "Mrs Burgess? My name's Rosie Holland, I work in the media in Skipley, outside Birmingham. Where a girl called Jackie Pickering used to work. You may have seen in the papers: she was killed a week ago."

Mrs Burgess frowned. "What has this to do with us?"

"Miss Pickering and your daughter Debbie were friends from university. I understand they talked on the phone a couple of times every week. There's a possibility that Jackie said something that would cast light on what happened to her. It's important that I get in touch with Debbie. Can you give me her number?"

Mrs Burgess didn't ask her inside; but nor did she ask her to leave. She was thinking, trying to work out what it meant. "You say you worked with Jackie?"

"Not directly. But everybody involved is anxious to find out what happened. You were aware of the friendship between her and your daughter?"

"Of course. Jackie came here quite often when they were at university. Until—" She strangled the sentence at birth. "We were upset when we heard the news, but we didn't know that she and Debbie were still in touch. We . . . don't see much of Debbie these days."

Rosie nodded understandingly. "They drift away, don't they? She'll have her own life now – job, friends, home. Does she still live in Nottingham?"

"No, she . . . " She stopped, eyeing Rosie speculatively. "Tell me again why you want to talk to her. Are you saying she's involved in Jackie's death?"

"No, not at all," said Rosie hurriedly, though that was exactly what she was hoping. "It seems likely she was killed because of something she was working on. No one at the office knew what it was – I hoped Jackie might have told Debbie."

"And why are you asking this, not the police?"

It was a good question. "Detective Superintendent Marsh from Skipley CID will want to talk to Debbie. If you're not happy about giving me her phone number, give it to him."

Something unexpected happened in Mrs Burgess's face. She was a respectable middle-class woman, not at all the type to come out in a rash at the mention of the police. But she flushed and her eyes hardened, and she shook her head crisply. "Thank you very much, but I've already seen enough policemen to last me a lifetime."

Rosie held her breath, aware that somewhere upstream a floodgate had given way. Mrs Burgess might not want to talk to her but if she went on standing here she would. The polite thing, of course, would have been to make her excuses and leave.

But Rosie Holland rarely, if ever, did the polite thing. "You're talking about the court case."

There had been a little time for the memory to lose its edge, not so much that the woman was surprised her visitor knew. "So you heard about that. Then you know that the court acquitted him." Her manner was both bristly and tired. She'd been through this so many times.

"Yes," nodded Rosie. "The jury believed him, not Debbie. I assume" – she waved a hand to indicate the reason, that the woman still lived with the man accused of raping her daughter – "you did too."

"That's right. Miss Holland, I knew long before the jury that my husband hadn't done what Debbie said he'd done. I knew he was innocent. Now everyone does."

"It must be every mother's nightmare," Rosie said softly. "Having to choose between her husband and her daughter."

Coals of anger burned deep in the woman's eyes. "It is. I've never regretted my choice, but I never go to sleep without praying that one day Debbie will come to terms with what happened and we can be a family again. Debbie was certainly a victim, Miss Holland, but she wasn't her father's victim. If you don't believe me, perhaps you'll believe him."

So involved in this conversation was Rosie that she had barely noticed, only as a minor irritation on the edge of consciousness, the idiot across the street trying to use his car horn as a musical instrument. Now, in a flood of understanding, she remembered what it meant. What it meant, and what she'd been meant to do when she heard it.

She spun on her heel on the Burgesses' front step and found herself eyeball to eyeball with an SAS-trained killer.

Seventeen

Between the back door of the building where he lived and the residents' car park Matt Gosling was mugged by a reporter from that newspaper known in the trade as the 'Daily Vomit'.

Traditionally such persons are small men in raincoats, ferrety faces decorated by narrow ginger moustaches. But time moves on even in the most retro division of the newspaper industry, and today's face of 'The Vomiter' was female, aged about twenty-five, attractive in a brittle sort of way, and about as dedicated to ethical journalism as her predecessor had been.

"Mr Gosling, how does it feel to know your paper's professional psychic murdered a girl working for a rival organisation over a ratings war?"

So the genie was out of the bottle, and nothing Matt could do now would squeeze it back inside. It was going to be in 'The Vomiter', and if 'The Vomiter' had it tomorrow morning the real newspapers would have it the day after. Their language might be more restrained but the story would be the same: Shad Lucas had confessed to killing Jackie Pickering.

What he said now, the precise words he used – assuming she quoted him precisely – were vital. He could cut his own throat, and the throats of all who worked for the *Chronicle*, or he could throw up a palisade they could conceivably defend.

He always found it helpful to define his problems in military terms.

It was an effort to smile at the little harpy, but he made it. "You're a bit late for a scoop, Miss" – she had to remind him – "Miss Moody. Six o'clock tomorrow morning you'll be able to read the full account in the *Skipley Chronicle*. I don't think you can get out before that, can you?"

She stared at him, emblazoned eyes suspicious, unsure whether to believe him. "You're carrying the story?"

"Of course we're carrying the story. I'd offer to run you off a proof, but it wouldn't be much help to you. Being full of facts and littered with accuracies, I mean."

She swallowed hard. "You could answer my question."

"Let me get my tape recorder from the car," he said, "and then I'll answer any questions you have. Only, regardless of what you write, let's at least get the questions right.

"Shad Lucas isn't a professional psychic for my paper or anyone else. Rosie Holland is the *Chronicle*'s professional counsellor; Shad is her gardener. The production company making *You've Been Had* is no more a rival to a proper newspaper than is your own. The ratings issue is equally spurious: they get viewers, we get readers, many of them are the same people. It's true there's been some animosity between our two organisations, but I'm happy to say their people and ours are cooperating fully with the police investigation.

"If you want confirmation of that, talk to Ms Holland or to Ms Frank at PVF. As a result of their cooperation, facts have emerged which cast serious doubt on Lucas's guilt. Naturally we're hoping he's innocent. But mostly we're hoping the killer of Jackie Pickering will be brought to justice."

"Even if the murderer was your employee? I'm sorry," she amended slyly, "your employee's employee."

"Oh yes," said Matt firmly.

"If Lucas didn't kill her, why is he saying he did?"

Matt breathed heavily. "He suffered a head injury. However he came by it, there's no doubt he suffered a severe blow to the head with concussion and consequent amnesia. Have you ever been concussed, Miss Moody? Because I have, twice. You're not at your best for quite a while afterwards. The first time I insisted on telling the MO how to play Charades. The second time I was convinced I'd lost my gun. It didn't matter how many people told me I hadn't, or how often they produced it, I was convinced I'd left something vital behind."

She was mesmerised. He was a good-looking man, with steady,

intelligent eyes in which still danced a glint of boyish humour; a strong man, competent and successful – he'd rescued a failing business and put it on a profit-making basis. Of course, that could change; particularly in the light of recent events. But even the prospect of bankruptcy didn't stop him being a damned attractive man. She said breathily, "And had you?"

Matt nodded and smiled. "My foot."

It wasn't the first time he'd thrown his missing extremity into a conversation deliberately to unsettle an opponent. But there weren't many advantages to being an amputee, he was damned if he wasn't making full use of any he came across.

Emma Moody didn't know where to look. A gravity well was dragging her eyes down to ground level and she hadn't the time to recognise that it would be more natural to look than to avoid doing. He'd raised the subject, she had nothing to be embarrassed about, but she was. Which was odd, because 'The Vomiter' and her own contributions to it embarrassed her not at all.

"That one," he said helpfully, pointing. He wasn't at all a malicious man, but there was a part of him which took an unkind pleasure in the colour flooding through her cheeks.

It wasn't quite the end of the interview but it might as well have been. The flustered reporter had trouble stringing together three intelligent sentences. Finally Matt took pity on her and gave her a statement; and repeated it when she pressed the wrong button on her own tape recorder. They parted civilly, and Matt continued his journey feeling oddly satisfied with the encounter.

At the *Chronicle* he went straight to Dan Sale's office. "You're going to have to remake the front page."

"What?!" There was still time. There was time until – and in real emergencies even after – the presses started to roll. But Sale hated surprises.

"We need to carry something on Shad Lucas and the Pickering girl. The 'Daily Vomit's onto it, and if they're going to have it we have to have it."

Sale looked at him over the wire-rimmed specs he wore primarily for that purpose. "Wouldn't you say that was an editorial decision?"

Matt nodded cheerfully. "Of course it is, Dan." While he was nodding he was calling up the front page on Sale's terminal.

"As long as we're agreed," sniffed the editor. With all the wonders of modern technology on the desk before him, he took up a biro and a sheet of paper. "Now, how much do we say? What we know, or what we think 'The Vomiter' knows?"

It took Sale no more than ten minutes to draft an unsensational but informative piece on the continuing investigation into the death of Jackie Pickering and Shad Lucas's involvement in it. Mention was made of Lucas's connection with the *Chronicle* and of his previous successes on behalf of the police. It wasn't entirely clear whether he was Helping Police With Their Inquiries, or just helping police with their inquiries.

"You don't think we're being a bit coy?" ventured Matt.

Sale glared at him. "Restrictions apply to the reporting of criminal cases where a person has been charged, is about to be charged or where charges may reasonably be anticipated. The Poison Dwarf from the 'Daily Vomit' may not be aware of that, you may not be aware of that, but I am a professional journalist and know exactly what we can and cannot say at any juncture of a criminal prosecution. Prejudicing a trial is a serious offence, and I don't intend for the highlight of my career to be reporting my own conviction for contempt of court."

"Plus, if that's all we can lawfully say, no one can criticise us for not saying more."

"Yes, there is that," admitted Sale. Scrutinising the front page layout, he selected an item on oil seeping into the Brickfields Park pond and consigned it to page three. "There. It's on the front page, nobody can say we tried to hide it; but it's amazing how things vanish when they're just below the fold."

Matt nodded his approval. "I don't see what more we can do. It meets our obligations without making things harder for either Shad or Rosie."

"No, we've covered our backs," agreed Sale. "But don't imagine that's the end of it. The 'Daily Vomit' will make up for being second with the story by blowing it out of all proportion, turning speculation into allegations and allegations into facts. You won't recognise yourself or anyone in it. We should be braced for trouble. People who mistake it for a newspaper may think we're in some way responsible for that girl's death."

"We'd better warn Rosie. Where is she today?"

Sale put a letter on the desk and waited while Matt read it.

The proprietor of the *Skipley Chronicle*, who could take slanderous accusations by the 'Daily Vomit' in his slightly uneven stride, paled at its contents. "She's gone? Dan . . . you accepted her resignation?"

"Of course I didn't," Sale said indignantly. "I put her letter in my drawer, as insurance against a major emergency. She's determined to leave if Lucas is charged. I said we could ride it out, but she wouldn't risk the *Chronicle*'s reputation. Unless and until this all turns out to be a hideous mistake, Alex is running The Primrose Path."

Matt didn't know what to say. He knew they were in trouble but he hadn't realised it could come to a choice between his newspaper and his star columnist. "So . . . where is she? At home?"

Sale shook his head. "I really don't know, Matt. Officially, at this moment, she doesn't work here any more. But if I was guessing, I'd say she's out somewhere trying to prove Shad Lucas didn't do what he thinks he did."

"Prufrock might know." Matt reached for the phone.

There was no reply. He found himself the recipient of one of Sale's knowing looks. "Where Holmes leads," he said, "can Watson be far behind?"

Ray Burgess was not a big man but he moved with a quiet authority that swept all before it. Rosie found herself borne up the steps and into the front hall, and Burgess shut the door behind him with a crisp, rather final click.

"Now then," he said quietly, "let's start again at the beginning. Who are you, and what do you want with my family?"

Long before she worked for an ex-soldier, Rosie had discovered that the best form of defence is attack. She drew herself up to her full, impressive scale and rapped out: "I'm Rosie Holland, I work for the *Skipley Chronicle*, and there are people who know exactly where I am and what I'm doing."

"Like the idiot in the Volvo?" Burgess failed to look alarmed. "Well, I wish somebody'd tell me."

"She was asking about Debbie," said Mrs Burgess. There was a sense of things unsaid in the timbre of her voice.

"Ah."

Rosie had reached the point of looking for the back way out. Any two normal people the size of the Burgesses she'd simply have shouldered past; but Roy Burgess was not just a former soldier, he was a former member of the SAS. He was also, possibly, a child abuser and murderer. Her sense of vulnerability was not soothed by knowing that Prufrock was in the car.

"Nothing much happened in Skipley this week?" asked Burgess grimly. "Having to rehash old news to fill the pages?"

Fear always made Rosie querulous. It would have been wiser to take some of the heat out of the situation. But, not being built for flight, adrenalin made her square up to her enemies. "Is it old news?" she demanded. "Or the reason a girl was murdered in Skipley a week ago?"

The silence was more than an absence of sound: it filled the hall like fast-falling snow or ash, creeping into all the crevices, setting hard, a thing without substance which, in enough volume, was capable of crushing out life.

Finally Burgess fought his way through it. "What are you *talking* about?"

"Jackie," whispered Mrs Burgess. "She's talking about Jackie."

Rosie was watching Roy Burgess like a hawk, and she still didn't see that Road to Damascus moment where the dominoes tumbled, the pieces fell into place, sudden comprehension flooded the eyes and he reached for his piano wire. If anything he looked more mystified than before. "Jackie Pickering?"

"Of course Jackie Pickering!" exclaimed Rosie. "She's dead, Mr Burgess! Murdered."

"I know she's dead," he snarled, "I read the papers. I still don't understand what you're doing here. Are you looking for Debbie? She doesn't live here any more. She *never* lived at my garage!"

By degrees Rosie was feeling less like somebody cornering a killer and more like someone who might have made a mistake. "Debbie knew Jackie better than anyone else. They were close friends for years, they still talked every week. Jackie was working on a story, a big story: she didn't tell anyone at the office what it was but I bet she told Debbie. It may have got her killed. I need to know what it was."

Burgess was beginning to see daylight. "And you thought of me. So you're here to accuse me of . . . what, exactly? Murdering Jackie? *Why*? Oh, I see – the judgement of the court wasn't enough, she wanted to take another crack at me." His voice developed a dangerous rasp. "Is that it – is that what you thought? That my daughter's friend intended to expose me for what she believed I did when Debbie was a child, and to shut her up I murdered her? That's it, isn't it? That's what you believe."

Rosie picked her words. "It was a possibility that needed exploring."

"By *you*?" He sounded incredulous. "Are you mad? You thought I'd already killed one person so you came here to confront me? Why didn't you tell the police, let them come? Why does it matter to you enough to risk your neck? Because let's face it, if the man who killed Jackie decided to kill you too, that living advertisement for Care in the Community out there in your car wouldn't be able to stop him. What . . . why . . . ?" Torn between fury and incomprehension, he was struggling to find the words. "Why do you care so much?"

"Because if I can't find out what happened to Jackie a young man is going to spend the rest of his days in a living hell," Rosie shot back. "I don't mean prison; I don't mean a mental institution. I mean, with violent, insane people inside his head."

She saw his expression, caught her breath and shook her head wearily. "I don't expect you to understand. But that's why I'm here."

He didn't know what to say to her. Of course he was angry; even so, he could see that she had a purpose beyond making capital out of his family's misfortune. He wasn't ready to help her. But he wasn't ready to throw her out either. "They've arrested someone?"

"Not exactly," said Rosie. She wasn't sure how much of this

she should be sharing, especially with him, but she was beginning to suspect it mightn't matter. "He found her. My friend. He was concussed, and now he thinks he killed her. I don't believe he did. I have to convince him."

"You need an alternate suspect."

She demurred, unconvincingly. "I'm just trying to contact your daughter. She may be the only person who knows what Jackie was working on."

"And you thought you'd find her here? Miss Holland, you do know what the court case was about?"

"Of course I do. I also know that you were acquitted. I needed to know if that was the end of it."

Mrs Burgess said softly, "You'd think it would be, wouldn't you?" She sounded close to tears. "That bloody man. That bloody, bloody man!"

It was Rosie's turn to practise the puzzled squint. What bloody man? Not Shad – who else?

In another moment she'd have asked, and then the dominos would have begun falling into place. But before she could shape the words all hell broke loose. What she initially took for a rock, but turned out on closer inspection to be a garden gnome, came flying through the pane in the front door surrounded by a halo of shattered glass. The gnome, who was cast in cement with his hat and his boots picked out in red, cannoned off the newel post at the foot of the stairs and dug a divot out of the parquet flooring. Shards of toughened glass spread out, glittering like frost.

The three people standing in the hall watched the progress of the ballistic gnome and for several seconds thought of nothing but keeping their feet out of his way.

None of them was looking at the door; none of them saw a pink hand come through the gap where the glass had been and grope for the latch. Neither Rosie nor the Burgesses had got beyond thinking of a flying gnome as a kind of natural phenomenon when Arthur Prufrock flung back the door, filling the aperture rather better from side to side than he did from top to bottom, and bawled, "That boy: stand still! Any more of this and someone's going home with a note!"

Eighteen

News travels fast. Even in the days before the printing press it had a way of getting around, and what it lost in accuracy it made up in colour. Since the birth of telecommunications it gets round virtually instantaneously, so viewers half a world away can witness events as they unfold in a mid-West playground or an Asiatic desert. But accuracy can suffer as much from speed as it did from delay.

Alex went out for an evening paper at four o'clock and found her progress observed, up the street and then back, by three pairs of sullen eyes floating like blobs of blackcurrant jam in the semolina faces of three fourteen-year-old girls. From the backpacks and the rudimentary uniform, they had come here after chucking-out time at the local comprehensive.

Her first instinct was to pass them without comment and get on with her own business. They were nothing to do with her or she with them. But close enough to the *Chronicle* to put her foot over the threshold she found herself wondering what Rosie would have done. Passed them by in silence? Allowed herself to be stared down by three pasty girls who probably still had Barbie dolls at home? She didn't think so. She tucked the paper firmly under her arm and turned back.

"I'm Alex Fisher," she said evenly. "Can I help you?"

The direct approach seemed to unnerve them. They looked away and mumbled, and pushed themselves off the wall they were leaning on and seemed about to leave. Then one of them looked up, sullen gaze touched with a mixture of defiance and prurience. "That's where he works, innit? Is he in there now?"

Alex felt her heart plummet, worked to keep the dismay

out of her face and voice. "Who's that?" As if she didn't know.

"Him as killed that girl." Emboldened by Alex's restraint – she appeared to have been ready to dodge a slap – she pressed for answers. "Was it really black magic? Do you know him? Is he really a gypsy?"

Alex Fisher had been blessed with a demeanour which always seemed cool no matter what the turmoil beneath. This wasn't the first time she'd had cause to be grateful. If nobody knew she was in a panic, perhaps it wasn't fair to describe it as a panic at all.

She breathed steadily for a moment before replying. "You're referring to the death of Miss Pickering. I'm afraid you've got it badly wrong. We don't know who killed her. The only thing I can tell you for sure is that it wasn't anyone who works here."

"Well, you would say that," said one of the other girls in a tone of deep scepticism.

"Indeed I would," said Alex briskly, "because it's the truth. If you want the full story I suggest you buy the *Chronicle* tomorrow."

"What – for a cover-up?"

Alex was keenly aware that she was Rosie's understudy, not her successor. It seemed incumbent upon her to react in Rosie's image as well as nature permitted her. She tried hard to bristle. "The *Skipley Chronicle* has nothing to cover up, and wouldn't if it had. I don't know where you got this story about black magic but it's nonsense. The man you refer to – who is a friend of ours but does not in fact work here – is helping Skipley CID. And I mean exactly that: he was a witness, he's helping them find out what happened to Miss Pickering and who's to blame."

"An' he's a gypsy?"

She was damned if she was going to lie: it was nothing to lie *about*, nothing to be ashamed of. Her back stiffened with disapproval. "I believe his mother is of Romany extraction." She winced to hear herself say it and didn't quite know why. Alex lacked Rosie's robust attitude to political correctness. She worked on the assumption that if anything was capable of offending anybody it was best to look for another way of putting it.

"*Told* you!" shrieked the first girl triumphantly, shouldering her bag and swinging off down the street with the others in tow. "*Told* you it was black magic!"

Alex watched them go in despair, and was only glad she had nothing heavy to throw at them.

She went to her office and sat down to check the paper for anything that would reflect on what appeared in The Primrose Path tomorrow. It was too late to change much, except in a dire emergency, but there was always the time-honoured remedy of rendering the offending material unreadable. A dab of acid in the right spot saved many a newspaper from a libel action. Before computer setting a trusty printer used to wallop the type with a hammer.

After a few minutes Alex found she was unable to concentrate on the paper for thinking of the exchange outside. It had left her uneasy. She didn't see how anything could come of it, but still . . . She left the paper spread on her desk and headed for the editor's office.

"I don't expect it's anything to worry about but . . ."

She hadn't realised Matt was in there too. Their eyes met, kindled and then sheered apart; Alex actually blushed. They were at that bashful stage of relationships where, without being prepared to lie about it, they quite hoped other people hadn't noticed. Other people, of course, knew exactly what they were up to and took a perverse pleasure in showing no discretion at all. Even Dan Sale, who had as much time for office gossip as the Mothers' Union has for King Herod, couldn't resist splitting a malicious grin between them. Recent developments could hardly have been more widely known if they'd been caught bonking on top of the photocopier.

Sale coughed the smile off his face. "Was it me you were looking for?" His gaze strayed towards his proprietor. "Or, um . . . ?"

Alex stiffened a perfectly formed sinew and summoned up some blood. "In fact, you should both hear this. It may mean nothing. But I was just talking to some schoolgirls who accused us of employing a practitioner in the black arts."

Matt had flashed his engaging grin before he realised she

wasn't joking. He looked quickly at Sale, and Sale wasn't smiling at all. "What did you tell them?"

"I told them the truth. And to buy the paper tomorrow."

"Always a sound response," nodded Sale approvingly. He looked as if he was going to say something else but then didn't.

Matt had known him just long enough to be able to fill in some of his silences. He raised an questioning eyebrow. "Is this what you were afraid of? The backlash – is this how it starts?"

"With three schoolgirls?" Sale gave a negligent shrug. "Unless their satchels are full of Molotov cocktails, how much damage can three schoolgirls do? They've probably gone home now anyway. Have they?"

Matt, who was closest, moved to the window. He answered with a sharp intake of breath.

Alex, frowning, said, "Well – are they still there?"

Matt cleared his throat. "Bit hard to say. I can't see them, but they could be with the gang from Threatening Crowds R Us."

"He used to be a teacher," explained Rosie, a shade superfluously, when the dust had settled.

"And what is he now?" asked Roy Burgess carefully.

She gave a rueful shrug. "My friend."

"You do have some interesting ones, don't you?"

When Prufrock armed himself with the cement gnome, he had no idea what he was going to walk in on. But he believed Rosie was in danger, and he could no more have hung back chewing his fingernails than ignore a rude limerick written in somebody's hymn book. Widely considered a mild-mannered, inoffensive little man, in fact Arthur Prufrock's scrubbed complexion and neat white moustache hid a soul of adamant. Break a window? He'd have stormed the Bastille for a friend in trouble.

But he didn't find what he expected to. No whirling fists or glinting knives; no air-thickening threats and obscenities; not even a vigorous trading of insults. Roy Burgess hadn't shut the door to keep his visitor from escaping: he'd done it to keep in the central heating.

Prufrock said stiffly, "I appear to have misread the situation.

In which case I owe you an apology, and the *Skipley Chronicle* owes you a new pane of glass."

"Never *mind* the glass," exclaimed Burgess in exasperation. "Can we please all stick to the point until, as an absolute basic minimum, I know what the hell's going on!"

But Rosie ignored him, her attention on his wife. "What bloody man?"

The gnome had interrupted her train of thought. Mrs Burgess stared at her visitor without comprehension. "What?"

"You said, 'That bloody bloody man'. What bloody man?"

"The one who started all this. The one who told Debbie she'd been abused."

A chink of daylight glimmered through the fog in Rosie's brain. "Someone had to tell her?"

"Yes. She didn't remember because it never happened."

The hall wasn't big enough for four of them and a cement gnome. Mrs Burgess sighed and opened the door to the living room. "Come inside. If we have to talk about this we might as well be comfortable."

It began in Debbie Burgess's second year at university. The course was demanding, she'd had trouble making friends, she became involved in a difficult and ultimately destructive relationship. She got behind with her work, became seriously depressed, went to her GP and was sent for psychotherapy.

Naturally concerned, her family took care to check out the practitioner first. Between psychiatrists and psychologists and therapists and counsellors, some of them properly trained, qualified and regulated and some not, there's scope for a crank or two and that was the last thing Debbie needed. The Burgesses were reassured to learn that the recommended therapist was a qualified MD. They believed their daughter would be safe in his hands. Their sessions began.

She was depressed, anxious, apathetic, her energies stultified and without organisation: in a healthy and intelligent young woman, clearly there was some reason for this. How did she get on with her family?

Fine.

She was, in fact, still living at home. Any particular reason?

Convenience and economy. Her home was convenient for the university, cheaper and more comfortable than digs.

But what was the real reason?

Debbie didn't understand. Those *were* the real reasons.

She got on all right with her mother and father?

Fine.

Both of them?

Both of them.

When did she lose her virginity?

That came as a surprise. But she answered honestly. Sixteen, with an assistant instructor at an outdoor pursuits centre. Under an upturned canoe, with him scared of losing his job and constantly peeping out from under the spray dodger.

Enjoyable?

Had better since.

But no lasting relationships. Why might that be?

Debbie Burgess pointed out that at twenty she wasn't ready to settle down. She wanted fun, not lasting relationships.

Then why wasn't she happier with her life?

She was too polite, too nicely brought up, to point out that this was his field of expertise and the reason she had come.

What was her earliest awareness of her sexuality?

She didn't know how to answer that. He seemed to think she was refusing to answer it.

Was she aware of research indicating that children were sexual beings much sooner than was often assumed?

Well . . . no.

Really? Or was she avoiding thinking about it?

There was something about his persistence she was beginning to find alarming. She had no reason to think about it, she said, since she didn't have any small children and it was a long time since she'd been one.

Did she remember being a small child?

Just about.

Not clearly?

Does anyone?

Oh yes, some people did.

Perhaps they had reason to.

And perhaps the others had reason not to.

She bridled at that. He was getting at something, she just wasn't sure what. Was he accusing her of something? She asked, What kind of reason?

And he said, "Why don't we take a look?"

She'd heard of regression therapy, had thought of it as something out of the drawer marked Weird, along with astrology and crystals, mostly pursued by earnest young women who also took pottery classes. She hadn't time for pottery classes and she didn't think she had time for this. She was surprised at him suggesting it. He was a doctor, with letters after his name.

So maybe she was wrong and it was a legitimate avenue of exploration. She shrugged off her unease and agreed; and when he said it would involve hypnosis, she agreed to that too.

Rosie got to the climax before the painful tale Mrs Burgess was telling. She'd heard it before, more than once. "And under hypnosis," she said flatly, "Debbie remembered being sexually abused by her father."

The woman's eyes dipped, hiding tears.

Roy Burgess's jawline was white. "She *remembered* nothing of the kind. The idea was planted in her head by someone she was meant to trust, and she was too young and vulnerable to fight it. He persuaded her it had happened and she believed him. But it never happened. Nothing like it ever happened."

"I know," said Rosie, "I know. The jury knew; and the medical profession is well aware of False Memory Syndrome. It's no comfort, I know, but yours isn't the first happy family to be broken up by it. Initially it was known as Recovered Memory, and treated as though what someone remembered under such conditions was the deepest kind of truth. The fact that they'd remembered nothing before was taken as further proof: the only reason people wouldn't remember details of their childhood was if there was something to repress. The family has to seem normal because of the devastating secret at its heart.

"There are cases where genuine abuse emerges from such

therapy. But psychiatry is the same as other branches of medicine: at its best dealing with real problems. If a patient presents from a dysfunctional background and complains of difficulty relating to other people on a wide range of levels, and then hypnosis brings up memories of abuse, that's a scenario where you have to listen to what she's saying. Or he – it's as likely to be a man as a woman.

"But Debbie? She was tired and depressed because her studies were harder than she'd expected and her first adult relationship had just ended badly. With a history like that, picking a decent family apart in the hopes of finding a rotton core is the psychiatric equivalent of vivisection."

She shook her head in grim wonder. "Your daughter was very badly served by my profession. You all were. Thank God the legal system did a better job."

Roy Burgess looked as if he'd been struck by a gentle thunderbolt. He was used to telling this story, or having it told. He was used to the cautious expressions of people who thought it was in everybody's best interests to assume that the jury got it right. He was not used to people understanding the mechanisms by which his family had been fragmented. The jury had believed him; his wife believed him; he wasn't sure there was anyone else who genuinely did, until now. If he hadn't had the honour of the SAS to uphold he might very well have cried.

"Not good enough to give me my daughter back," said Mrs Burgess thickly.

"Does she still believe . . . ?"

"I don't know that she believes it; but she still *feels* as if it happened. She *remembers* it. I think she accepts, logically, that the jury were probably right when they decided her memory was unreliable. But when she's in a room with her father she *feels* she's standing next to a man who raped her when she was too young to stop him or even ask for help. She feels violated."

"She *was* violated," Rosie agreed hotly, "just not by the man she blames. I hope you made an official complaint."

"Oh yes," said Burgess wearily. "Fat lot of good that did us. The powers-that-be decided that the relevant guidelines had not been breached. That, however regrettable the consequences, Debbie appeared to have been treated in good faith and in line with current practice."

Through her anger Rosie was aware that they'd drifted off the point. She'd come looking for Debbie Burgess, and to see if her father made a plausible villain. She'd found, inconveniently enough, that he didn't; which left her with her original purpose. To find Debbie, talk to her, ask what Jackie Pickering had talked about last time she phoned.

And Rosie rocked in her chair as the answer that had been staring her in the face finally resorted to slapping it to get her attention.

Jackie wanted a big story that nobody else knew about. She also wanted vengeance for her friend on the man who abused her. Not her father: even Debbie knew that, Jackie certainly did. No, the blame lay with the man who made Debbie Burgess believe she'd been the victim of her father's carnal desires when there wasn't the least fragment of evidence to that effect.

Now Jackie was in a position to do something about it. When she confronted him with the consequences of his mind games in front of a television audience, she would launch her own career and end his. He was a successful professional man with the confidence of the medical establishment – but only until Jackie Pickering made her programme on False Memory Syndrome.

So who had a motive to murder Jackie Pickering? A young man with a curious talent for whom exposure might mean mockery, mistrust, a few vacancies on his round as a jobbing gardener? Or a psychotherapist with a lucrative practice entirely dependent on his reputation, his good standing with his profession and his ability to avoid being publicly denounced?

Rosie stared at Prufrock; and Prufrock, using that radar for trouble which had served so well in his own career, picked the kernels of understanding as it were straight from her brain. "You think . . . the therapist . . . ?"

But Rosie's thoughts had already leapfrogged ahead. A man who had killed to protect his reputation had nothing to lose. "What's his name?"

It was just enough of a non-sequitur to make Mrs Burgess blink. "Who – Debbie's psychiatrist?"

"Of course Debbie's psychiatrist," growled Rosie. "He's the key to all of this. Not just to your tragedy – to Jackie's. Who is he, what's his name?"

The Burgesses exchanged a glance, shocked and horrified and yet not altogether displeased if it should be so. This man had put them through hell. If their daughter's friend had died trying to prove it, that was appalling. But if the fat woman with the home perm hairdo could finish the job – if he was going to pay for Jackie – he could pay for them all.

Neither of them needed to look it up: it was engraved in their memories. Roy Burgess's voice was thin but sure. "Cunningham. Andrew Cunningham. I can get you his address . . ."

But Rosie was already diving for the phone. "No need," she gritted as she dialled. "I know where to find him."

Nineteen

Detective Superintendent Marsh was not in his office. Rosie had had difficulty composing a message that *he* would understand and act on with sufficient urgency; she had no idea what to say to his sergeant.

"Get hold of him as soon as you can," she said tersely. "Tell him I have to speak to him – nothing he's doing is more important."

Of course she didn't know then that what Marsh was doing was trying to prevent a hostile crowd from burning down the *Chronicle* building.

She gave him her mobile number. "In the meantime, get Shad Lucas out of Fellowes Hall and into protective custody. Don't call ahead, just go and get him. Don't take no for an answer."

"But . . . but . . ." Detective Sergeant Burton wasn't used to being browbeaten like this by his superior, let alone a member of the public.

"*Please*," she growled, "there is absolutely no time to discuss it. It's a matter of life and death, and I promise you Superintendent Marsh will not have your guts for garters if you do as I say!" She took his stammering as acquiescence and put the phone down.

"Arthur, time we left."

Even with motorways most of the way – even with Rosie driving – they were ninety minutes from Fellowes Hall. Ninety minutes in which, unless Sergeant Burton was prepared to act on his own initiative, Shad Lucas would be at the mercy of a man who needed him dead. Or if not dead then destroyed: his mind shattered, his memory past retrieval.

Rosie could guess, could frame a theory, could maybe cast

enough doubt to shift suspicion from Shad on to the man treating him, but only Shad himself could know what happened in Skipley railway yards. Maybe he couldn't get at the information right now, maybe he was confused – maybe strenuous efforts had been made to confuse him – but somewhere deep inside the knowledge existed. He knew what had happened to him and what had happened to Jackie.

And the man who killed her needed nothing in the world so much as to bury that knowledge where it could never be found. He needed a scapegoat, and who more plausible than a young man who was known to be peculiar, who could be convinced that he himself committed the murder, who would say so to the senior investigating officer before letting his damaged mind slip off the cusp of reality altogether? And if it wasn't ready to slip, it could be pushed.

Their best hope now was that Cunningham had no idea how urgent the matter was, how close to his heels the hounds snapped. If he thought he had time – and for the past several days Marsh's only access to the suspect had been through his psychiatrist – he could chart convincingly Shad Lucas's descent into madness. But if time ran short the job could undoubtedly be done in five minutes with a syringe of something that would fry his brain. As long as he didn't die, as long as an autopsy wasn't an option, he'd get away with it. As far as Cunningham knew, no one had any reason to suspect him. With Shad insane, no one ever would.

"I still don't understand," Prufrock said thinly as they travelled, "why Shad thinks he killed Jackie Pickering. Amnesia is one thing, but why does he think he remembers something that didn't happen?"

"That's exactly what false memory is," gritted Rosie, bearing down on a rep cruising in the outside lane until he crossed himself and veered out of her way. "Once planted, a false memory is indistinguishable subjectively from the real thing. Those affected believe in it because they remember it happening – they were there. Debbie Burgess may *know* her father never raped her, but she *believes* he did because she remembers it. Shad believes he killed Jackie Pickering because an expert in Recovered Memory got hold of him when he was at his most vulnerable and coached him into remembering what he needed him to remember."

"But . . . it's so *real* to him!"

"Of course it's real, Arthur! It was real to Debbie Burgess, and she's like you and me. Shad isn't. He's a powerful natural psychic: he can pick other people's thoughts, feelings and memories clean out of their heads. He was there, or nearby, when Jackie died – he *knows* what she felt. He also knows what her killer felt. With that to work on, someone much less experienced – and much less motivated – than Cunningham could have made him think those were *his* memories, his reasons. It only needed a little careful manipulation to make him confess to the crime. And the real murderer is safe."

Prufrock thought about that. "Not entirely. Not while there's any chance of Shad starting to recover – to recognise the difference between adopted memories and real ones. He'll only be safe when . . ." The glance he shot her was sharp with fear. "When he's rendered Shad incapable of stringing two coherent thoughts together. Permanently."

"We'll be there in half an hour," Rosie said in her teeth. "If Marsh got our message, he's already safe."

"If Marsh had got your message he'd have phoned."

Rosie thought so too. "Or maybe Sergeant Burton will have dealt with it himself?"

Prufrock looked doubtful. "I don't think that's how you make Chief Constable – using your initiative." But he was thinking of something else. The word 'message' was running round inside his head looking for something to connect with. "Oh no!"

"What?" She cranked round so quickly the car swerved.

"The message we left for Shad. If Cunningham's seen it – and he will have seen it, he'll be making sure he sees everything to do with Shad – he knows we're on to something. He'll assume we're on to him. We weren't, then, but he'll think we were. He'll think he's out of time. He'll do whatever's necessary to break the trail between him and Jackie Pickering."

Rosie glanced at the speedometer. The big car was already way over the speed limit. She pumped the pedal some more and the clock edged towards ninety.

"It's nothing to worry about," said Andrew Cunningham calmly. "ECT was routine therapy when I started in this business. It was practised in every psychiatric ward in the country. It was considered safe and beneficial, and it achieved some excellent results. It was only as the new generation of psychotropic drugs became available that it was sidelined. But there have always been some patients who respond to it after the drugs have failed. Let's hope you're going to be one of them."

"Will it hurt?"

"You won't know a thing about it."

After five o'clock, when the offices closed and the factory shifts changed, the crowd in Moss Street swelled until you couldn't have got a bicycle along it, much less a newspaper van. The pages for tomorrow's *Chronicle* were ready to go to the press, stacked up inside the back door like charter flights waiting to land.

Dan Sale was pacing up and down beside them, making everyone nervous. He'd brought papers out late before – strikes, power cuts and, on one memorable occasion, an unexploded bomb had torn up the schedule and thrown it on the fire – but he'd never missed an issue and he didn't mean to start now. He had his phone in his hand as he paced, contacting everyone he could think of who might be able to help. At one point he called the airfield to see if a helicopter could land in the back yard. But there wasn't enough space for safety, and while the pilot might have risked it to pluck someone from the jaws of death he didn't view Sale's batting average in the same light.

Even if he'd been willing to try, Harry Marsh would have vetoed it. It was the date on a damned newspaper they were talking about, for heaven's sake! If a helicopter touched an overhead wire and came down on the crowd it would kill scores of people.

"Then move them!" snapped Sale.

"If they don't disperse we will move them," promised Marsh.

"But if you're expecting me to whistle up a squadron of Cossacks to charge them with drawn sabres you're going to be disappointed."

"Then what *are* you going to do?"

"Wait," said Marsh, unperturbed. "Boredom clears more streets than force. Keep telling them there's nothing to see, that neither Lucas nor Rosie is in the building. If nothing happens for an hour, most of them will start wanting their tea."

"An hour?" Sale could live with an hour's delay. An hour's delay had been nothing in the days when an apprentice printer could trip over the shop cat and send a day's work fountaining into the air in a thousand slugs of type.

"Two, tops," Marsh nodded encouragingly.

"What, actually, do they want?" Matt thought it might be a naive question but somebody had to ask it.

"Mostly they want not to miss anything. They've got wind of something unusual, they know the *Chronicle* is involved, and it's a nice handy place to picket. Part of the price you pay for a town-centre location, I'm afraid."

"They're not friends of Jackie Pickering's then."

"I doubt if half of them would recognise her name. No, they know a girl was killed; they know she worked for a television company that had a dispute with the *Chronicle*; they know there's a suspect who also has a connection with the *Chronicle*. A mob is like an amoeba: it can only process information in the simplest of terms. Lucas being a friend of Ms Holland's implicates the paper. Where is she, by the way?"

Sale shrugged. "Nottingham. Don't ask me why – I never have more than the vaguest idea where Rosie is and what she's up to."

"It hardly matters," said Marsh, "as long as she's not here. As long as neither of the people they want to throw stones at is available, sooner or later they'll get bored and go home. Rosie waving at them from a window just to prove she's not afraid could be enough to start a riot."

"They were talking about black magic," said Alex faintly.

Marsh grunted derisively. "Amoeba thinking. Slap a sexy label on something and you don't have to bother working out why it was done, or why it was done that way. Black magic – explains everything, doesn't it? Nobody expects to understand it so it isn't a problem when they don't."

"It means they know about Shad," said Alex tautly. "Not just that you have a suspect, not just that he's a friend of Rosie's, but who he is and what he does. If they thought I'd killed Jackie Pickering, or Matt had, nobody'd be talking about black magic. It's because Shad's a psychic. It's because of what he's done for the police in the past that there's a mob baying for his blood right now!"

This was an exaggeration but nobody said so. There was a general recognition that if it wasn't strictly true now it might be later.

"We won't let them hurt him, Miss Fisher," Marsh said quietly.

"I don't doubt your good intentions, Superintendent. But this thing is going one of two ways, and I doubt your ability to protect him in either eventuality. If he did it he'll go to prison. The talk will follow him. A police nark who sacrificed a young girl in a black magic ritual? – they'll crucify him.

"Or you'll find someone else did it – or anyway you won't be able to prove Shad did – and you'll let him go. You think that'll be the end of it as far as these people are concerned? They'll think he got away with it. Because he helped you in the past, you let him go. They'll drive him out of town. This is where he lives, where he works, but not after this. He's a dead man in prison, a pariah out of it. I don't know how anyone can protect him."

Harry Marsh would have liked to dismiss her concern as hysterical, but he knew better. Guilty or innocent, Shad Lucas was going to pay for Jackie Pickering's death, and go on paying probably for the rest of his life.

Lacking an adequate reply, he turned back to the window. The crowd had stabilised at perhaps three hundred people. For every new arrival now, someone else sloped away to see what was on the TV. As long as nothing happened to hold their interest he was going to be right. At least about that.

"You'd better get hold of Ms Holland, let her know what's going on. She doesn't want to walk into the middle of this."

Alex nodded. "I tried her mobile earlier, couldn't get through. I'll keep trying."

"Good enough. I'll be at Brickfields if anyone wants me." The police station enjoyed one of the most desirable locations in town, overlooking Skipley's answer to Central Park.

Dan Sale raised a surprised eyebrow. "You're leaving?"

"Crowd control isn't a CID matter," Marsh reminded him. "Chief Inspector Gordon has it in hand; if he needs reinforcements he'll call for them. My time'll be better spent on my own case: trying to find out what really happened behind the station. Maybe, right now, that's the best anyone can do for young Lucas."

He found Rosie's message waiting on his desk. He stared at it; then he put his head on one side and stared at it some more. It didn't help. He called Sergeant Burton. "What's all this about?"

"Your friend Miss Holland. She was hot under the collar about something – I couldn't make out what. She wanted Lucas in custody. I don't know why. Maybe she's changed her mind, decided he did it after all? But he's not going anywhere – there are as many locks there as there are here."

"She must have had something in mind." Marsh frowned. "Get her on the phone, will you, let's find out what."

Sergeant Burton returned shaking his head. He'd had no more luck than Alex. "I'll try again in ten minutes."

But Marsh couldn't shake off the feeling that there was a degree of urgency here. Not just because Rosie Holland was telling him how to do his job again – he was getting used to that. But mostly she paid him the courtesy of doing it face to face. Phone messages via his sergeant were a new departure. Something had happened, and she hadn't time to get here and discuss it with him, and she hadn't even time to wait for him to return her call. She wasn't a stupid woman and, in spite of the schoolboy sense of humour, she wasn't a frivolous one. If she was worried there was probably good reason.

He hadn't been at his desk for five minutes before he got up again. He had plenty of work waiting, not only on the Pickering case, but he was too uneasy to settle to it.

"Get your coat," he decided, "we're going out there. Fellowes Hall. See if everything's all right."

"Are we bringing Lucas back with us?"

But the Superintendent didn't know. "Depends what we find. And whether we can work out what the hell Rosie Holland thinks *she's* found."

"Only if we do, we'll need more bodies," said Burton.

Marsh scowled. "I really don't know what's wrong with police officers these days. When I was a young detective we thought nothing of wrestling a suspect into the back of a squad car single-handed and handcuffing him to the seat. We'd have been laughed at for wanting help to arrest one man. You're all so precious these days. I don't know when I last saw a constable with a seriously good black eye."

DS Burton was a quiet, thoughtful man but he wasn't the pushover people sometimes believed. "How fortunate for me then, sir," he murmured, "that you'll be able to show me how to do it."

When electro-convulsive therapy was first used in the 1940s in the treatment of depression and agitation, it was given without either anaesthetics or muscle relaxants and the resulting convulsions could be violent enough to cause fractures. Although there should be no memory of the shock travelling across the temples, it also managed to frighten many patients. This, together with a comparatively low success rate, relapses in some patients, memory loss and confusion in others, and the development of drug regimes with better results and fewer side effects, led to ECT being demoted from the front line of psychiatric medicine to a treatment of last resort. It still has its uses in obdurate cases: in certain types of schizophrenia, for instance, it can produce improvements.

It is not, however, a useful treatment for amnesia, and never was. But Shad Lucas, despite owning one of the most interesting minds on the planet, knew nothing about psychiatry. He knew about cinerarias. He was given a consent form and a biro, and he signed.

Andrew Cunningham was a belt-and-braces man. He hoped he would never have to produce that form. He was a consultant at a reputable clinic: when he said that a patient being treated for a personality disorder so serious it had led him to commit murder suddenly deteriorated and lapsed into a near vegetative state, he expected to be believed.

The consent form was in case he got the voltage wrong and Lucas died. In that event, his best defence would be that the patient was determined to try anything that might conceivably help and Cunningham, knowing what the price of failure would be, was persuaded to help. That death resulted from what should have been a safe procedure he would attribute to the abnormality of the patient's brain. He would say that he kept within the clinical recommendations of 70 to 150 volts at very low amperage for up to half a second. There would be no one to contradict. He didn't need a nurse to prep the patient because preparation would be superfluous and – if he got it right – he didn't want to be asked what the needle holes were.

There would be criticism of his judgement but he'd survive it. Every one of those who might review the case would have made mistakes in the past. Honest errors in desperate cases are generally accepted as having been made with the best of intentions. Whatever the Holland woman thought she'd found, it would count for nothing once the only witness to the death of Jackie Pickering was silenced.

"All right, Shad? Are you ready?"

"As I'll ever be."

But he wasn't. Nothing could have prepared him for the jolt of pain that went through his head like an ice pick driven by a poleaxe. Pain and terror ripped through him; convulsive spasm threw his body against the restraints with all the power of his strong young muscles. His brain and his body wailed in terrible harmony, and only the leather gag preventing him from biting his tongue kept his agony in the back of his throat.

Chaos took him. A whole new spectrum of colours spun

vertiginously about him: the colours you get from splitting darkness with a prism. Sounds as primitive as a scream, sounds wrenched from the birthing of the world, bathed him like fire. Dimensions split apart and coalesced in new, vibrant combinations and he fell through them as a hailstone falls and rises in the convection of a storm, skin and muscle and mind flayed in the turmoil by exquisite crystalline knives.

He felt himself butchered and was helpless to resist. He felt himself ravelled out – sinews stretched, nerves exposed – and folded afresh like origami. The blood in his veins turned to vitriol, burning as it coursed.

The shattered wreckage that had once been Shad Lucas – gardener, unreliable clairvoyant, decent human being – torn apart at a molecular level, waited, breath abated, for the grace of death; and waited in vain.

Twenty

Harry Marsh preferred driving to being driven. When he was in a rush he compromised by letting DS Burton park the car. He enjoyed driving and saw no reason to give up one of the perks of his job. Today, though, he drove for a different reason. He was haunted by a feeling of urgency and, though he had no reason to order a driver to ignore the speed limits, he could ignore them himself without attracting comment.

Sergeant Burton kept trying Rosie Holland's number, finally got a reply. Marsh didn't want to stop so relayed the conversation through Burton. This left him free to concentrate on getting past a grey estate that was blocking the lane ahead.

"Detective Superintendent Marsh says, where are you? He's been trying to get hold of you for fifteen minutes."

Prufrock held the phone up so Rosie could snap back for herself. "Fifteen minutes? It's an hour and a half since I called – I thought you'd have everything under control by now! Do you mean you haven't been to Fellowes Hall yet?"

"Detective Superintendent Marsh says he's on his way there now," reported Sergeant Burton dutifully. "He says your message made no sense."

"If it didn't make sense," snapped Rosie furiously, "it's because you gave it him wrong! Shad Lucas is in danger. I told you ninety minutes ago that you had to get him out of there. What have you been doing since then – playing Fantasy Felons?"

"Detective Superintendent Marsh says—"

There was a crackle on the line as Marsh lost patience and took the phone. He wasn't getting past the estate anyway: the lane was too narrow and the thing was bucketing from side to side as if it was already going as fast as it could. "Ms Holland, what the hell's going on? I'm on my way to Fellowes Hall now, I'm five minutes away. Where are you?"

"I'm . . ." There was a pause. "Are you a navy blue BMW?"

Marsh blinked. "Yes."

"'Cos I'm the grey Volvo in front of you. OK. It's Cunningham. Andrew Cunningham killed Jackie Pickering because she was going to expose his methods as dangerous on television. His career was heading down the tubes. He needed a scapegoat for the murder and by God he got one. We have to get Shad out of there while there's still a chance he can tell us what really happened."

Too many questions were racing round Marsh's head looking for answers. With Fellowes Hall – and apparently some kind of confrontation – two miles down the road he hadn't time to organise them into words. Instead he said baldly, "I don't understand."

"You don't *have* to understand," Rosie shot back impatiently. "I'll explain later. All you have to do now is get Shad away from Cunningham and into the hands of someone who actually, genuinely wants to help him. If it isn't too late already."

"Too late? What are you saying – that Cunningham could harm him? Kill him?"

"Superintendent, he's already killed once! A girl who threatened his reputation. Shad threatens his freedom. He has nothing to lose. If he can make himself safe by killing again he'll do it without hesitation. He crossed the Rubicon back at the station. Shad isn't a patient, he's a witness. He'll deal with him any way he has to."

Marsh thought for a second. "Then will you either drive that hearse a bit quicker or pull over and let me pass?"

But there was no opportunity and soon there was no need. The gates of Fellowes Hall appeared round a bend and the two cars flashed – well, the BMW flashed, the Volvo lurched – down the drive.

They pulled up in a chorus of spitting gravel outside the main door, beside Cunningham's silver Jaguar. Sergeant Burton, with the benefit of youth, was first up the steps, Superintendent Marsh close in his wake. Rosie lumbered after them like a bulk carrier, Prufrock bobbing behind her like a Clyde puffer.

Inside they split up. Burton engaged the receptionist, Marsh headed for Cunningham's office. But it was empty. Frustrated, he turned on his heel, looking up and down the corridor as if his quarry might chance into view.

Rosie had headed for Shad's room. That was empty too. She saved Prufrock the trouble of catching up by heading back to reception.

Burton had fared no better. The receptionist didn't know where either man was. She offered to bleep Doctor Cunningham on his pager.

Just then the intercom on her desk buzzed. Marsh stayed her hand from answering. "If that's Cunningham, don't tell him we're here." She stared at him uncomprehendingly but nodded compliance.

It wasn't Cunningham. It was a nurse who'd found the door of the ECT room unlocked and wanted to know if the facility was supposed to be in use.

"ECT?" mouthed Superintendent Marsh.

All the colour had drained from Rosie's face. "Oh my God. That's how he's dealing with it."

"ECT?" said Marsh again, aloud this time.

"Electro-convulsive therapy. They pump electricity through your brain. It's supposed to do you good. Except in certain American states, of course, where they do it because they're really pissed off with you." She was talking like that because she was scared, and she wasn't looking at Marsh, she was looking at the receptionist. "Where is it? Quickly! Where?"

The ECT room was hidden in the bowels of the building like a guilty secret. They'd never have found it without directions. A reeded glass panel in the door was back-lit but it was impossible to see anything through it.

"That's what caught my attention," said the nurse who was waiting for them. "They don't use it very often, and when they do it's usually me does the prep. But you don't like to barge in . . ."

Rosie didn't wait for the end of his explanation. It was reasonable enough, but Rosie Holland never had trouble barging in anywhere. She shouldered past and threw the door wide.

Marsh was right behind her. He'd have been in front if she'd given him time or – again – if there'd been room to pass. "Be careful. If you're right, there's a dangerous man in here."

She dismissed his concern scornfully. "It's not *him* I'm worried about. You can have him. But there's a young man with a remarkable brain in here too, and either that brain's about to be connected to the national grid or it already has been. There's no time left to be careful *in*."

Or perhaps there was all the time in the world. As they pushed together through the inner swing doors a faint tangy smell like ozone hung in the air. Marsh didn't recognise it, simply sniffed, frowned and pressed on. Rosie did, and it stopped her in her tracks. "We're too late."

Prufrock finally caught up, breathless and anxious. "Is he here?"

She shook her head wearily. The room's main piece of furniture – a high couch chiefly remarkable for being equipped with padded straps – was unoccupied. But it had been used: the straps dangled untidily.

Shad Lucas had lain down on that couch, afraid but doggedly determined, believing that the man who told him to was trying to help, and suffered the straps to be secured about his body. Rosie could only guess how frightened he must have been, but he'd done it because it was his last hope. Of preserving his liberty, of saving his soul; of finding an explanation for what happened that he could live with.

He'd lain there, helpless, and watched while Doctor Cunningham coated a pair of electrodes in saline and probably jumped, his nerves screwed tight as guitar strings, at the cold, clammy touch of them to his temples. He'd gritted his teeth to silence them and watched Cunningham turn his attention to the machine beside the couch. It was just a box with buttons and dials, but it was connected to his head now with wires. He couldn't read the dials, and it would have made no difference if he could. He had no way in the world of knowing they were turned up way above therapeutic levels.

"He did it," she whispered. "The *animal*. He said to Shad, 'Trust me, I'm a doctor.' Then he tied him down and pumped raw electricity through his brain." Her head rocked back on a moan of pure grief and a slow tear formed in her eye. "That marvellous brain, that we were only beginning to see what it was capable of. Now we'll be lucky if it still knows which hole in your face your dinner goes in."

Prufrock was as white as a sheet, his eyes the colour of daybreak on icicles. His voice was a mere breath, but a breath straight from Siberia. "Deliberately? You mean, he's destroyed Shad's mind in order to cover his tracks?"

"Yes," whispered Rosie.

Harry Marsh had ducked down behind the high couch; now he reappeared. "Well, maybe," he said tersely. "Ms Holland, look at this."

There was a body on the floor, limbs sprawled and tangled with the equipment, long and narrow and clad in what had been a white coat until it got bled on. It groaned as she bent over it. It wasn't dead; and it wasn't Shad.

"And tell me," continued Harry Marsh, a thread of hope just audible in his voice, "how someone whose brain was burnt to a crisp managed to deck the bastard who did it when he came to untie him afterwards?"

He ran. Running felt good. His bare feet were cut and blistered, lactic acid burned in his muscles, but that just meant he had a body again and after where he'd been any body, even one that hurt, was welcome. He couldn't think. He couldn't remember why he was running. He didn't know where he was or where he'd been. He recognised the sensations of pain, of fear and, increasingly, of exhaustion, and for a spell he had no way to measure that was all the universe he knew. He didn't know his own name.

He stayed off the road. He knew that was important although he didn't know why. Bramble hedges tore at his shirt and at his skin; crossing a stubble field was like running on nails. But he had a body again, and as long as he could feel it he could hold on to it. That was all that mattered: not the blood trails across his arms and chest, not the tattered soles of his feet, not even the violent beat – like pain but not pain exactly; like stroboscopic lights but not exactly that either – pulsing across his temples. He was alive, and he was putting distance between him and whatever had hurt him. That was what mattered.

An unconscious man can be neither cautioned nor questioned so no dilemma arises. As regards a suspect in the process of regaining consciousness, rules of procedure codified in the Police and Criminal Evidence Act specify that he cannot be questioned until he is capable of understanding the caution. Responsible police officers abide by the rules: partly because they're fair and partly because failure to do so gets good cases slung out of court.

There is nothing in PACE relating specifically to the role in these circumstances of newspaper columnists who used to be doctors. Rosie hauled Andrew Cunningham out from under the couch, gave his bloody head a cursory examination and said, "He'll live". Then she filled a kidney dish from the tap.

Doctor Cunningham had been grabbed from behind and had his forehead bounced off the wall. It was a nasty injury rather than a dangerous one and he wasn't far away. Voices and the touch of hands were already recalling him when the shock of cold water in his face pulled him back like an over-stretched elastic band. He blinked and put up a belated hand to defend himself. When his eyes cleared he was nose to nose with a plump face red with anger in which burned the eyes of Genghis Khan.

"I know what you did," she said in her teeth. "I know why. I need to know how much damage you did and how long ago he left here."

Concussion is a funny thing. It's possible to regain consciousness, immediately remember everything up to the moment of the injury, and be able to pick up the threads more or less where they were dropped. Or you can be away on Planet Weird for hours, and sometimes much longer than that. Andrew Cunningham came round shaky and woolly but still with a pretty fair grasp of what had happened, who these people were, and why he had to be very careful what he said next.

He said, "Who?"

"You know very well who!" snarled Rosie. "Shad Lucas – the poor sod you meant to carry the can for you. You told him there was a way of getting through his memory block, didn't you? You brought him in here, strapped him down, wired him up, turned up the power and cooked him. You thought we'd never know. You'd say he'd gone into spontaneous fugue, it must have been the guilt catching up with him, and nobody'd ever be able to prove otherwise.

"Only it didn't go quite to plan, did it, Doctor? When he was somewhere between dead and alive you turned the machine off, unstrapped him and went for a wheelchair" – it was standing abandoned just inside the door – "so you could get him back to his room. But he wasn't where you left him. He shouldn't have been capable of any activity, beyond maybe curling up in a ball and sticking his thumb in his mouth; but somehow he'd clawed together enough physical control to get off the bed. You thought he'd fallen down behind it, didn't you, and went to check. But he must have been" – she glanced round – "waiting behind the door. As you passed he grabbed you and ran you into the wall. Then he got the hell out.

"So when was this? How long's he been missing? What kind of a head start does he have?"

Cunningham shook his head bemusedly but he understood well enough: he was playing for time. Time to be sure, to make his woolly head focus on what he had to say and do to protect himself. "The clipboard. Pass me the clipboard."

It was hooked over the bottom of the couch. She did as he asked.

"You've got it wrong," he said, enunciating carefully. "I discussed ECT with Shad as a last resort and he wanted to try it. He signed a consent form. See? He wanted answers more than anyone. But something went wrong. Not because of anything I did, but because Shad's brain is different to yours and mine. He should have slept it off peacefully. Instead he woke in a panic, lashed out at me, and now I gather he's missing. That's unfortunate, Ms Holland, but it isn't anyone's fault."

"No one's *fault*?" she exploded. "Cunningham, if you want to pass that kind of power through somebody's brain and get away with it *you have to turn the damn machine back down when you've finished*! This wasn't therapy that misfired – it was attempted murder. And the only reason you'd try to murder Shad is if you murdered Jackie Pickering. You're going down, Cunningham. All you can do to make things easier for yourself is to cooperate. It's five past six now: how long has Shad been missing?"

She watched as Andrew Cunningham thought about confessing. There were things he could have said, not to justify his actions but to explain them. 'I'm not a bad man,' he could have said. 'I'm a doctor. Debbie Burgess and the others – I treated them to the best of my ability. The False Memory phenomenon only came to light as a result of these cases – I wasn't flying in the face of known hazards, I was working at the sharp end of psychiatry, breaking new ground, making as I believed important advances.

'When I realised I'd been deceived,' he could have said, 'I was horrified. But I'd been doing my best in the light of current knowledge – I shouldn't have been pilloried for it. Ground-breaking surgery fails again and again before it succeeds. Organ transplants would still be an impossible dream if the surgeons hadn't had the courage, and the support, to try again. I was entitled to the same support. *I hadn't done anything wrong.*

'Instead of which she set out to destroy me,' he might have said. 'The Pickering girl. She was going to build her career on the ashes of mine. She worked in entertainment, my job is mending sick minds, but she had the power to ensure I would never work again. It wasn't fair and it wasn't right, and I went to that meeting to make her see that. But she wasn't open to reason – she knew what she wanted and she was going to have it, whoever suffered. And the sense of outrage burgeoned inside me and, in a moment of madness, I put a stop to her. Everything that followed derived from that one eruption of righteous fury.'

It didn't explain the knife he had been carrying; it did nothing to justify how he used the innocent man who stumbled into his hands; but it would have won him a little sympathy. Poor Doctor Frankenstein, who tried to distil perfection from corruption and instead created a monster.

But he didn't want sympathy, he wanted to get away with it, and he still thought there was a chance. Rosie saw the moment he decided to go for it. Lucas was on the run. None of them knew how badly his brain was damaged. He might run under a bus or off a bridge; he might simply disappear and turn up months or years later as a rotting corpse that had tried to bury itself in some undergrowth before it died.

Even if they found him alive, what could he tell them? Probably nothing at all. Even if he could still communicate, nothing he said would alter the fact that he had signed a consent form for electro-convulsive therapy. The power output? He must have stumbled into the machine, knocking off the settings, as he fled. Who could prove otherwise?

"I don't know," said Doctor Cunningham.

Rosie snatched back the clipboard. For a moment Detective Superintendent Marsh, who had been holding his tongue while there was a chance Rosie could get answers to questions he couldn't even ask, thought she was going to hit the man with it and he moved, reluctantly, to intervene. But she wanted to see the paperwork.

She was right. He'd been so intent on covering his back that he'd filled in the forms as he would have done for any patient. He'd lied about the voltage – he'd entered it as 85 – but there was no reason for him to fabricate the time of treatment and he'd entered it as commencing at 5.45 p.m. He'd been on the floor, and Shad on the run, for perhaps fifteen minutes.

"We have to find him," said Rosie, turning to Marsh.

"Of course we do. Where do we look?"

She gave an elephantine shrug. "He shouldn't have been able to get off that bed, or walk across the room. But plainly he did, so an excess of electricity flashing across his temples didn't have the same effect on him that it would on you and me. Well, we know his brain's different to ours. We still don't know how different.

"I don't know how far he could have got. Maybe he's still in the building, or the grounds. Or maybe he's running like a scalded cat because he knows something terrible happened to him here and he has no idea what. Superintendent, we have to find him! He desperately needs help."

Twenty-one

Matt didn't want Alex to go home to an empty flat. "Who knows what Rent-a-Mob'll do next? It wouldn't take much ingenuity to follow your car. I don't like the idea of you being in on your own."

If she was honest, Alex wasn't keen either. It was the middle of the evening now, all but the most persistent of the crowd had gone home and Chief Inspector Gordon had indicated that the risk of a confrontation had passed and they could leave in safety. In fact, there were now more policemen in Moss Street than there was crowd to control. But the episode had left a nasty taste in her mouth, and Alex wasn't someone who shrugged off unpleasant experiences. She worried. Mostly she worried that she hadn't handled matters as well as she might have. Tonight, though, she was worried about getting a brick through her window.

Her hesitation was all the encouragement Matt needed. "Let's go and get some supper. Then we'll go back to my place." Matt's flat was the top floor of the old Warwick & Worcester Assurance building, higher than even Tessa Sanderson could have hefted a brick.

The hesitation was still there. He smiled. "I'll sleep on the couch if you'd prefer."

Alex thought about it, then she shook her head. "No, I don't think I'd prefer that at all."

They went out to his car in the yard.

The restaurant was just round the corner from the WWA building so Matt parked in his own space in the courtyard. He helped Alex out of the low car – she didn't need help but was gracious enough to accept it anyway – and they headed for the wrought-iron gate on to the street.

Three men came in through it, closing it behind them.

All Matt's instincts yelled, 'Trouble!' He knew everyone who lived in the building and most of the people who visited, and he'd never seen these three before. But even if he'd been a stranger here he'd still have known they meant trouble. Army officer training isn't primarily about using the right cutlery. It isn't even about weaponry: on any battlefield the senior NCOs know more about the armaments, their own and the enemy's, than the officers. No, the greatest skill an officer can master, the greatest contribution he can make, is learning to read a situation. Knowing how to fight is useful; knowing what to fight with is useful; but knowing when to fight is vital.

Matt Gosling had excelled at the practical aspects of soldiering, but he hadn't been bad at the theory. Leading patrols in Bosnia and Northern Ireland honed the theory into a reliable sense of when he was likely to get shot at and when he wasn't. He knew these men were trouble because once it had been his job to know.

Neither the car nor the back door to the building were close enough to be of help: Matt didn't run too well these days and Alex was in high heels. The street was only a few metres away but three men and a shut gate blocked the way.

Matt slipped Alex his car keys. "If you get the chance," he murmured, "call the police."

She stared at him as if he were mad. "*Why?*"

There was nothing remarkable about any of them: aged in their late twenties, dressed in denims and jackets, they might have been on their way home from any of the town's factories via a handy pub. They were decent-looking men, not dirty or drunk or wild of eye, but they blocked the exit as if they meant it.

The nearest of them stepped forward. He had short sandy hair and a stubborn expression, as if what he was doing embarrassed him but he thought it needed doing anyway. "You're from the local rag."

Matt breathed steadily. "Most of our readers call it the *Chronicle*. I take it you're not a fan?"

"'S all right," muttered the second man, staring at his boots.

"Sport's good," offered the third helpfully.

The first man glared them to silence. "Where is he?"

Matt knew exactly who they meant. But he wanted them to say it for any additional information it would give him. "Where's who?"

One of them said, "Shad Lucas," and another said, "The freak."

Alex breathed lightly. Matt breathed slow and deep, feeding oxygen to his muscles. "How should I know?"

"He works for you."

"No," said Matt, "he doesn't."

The man clucked impatiently. "All right – so he works for Rosie Holland and she works for you. And there's a girl dead because of a feud between her TV station and your rag, and when she was found that freak was standing over the body. Now, to any fair and reasonable man that sounds awfully suspicious, and you'd think he'd be sweating under interrogation down at the police station.

"But he isn't, is he? He's not under arrest, he's not being grilled, he's not even helping police with their inquiries. Why not? Because he has influential friends. Because the *Skipley Chronicle* thinks he's something special. Because you've used him in the past and now you can't afford to have him recognised as the dangerous freak he is. That's why I think you know where he is. Someone's protecting him, and nobody else has a reason to."

"You're wrong," Matt said calmly. "I'm not protecting him. He's sick, he's in hospital – and don't ask where because I'm not going to tell you. In spite of that, he *is* helping with police inquiries, and they haven't arrested him because they don't believe he killed anyone. He wasn't found with the body. They only knew the girl was dead because he told them. Any fair and reasonable man," he added sardonically, "would wonder if that was the action of a murderer."

"Well, you would say that," snarled the man. "Tell you what – I'll visit him in hospital, talk to him myself. If he can persuade me he's innocent we'll send him some grapes."

Matt laughed out loud. Alex was startled by the roughness in his voice. "You can't really be that stupid. You can't really think I'm going to let you and your thugs torment a sick man. I'll tell you one thing: he's no longer in Skipley, he hasn't been for days. You're not going to find him; and if you did you still wouldn't have the man who killed Jackie Pickering. Leave it to the police: they know what they're doing."

"As far as I can see," retorted the man with sandy hair, "what they're doing is bugger all. I think they know who killed her. I think it just suits them better not to say. I think they're scared of dealing with him. Well, we're not."

"Fine," snapped Matt, "then go and do it. But don't do it here – you're on private property, and you're in my way." Grasping Alex's hand he took a step towards the gate.

It wasn't a good move. He was putting them in the position of having to either step aside or stop him, and it was too soon, they were still too wired up to step aside. The man with sandy hair spread a broad hand against Matt's chest. One of the others gripped Alex's arm.

He wasn't hurting her but it was an escalation. She favoured him with her coolest stare, determined that he shouldn't see her fear. "I don't understand," she said. "Why is this so . . . personal to you? Crime happens all the time, even terrible crimes – even murder. Three weeks ago an elderly man was beaten to death in his own flat by thieves who got away with his television and his toaster. Where were you then? What is it about this particular episode that brings people who don't know Shad and didn't know Jackie on to the streets?"

The man who was holding her arm said it again. "He's a freak."

She stared at him. "That's it? That's all there is? He can do something you can't, so you want to tear him limb from limb? I can do something you can't: I can knit Fair Isle. Does that make me a freak too? Do you want to hurt me because of it?"

"Don't be stupid," he growled; but there might have been a note of uncertainty in it.

"Shad is a dowser," explained Alex patiently. "He finds water – for farms that need it, for industry, for anybody who needs a well. That, essentially, is what he does. That's what you're scared of?"

"What about them bodies?" asked the third man.

Alex drew a breath and then nodded. "That's right. If somebody needs him to, he can find other things. That's how he's been able to help the police in the past. The case you're referring to, they had a man in custody for the abduction of several small children. But without bodies they were going to have to let him go. Shad found the bodies for them and the man went to prison. Now you tell me: how does that make Shad Lucas public enemy number one?"

Almost, she won them round. She was so plainly a good and honest person that it was almost enough for them that she said Lucas had done nothing wrong. Perhaps if she'd been alone it would have been. Perhaps they would have let her pass if the only alternative had been roughing her up.

But that wasn't their only choice. There was Matt too, and though Matt was also an honest and decent person he looked robust enough to take a little pushing and shoving if it meant they could go back to their friends with a swagger in their step.

The one with sandy hair still had his hand on Matt's chest. He looked at it as if he'd forgotten it was there. Then he looked up at Matt, who was taller, and flicked a humourless smile. "Sorry, not convinced. It's too much of a coincidence that every time your freak shows his face somebody ends up dead. You're going to tell me where he is. You're not leaving here till you do."

"Don't call him that," said Matt quietly.

The man blinked. "What?"

"A freak. He finds it offensive. So do I."

Alex's eyes widened at him. The situation had been coming under control. All they needed to do was hang on to their patience and not make things worse. Now Matt was stoking the quarrel over a word. She didn't like it either, but this wasn't the time or place to make an issue of it.

The man barked a surprised laugh. "Offensive? Really?" He pushed hard with the heel of his hand so Matt staggered back a step, off-balance. "Gee, I wish you'd said before . . ."

Afterwards Alex tried to tell herself that the situation had been on a knife edge, it could have spiralled out of control whatever she and Matt did. The men would have become more offensive and more aggressive and ultimately they would have resorted to violence however little provocation they were given. But the fact was, they didn't have the chance to because Matt had had enough.

He brought a clenched fist up sharply under the elbow of the man's extended arm. There was a nasty clicking sound and a howl of startled agony. In the same moment Matt gripped the hand now locked against his chest, twisted and forced it up the centre of his opponent's back. The man was still snatching breath for a second yell when Matt pivoted – less than graceful on his prosthetic foot, but a model of ruthless efficiency compared with anyone who has not had professional training – and landed his good foot in the small of the other man's back. There was a third and diminishing cry as the man cannoned away from him and crashed to the ground. By then Matt had moved on to the next.

The man holding Alex's arm knew that dropping it was the most urgent item on his agenda; even so he couldn't get it dropped fast enough. Matt repeated the hammer blow to the elbow, so that the man's hand shot up into the air, and in the same move kicked out sideways to his shin. Another satisfying clunk, another gratifying wail, and the odds were down from three-to-one to evens.

No – the numbers were, not the odds. The odds had been near enough fair at the start: three macho men from the Skipley Sheet-Metal Works versus a trained soldier missing a foot. But for that misfortune Matt might have felt constrained to fight with one hand tied behind his back and the outcome might have been in doubt for a good thirty seconds longer.

With his companions in mid air the third man did a swift reassessment of the situation and very nearly came to the right conclusion. He cast a fraught glance Alex's way, and she saw in his eyes the knowledge that the best thing he could do now would be to run like hell. He was betrayed by a sense of loyalty to his comrades and a fear of cowardice that was greater than his fear of being hurt. He backed a couple of paces, then steeled himself and thundered in like a charging bull.

Matt met the assault with a jab from the heel of his hand to the centre of the man's face. Blood fountained, but even through it Alex could see that the man's nose had been not so much broken as pulped. A moment later the man realised that too and sat down with a thump in the middle of the car park.

Matt held out his hand – then, seeing the blood on it, quickly withdrew it and held out the other. "Can I have the car keys? I'll phone the police."

Alex stared in horror at the mayhem he had wrought and felt sick and ashamed. She didn't know what to say to him. She reined her voice in tight and stuck rigidly to the point. "And the ambulance."

He raised a slightly puzzled eyebrow. "Ambulance?" He was barely out of breath.

Her cheeks flushed and she panted at him in disbelief. "Look at them, Matt! Look what you've done. You've broken their bones. They were unpleasant to us and you responded with deadly force!"

"Deadly force!" he echoed scornfully; but his eyes were perplexed. Plainly he'd upset her: he wasn't sure how. "What did you expect me to do? Wait till one of us got hurt?"

"Matt, that's exactly what I expected you to do! If you could deal with them that easily you could afford to wait. You had no right to strike the first blow."

The three men were moaning and bleeding on the tarmac but no one was paying them any heed. A conflict of ideologies was being played out between the strong young man who, but for malicious fate, would still be a soldier and the elegant young woman whose career and personal successes were founded on the principle that differences can be resolved by discussion and diplomacy. This was the woman who, in her time as a hospital secretary, was regularly called down to mediate angry confrontations in A&E because even tiddly football fans tended to do what she asked when she asked so nicely. She had prevented more riots than hospital security and Rosie Holland combined, and had done it without getting her front teeth knocked awry.

The events of the last few minutes had shown her that the man she was contemplating spending her life with was a quite different type of person. An activist, not an intellectual; a warrior not a diplomat. He was a nice man, a kind man, thoughtful and considerate, but if push came to shove – particularly if either of them was being pushed or shoved – he would always respond with his fists. And she was shocked.

Typically, she blamed herself. She knew Matt Gosling's background: it had been an error on her part not to see that behind the good nature and the nice manners was a man who had chosen a violent career. He hadn't acted out of character: she had failed to recognise that among the elements of his make-up which she liked and admired were some less attractive ones.

She felt she had made a serious mistake, and come close to making a worse one.

Nor was her mind set at rest when Chief Inspector Gordon arrived to take charge. He listened to an account from each of them – and they agreed absolutely, neither of them had any interest in lying, Matt because he believed he'd done what was necessary and Alex because she thought the truth was quite bad enough – quickly realised he'd have to wait to talk to the injured men and packed them off to Skipley General.

Then, to Alex's dismay, he congratulated Matt on his performance. Matt didn't preen in the glow of his admiration; but even now the heat of battle had died there was no sense of regret in him, no awareness that responding to a shove in the chest by putting three men in hospital was a case of overkill.

She said nothing more, waited for the formalities to be completed and the police to leave. Then Matt went to steer her on to the restaurant as if nothing had happened.

Alex stood her ground. "No, Matt," she said quietly, "I don't feel like eating now. I'd like to go home."

He stared at her in amazement. "After what happened here? You want to be alone?"

She refrained from saying that, in her opinion, very little would have happened here if she *had* been alone. "That's right. Please, Matt, take me home. Or I can walk."

He knew he was missing something but he didn't know what. Now his eyes were clouded with concern. "I'll take you. I'll stay with you."

"That won't be necessary."

Twenty-Two

"He decked Cunningham, he got out of the clinic and he ran," said Harry Marsh. "Whatever's happening in his head, he worked that out well enough: he needed to get away from here. Where would he go?"

They were sitting in his car in front of Fellowes Hall. The dashboard clock said eight twenty; by the stars it was night. A thorough search of the building and the grounds had yielded nothing. There was no point trying to search further until sunrise. It's hard enough to conduct a proper search by daylight, impossible in the dark.

"His flat," said Rosie, counting on her fingers. "Prufrock's house. Maybe mine. Or maybe my office or yours."

The detective nodded. "I've got his flat covered, and Prufrock's been home for the last half-hour so he isn't there. I'd have heard if he'd gone to Brickfields, or to Moss Street." Her puzzled glance reminded him he hadn't had time to tell her about recent events at the *Chronicle*. He told her now. "That leaves your house."

"Let's get round there."

While he drove the Superintendent formulated a question. "Ms Holland, what condition are we going to find him in?"

There had been a time when Rosie Holland knew as much about the physical structure of brains as anyone, and even that hadn't been much. You looked at the convoluted lump of grey tissue in your hand, you put it on the scales and weighed it, you noted any obvious lesions, you took sections for microscopic analysis – and then you looked at everything that had originated in that brain, everything it had caused to happen, everything it had known and governed and thought, and you felt dwarfed by the majesty of it.

How did it do it? You could talk about neurons and ganglia and synaptic gaps, and chemical activity and electrical activity, and all you were doing was defining what it was you didn't understand. The working of the human brain could be described, its physical structure mapped, its operations observed. But as to *how* a brain works, let alone how a mind works, even experts don't claim to know much. A Unified Field Theory reconciling quantum physics with general relativity and thus explaining everything about the physical universe would be codified long before the last question about the human brain was answered.

And even answering the last question about the normal human brain would leave queries relating to the mind and brain of Shad Lucas.

Rosie heaved a substantial sigh. "Superintendent, your guess is as good as mine. Cunningham stretched that machine further than it was designed to go – volts, amperage, duration – to do a job it was never designed for. To inflict brain damage. He meant Shad never to wake up, or to wake up profoundly disabled.

"But if it had worked we'd have found Shad either unconscious on the couch or dribbling down his shirt in the corner. He had no business coming to with enough mental and physical command to flatten Cunningham and make his escape.

"So what kind of a state is he in? – better than he should be, but that isn't saying much. His memory could be gone. His entire personality could be gone. That may be little more than a zombie out there, a body powered by animal instinct and not much else. If that's what we find, Cunningham will have destroyed Shad as utterly as he destroyed Jackie Pickering."

Marsh didn't look at her. "This is my fault. I sent him there."

"Don't be silly," said Rosie tiredly. "You did what you thought was best. You were lucky enough to know an expert in memory-related psychiatric illness – it would have been negligent *not* to seek his opinion. Don't flay yourself, Superintendent, you had no reason to suspect Cunningham while there was time to stop him. You thought Shad was in good hands. So did I."

And now they knew better. While uniformed constables were beating the shrubbery around Fellowes Hall, Harry Marsh was on the phone – first to the Burgesses, then to their daughter. Debbie was still mourning her friend, inconsolably tearful; and that was while she still thought Jackie the random victim of a stranger. When she began to realise, from the direction of Marsh's careful questions, that she herself was the catalyst for the tragedy, grief turned to hysterics and she screamed and wept down the phone at him.

Only when she grew quiet was he able to get some measure of what she knew. Yes, Jackie had set her sights on Cunningham almost as soon as the extent of the damage he'd done became clear. For two years the girls had talked of making him pay: at first as a kind of fantasy, therapeutic in a way, like painting his face on a football and kicking it around. Later Jackie began to talk of it as a real possibility. She found a job in the town where he'd surfaced. She worked for the advancement that would empower her to make programmes. She tracked down other patients with similar tales to tell, lined up other psychiatrists to speak on the pitfalls of regression therapy and recovered memory.

The last time they'd talked Jackie had been elated, almost as if she were high on something. Debbie was anxious about her. Jackie shrugged off her concern, told her to be patient only a little while longer. The waiting was almost over, she promised. She wouldn't say more than that.

Debbie wasn't entirely sure if it was Cunningham she was talking about, even if she was in earnest or still fantasising. When Jackie was found dead three days later, and some kind of half-crazed vagrant was said to be helping police with their inquiries, it seemed suddenly irrelevant. Debbie never suspected a connection to the cause her friend had been pursuing since university, not until Marsh himself suggested it.

"Jackie was after him for two years," growled Marsh. "I wonder how long Cunningham was after her." He'd seen a lot of crime and a lot of criminals, had developed a certain understanding of some of them. Some crimes were just hanging around waiting for an incautious passer-by to commit them. Almost anyone could find himself on the wrong side of the law by carelessness or stupidity. But he didn't like people who planned crimes in cold blood, preferred a spur-of-the-moment axe murderer any day.

Rosie shrugged. "I suppose, since one of the psychiatrists Jackie approached warned him what she was doing. Her programme was almost ready, all she needed was his contribution. He may have known for months. Certainly he had time to plan his response."

"It wasn't panic, then – he really did intend to murder her?"

"She meant to break him," said Rosie. "He destroyed her friend's family, and he did it in a way in which there was legitimate public interest. The personal desire for retribution found common cause with her professional need to make a name for herself and they blinded her to the dangers of what she was doing – driving a man with so much to lose into a corner.

"Everything he'd worked for was heading down the tubes. Jackie had manoeuvred herself into a position where she could subject his professional conduct to a degree of scrutiny he couldn't survive. Don't underestimate the motive that gave him, Superintendent. Nothing in the world is so unemployable as a struck-off doctor. Defrocked vicars and disbarred lawyers can use their talents in other ways, but a doctor forbidden to see patients is finished."

Marsh pictured the big house up on The Brink, imagined the mortgage that went with it and found his eyes watering. "I assumed he came here because Fellowes Hall made it worth his while. But that wasn't it. After the Burgess case he had to start again somewhere, and in some field, where he wasn't known."

Rosie sniffed. "I thought it was a funny job for a memory specialist. He made it sound plausible enough, but I should have queried it then. The only reason he's working in an addiction clinic is that his old speciality was too hot for him. When did he come here?"

"About eighteen months ago."

"And three months later Jackie Pickering followed and began demolishing what he'd saved from the wreckage. She was obsessed, she was never going to give up. It was him or her: Skipley wasn't big enough for them both."

"She was planning his humiliation and he was planning her death."

"It was the only way he could shut her up. She was fired with a sense of righteous indignation, and she just kept coming. When they arranged to meet at the station, Cunningham was determined to come away safe. He'd survived one scandal just barely, he couldn't take another. It was dark, he could take her somewhere no one would see them, and he had the knife strapped to his ribs."

Marsh blinked. "Shad said *he* . . ."

Rosie cut him off impatiently. "Shad said what he was coached to say. *Everything* Shad said he got from Cunningham, either in their sessions together or straight from his head at the scene of the crime. The knife, and the knowledge to use it, were Cunningham's. He was a physician before he was a psychiatrist – he knows his way round the human body."

"And Shad had the bad luck to be passing."

Rosie shook her head. "Luck had nothing to do with it. He knew someone was in trouble. Fear made Jackie radiate like an emotional pulsar. He may have felt it before he left the flat – maybe that's why he was out late without much money. Or maybe he needed a pint of milk but her terror grabbed him before he got to the shop. I don't expect, now, we'll ever know."

"Don't be in too much of a hurry to write him off," Marsh advised softly.

Rosie appreciated his kindness though he didn't know what he was talking about. "However it happened, he knew she was in trouble and he tried to help."

"Cunningham must have wondered where the hell he came from," said Marsh. "There's no gate at that end of the station. Shad must have climbed over eight feet of wire netting."

"He would," murmured Rosie. "No wonder people are scared of him – he doesn't behave normally at all. Most of us would tell ourselves we'd imagined the cry for help. Only a freak would go to so much trouble to make sure."

Marsh frowned. "Who says he's a freak?"

"Just about everybody, sooner or later." Rosie sighed. "What he does, what he can do, is so far outside normal experience that people feel threatened by him. He's the alien in their midst: they don't understand so they're afraid. If I'd been found with the body, some people would have thought me innocent and some would have thought me guilty but none would have cared enough to picket the *Chronicle*. If you'd found Jackie they wouldn't have marched on the police station. But Shad's different. People treat him differently. Now a man he hardly knows has tried to burn his brain out. He must be a freak: people don't treat other people that way."

Marsh returned to the script they were hammering out. "So there was a witness after all. Cunningham had done everything he could to avoid being seen and heard, but he couldn't anticipate a witness who knew what was going on from streets away."

Rosie nodded. "I expect he took Shad for a wino or a junkie – if you've seen him in his work clothes you'll understand why. He knocked him out and left him with the body. If he woke up next to a corpse he'd run off and never say a word, but his fingerprints would be on the knife and the police would ignore any suspect whose prints didn't fit. And if he was found at the scene, no one would ever believe he didn't kill the girl.

"But Shad isn't a junkie, and he has friends who do believe him. Mostly, anyway. Only, when he woke up his memory of the critical period was lost. Thus far Cunningham was still safe, if nervous.

"But his luck held. When you sought his help he was suddenly able to protect himself. He knew how false memories can be planted in vulnerable people – that's how he got into this mess. Once Shad was a patient he could manipulate his recollection. If he could make Shad feel guilty about what happened he was safe. He'd confess; and when a little later Cunningham had to report that the murderer's wits had finally given way, he thought somebody'd make a note on the file, drop it in a drawer and that would be that.

"But he wasn't quite that lucky. When he realised the police weren't about to grab a confession, any confession, and rubber stamp it, the risk of discovery loomed again. And when I left word at the clinic that we were going to get Shad off the hook,

Cunningham assumed I knew the truth and decided he had to finish the job. Dispose of the only witness."

Marsh was nodding slowly. His voice was gruff. "You can't fault his logic."

Rosie blinked. "What?"

"I have no doubt," he said carefully, "that he did what we think he did, pretty much how we think he did it. It makes sense: it explains everything that happened. But it's purely circumstantial. We don't have any evidence that Andrew Cunningham has committed a crime. If he treated Debbie Burgess inappropriately, that's a matter for his professional body. Debbie can say that Jackie planned his downfall, but only Lucas can put him at the station, bundling her on to a train and stabbing her."

"But – what he's done to Shad! If he didn't kill Jackie, why on earth . . . ?"

"There's also no evidence that he did anything to Shad beyond trying to treat him. The dials? You can only say what they read when we went in there. There was a scuffle – either of them could have knocked into the machine and altered the settings. They were alone, the only one who can say different is Lucas. We need his testimony. We need him in his right mind."

It sounded to Rosie an impossibly tall order. But it wouldn't help to say so. "Maybe he'll be at my place."

But Shad wasn't there. "Now what?"

Nothing more could be done until morning. "Try and get some rest," said Marsh. "We'll start again at daybreak."

For as long as he could, until sheer bone-grinding exhaustion intervened, he moved as the rods move in a dowser's hands, a visible response to an invisible compulsion. When he was pointing the right way there was a little island of stillness in his head; when he wasn't it tugged at him as an agitated child tugs its mother's hand, dragging him back on course.

While he was moving – at first away from the terror and later towards whatever was drawing him – he was able to ignore the wider implications of his situation. There were too many things to do – he needed boots for his bare and bloody feet, a coat for his chilled body, food for his empty belly even if it was only carrots fresh from the fields and water from a trough; most of all he needed to put miles behind him – for him to dwell on what he had become and what he had been before. The very idea of 'before' was beyond his comprehension.

But it kept pace with his travels, stalking him like a panther, biding its time; and whenever he glanced back in trepidation, aware by the crawling of his skin that something was hunting him, it was that: the knowledge that before he was like this he was different. Things were different; life was different.

As long as he could keep moving he could avoid thinking about it. But finally he had to stop. He could hardly put one foot in front of the other. He was on the edge of a town: fields and hedge-lined lanes at his back, lights and angular buildings ahead. But he was too tired to continue. He smelled the sweet musk of hay and found a barn.

The smell meant something to him: he'd been somewhere like this before. He didn't know how that was possible: so far as he knew his life began mere hours ago. It hinted at a prior existence somewhere. That troubled him because he could find nothing in his head relating to it, but it also gave cause for hope. If there was more, perhaps the world made more sense than it seemed to. Perhaps there was some reason for him to run until he dropped. He didn't know what, but then he couldn't remember sleeping in a barn before.

Perhaps he would remember tomorrow. He climbed high enough off the ground to evade the draughts and surrendered himself to the spiky embrace of the hay. He wrapped his purloined coat around his aching body and waited for sleep to take him.

But it came too slow. Between exhaustion and oblivion there was a crack of time for thought to insert a crowbar. On the cusp of night, his defences down, the amok past swarmed over him.

From having no history, in the blink of an eye he went to having too much, swamped under a tidal wave of the stuff. Faces to which he could put no names, sensations he couldn't dignify with a context, emotions that left their mark in pain and loss but seemed to come from nowhere like desert plants blossoming after rain. Was this what memory was – glittering fragments of a mosaic with no frame of reference, nothing binding them in time or space? It made no sense.

He tossed on the hay and moaned, raking his temples in an attempt to get it out of his head, longing for the nothing that went before because nothing wasn't supposed to make sense and nothing couldn't hurt. This maelstrom of disconnected information racked him. He was supposed to understand. It was supposed to mean something. If he could understand what it all meant, where it came from, he could begin to make sense of where he was, who he was, what he was doing here. Until then he was trapped in a hall of mirrors, unable to distinguish between true and twisted reflections, the way out and mere echoes of the way out. He was still lost, still adrift on a raft of stars in an alien sky, still alone – the only difference was that now he knew it. And knowing made it worse.

Overwhelmed, whimpering with fear – because if this was what his life was going to be he didn't want it, didn't want anything to do with it – he packed his arms around his head like a soldier under bombardment and ached for release.

Twenty-Three

Rosie kept expecting the phone to ring and someone to say, 'We've found him'. But it only rang once, and that was a stringer for one of the nationals wanting her comments on the day's events. He got a comment all right, but not one he could print.

With Shad still lost out there in the dark she couldn't bring herself to go to bed. Sometime after midnight she fell into a ragged, restless sleep curled in her chair.

At half-past one she was suddenly wide awake, snatching for the phone. When the night sergeant at Brickfields said Detective Superintendent Marsh had gone home she demanded they get him back.

After six minutes the phone rang again and this time it was Marsh. "What's happened?"

"I know where he is."

"What?!"

"I know where he's gone. Pick me up."

The door opened as he reached for the bell. "Where?"

"Where does a murderer always return? Axiomatically?"

There aren't many police officers who know what 'axiomatically' means. But Harry Marsh was one. "The scene of the crime? But Lucas didn't . . ."

"I know that," said Rosie impatiently, bundling him back down the path to his car, "and you know that, but Shad thinks he killed Jackie Pickering. However little of his mind is functioning, that thought will be at its heart. He's at the sidings."

Marsh's first thought was that he couldn't be: that end of the station had been turned into an exclusion zone by DO NOT CROSS tape strung up by the Scenes of Crime Officer, anyone trying to enter would have been stopped. But time had moved on: SOCO had completed his work and wound up his tape two days ago, returning their goods yards to a relieved railway. He reached for his radio. "I'll get some help."

But Rosie stopped his hand. "Just us. Superintendent, he must be so scared already. If he sees a dozen men in uniform coming for him there's no telling what he'll do."

Marsh looked politely sceptical. "I doubt he's up to hurting anyone."

She cast him a withering look. "I'm worried he might hurt himself. It's a goddamned station, if he wanders in front of a train you'll need to scrape up what's left with a shovel!"

Marsh made no reply, but he did drive faster.

Rosie wasn't climbing any eight-foot wire fences. They drove to the main entrance and a night watchman let them in. There were no passengers on the station at this time of night, but the distant rumble and grunt of machinery indicated where wagons were being marshalled for the next goods train.

There were lights on the platform and lights across the yard where the wagons were, and between yawned a great gulf of darkness. Rosie felt a sudden tug at her heartstrings. Jackie Pickering had walked along this platform, arguing fiercely yet with a kind of bitter triumph with the man beside her, and didn't notice when she'd stepped off the end of the pier into the cold black ocean. By the time she realised her danger the darkness had swallowed her: she was out of sight and earshot of any who might have helped.

But there was still someone who could have helped, who tried to help. Rosie hoped she'd known she wasn't entirely alone; that even though it was too late, she hadn't died thinking her killer was the only one interested in her fate.

"Where would he go?" asked Marsh. The powerful torch was standard issue, but in a space this big it turned into a pale pathetic worm and quickly dissipated. All it achieved was to blind them to the light of the stars.

But Rosie had never been beyond where the platform ended. "I don't know. Where did he go before?"

Marsh had not seen it in the dark. It took him a moment to get his bearings. "Over there – no, over here. The wagons were on this track, waiting for the Holyhead train. Mind where you step." It had been rough enough by daylight.

"Is it electrified?"

He couldn't remember the subject coming up. He hunched his shoulders and repeated gruffly, "Just mind where you step."

The night watchman had offered to come with them. Already Rosie was regretting saying no.

There was nothing on this length of track tonight. They followed it to the buffers and glimpses of Railwayview Street through the wire netting beyond. A week ago Shad's Land Rover was sitting there, though Shad himself was in Crewe.

They stood for a minute, waiting. Then they stood for another minute with a growing sense of anticlimax. "Call him," suggested Marsh.

It seemed odd raising her voice in such a place at such a time. But there was no point keeping their presence secret: they weren't going to find Shad if he didn't want them to, the best they could do was persuade him to find them.

"Shad, it's Rosie. I've come to take you home. Don't worry, you're not in trouble. We know what happened and none of it was your fault. Everything's going to be all right."

She waited again; but she didn't expect him to say, 'That's all right then, and walk out of the shadows, and he didn't.

Marsh murmured, "Keep talking. I'll have a look round."

"Don't scare him off."

He passed her the torch, so when he moved away after three or four paces the darkness swallowed him up.

She tried again. "I don't know if you even remember me, Shad. You've had a bad time, it may be that right now nothing makes much sense. So I'll fill you in. Stop me if you've heard it.

"I'm Rosie Holland. We've known one another about five months. We have a mutual friend in Arthur Prufrock. He has a cottage in Foxford with topiary peacocks along his back hedge. He thinks they're whimsical; you hate them.

"The only problem with Arthur as a friend is that he doesn't drive. If you need a lift you need to call someone else. You needed a lift back from Crewe. You called Arthur, Arthur called me and we picked you up at the station. Just a week ago.

"You didn't know how you got there. Well, we know now. Somebody knocked you out and left you in a goods wagon. Right here. You stumbled on to something terrible: a man killed a girl. If you'd seen his face he'd have killed you too; but you only saw her before he dropped you. Afterwards, when you started to remember, you thought you did it. But you didn't, Shad. The man who killed her is in custody now."

Across the yard a distant light flickered as something passed in front. Rosie couldn't see if it was one of the railway workers, or Marsh, or the man they were looking for.

"Shad, I know you're afraid," she called out. "You've been through hell these last few days. But it's over. Where are you? Shad, tell me where you are."

Someone spoke then but it wasn't Shad. Harry Marsh, fifty metres away in the darkness, raised his voice. "Ms Holland, come over here. I think . . ."

She waited but he didn't finish the sentence. "Think what?" she prompted, but still he added nothing more. Irritably, Rosie went to see why not.

The torch picked up the side of a building: tar-black corrugated iron, some kind of shed. She walked round the corner and found a door. The door was open. She flashed the beam of the torch inside.

The first thing she saw was Harry Marsh, on his knees on the cinder floor, his face above the muffler white and startled in the torchlight, his eyes stretched, his body twisted awkwardly as if . . . as if . . . Rosie couldn't think of a single reason why he'd be kneeling there like that.

As if someone had a knee in his back, an arm across his throat and a blade under his jaw. What she'd mistaken for a scarf was in fact a sleeve. She looked past Marsh into the shadows, and someone else was there.

It was Shad, no question about it. Even in somebody else's

coat, with his hair tangled and seeded with hay, with his cheeks sunken and sallow, with a day's growth of beard on his jaw and nearly enough dirt to count as camouflage over the top of it, there was still no doubt that the man crouching behind Detective Superintendent Marsh, bending his spine across his knee as if he meant to break it, was Shad Lucas. But he looked back at her out of a stranger's eyes, wild and without comprehension.

Rosie gasped his name. But there was no recognition in the black pits of his gaze. He might not have heard her; or she might have hailed him in a foreign tongue; or language itself may have had no meaning for him. He went on watching with the fathomless stare of an autistic child. Her heart surged once and then fell.

"Shad," she said again, fighting to get the words out calmly, "it's Rosie. It's all right – you're safe now."

He still didn't move. Nothing flickered in the abyss of his eyes.

In moments of stress people tend to go back to what they know best. Matt Gosling saw his problems in terms of military strategy. Rosie became a pathologist again.

She couldn't see exactly what Shad was holding against Marsh's carotid artery, only that it was metal and winked in the light. She presumed it was a knife he'd got hold of somewhere, perhaps with the coat he'd stolen. It wasn't a big knife, but then it didn't need to be. If he used it in a determined scything motion, starting under one ear and finishing under the other, the presence of a doctor would not be enough to save Harry Marsh's life. She'd lose them both then: the policeman who'd done his best to help, to get at the truth even when the lie was easier, and the profoundly damaged young man who was going to end up after all as the killer he'd been made to think himself.

When all was told and understood, the law wouldn't blame him for that. He wouldn't be tried as a murderer. But if he escaped jail on the grounds that he had no control of his actions, a secure hospital was the likeliest alternative. It would be Fellowes Hall multiplied by a factor of ten. His remarkable brain would go nova then shrink to a white dwarf. Nothing that was recognisably Shad Lucas would remain.

Rosie was all that stood between either man and destruction. She was finally where she'd thought she was when she entered the house at Brindley Road, facing a young man with a knife and a head full of demons.

She backed slowly away from the door, lowering the torch so as not to blind him. She must, at all costs, avoid panicking him. She strove to keep her voice steady. "Shad, listen to me. This man has never hurt you. No one wants to hurt you now. Let him go, and let me look after you."

Her only reply was a desperate grunt from Marsh as the strong arm tightened across his larynx.

"I'm not going to jump you, Shad," Rosie promised, taking another backward step. "I'm too old, too fat and too tired. I'm also your friend. I know you. I know what you're capable of – and you're not capable of this. So I can wait while you think it through, decide what you want to do. Take as long as you need, but get it right. It's too important to make a mistake. No one'll disturb us: me and Harry are the only ones who know you're here." They hadn't been on first name terms but now didn't seem a good time to give the policeman his title. "You need to trust someone. Trust me."

That finally provoked a spark of recognition. Shad's head came up like a spurred horse's and a rush of breath, half indignant, half afraid, escaped him. The point of the knife jerked against Marsh's skin, drawing a bead of blood. Too late Rosie remembered where Shad must have heard those words last. Her insides flinched.

"God in heaven, Shad, I don't know what to say to you! I know what you've been through; better than you do. I'll tell you about it. But please, please don't do anything you're going to regret. Stop now and it's over. Put the knife away and we can go home. Please come home."

Things were happening in his face, expressions trying to find a way through the storm-torn pathways of his brain. His heavy brows gathered and his lips moved as if he were searching for words; but the effort proved too great and he looked away, defeated, surrendering to the nameless pain.

"All right," said Rosie, and now the shake in her voice was plain. "Let's get back to basics. I've told you who I am. Do you know who you are?

"You're a gardener. Other things too, but most of the time you're a gardener. You carry your gear in the back of a Land Rover. It's a rather elderly Land Rover and the doors don't match. The body's green, one door's cream and the other's orange. You keep saying you're going to paint it but you never have time.

"You live in Skipley, over a shoe shop in the High Street. There are steep stairs up to your flat – any time I visit you have to pull me up the last three." She paused, trying to think what other aspects of his life she could reintroduce him to without straying into danger areas. "Your mother doesn't have the same problem. She's my age but she's got the legs of a dancer. She's very dark, very striking, and she always wears red. She works in an end-of-the-pier show. You always say she's the worst clairvoyant in the world."

That was a mistake. Rosie saw him recoil as if she'd slapped him. The bent body of Harry Marsh jerked too. His face was wet with sweat.

But he was holding himself together. He knew Rosie was their best hope of all of walking away from this. He could put up with the pain in his back, and the knife at his throat, and wait stoically while there remained the chance that she could talk the crazed boy back to reality. He didn't blame Lucas; he was afraid of him but he didn't hold him accountable. How could you blame him for what he had no control of? Even before Cunningham got hold of him he wasn't entirely . . . He recognised where that thought was going and, shocked, stopped dead. It was as Rosie had said: sooner or later everyone called him a freak.

Right now, and for as long as his throat was intact, Rosie wasn't concerned with Marsh. All her attention was on Shad. It might have been a mistake, what she'd said, but at least she'd got a response. That meant something to him, connected with something. She pushed ahead, carefully.

"You, on the other hand, are pretty good at it. Not perfect – if you were you could save us all a lot of trouble – but still pretty good. You've helped me, and you've helped the police. Harry's a policeman. He knows you're one of the good guys."

For an instant Shad glanced at his hostage, and Rosie saw in his eyes that he'd forgotten he was there. His mind was in such turmoil that he could hold a man on the cusp of death and lose track of the fact.

He blinked and his gaze came back to her. He spoke for the first time. It was a mere growl, even lower than his normal speaking voice, but it was a recognisable word. He was understanding at least something of what was said to him, processing it and formulating a response. "No."

"Yes," Rosie insisted. "Nothing that happened was your fault. Unless you use that knife, you have nothing to regret."

"How can you *say* that?" he stumbled, grief twisting up his voice. "I *killed* someone."

Rosie shook her head emphatically. "No. Someone made you think that, but it never happened."

"I *remember*!"

"It's a false memory, Shad. It was planted there by someone who needed a scapegoat. Precisely because of what you are – a clairvoyant, someone who can tune in to other people's thoughts – he succeeded better than he could have hoped. But that isn't your memory: it's his."

It was a bizarre notion to inflict on someone who was only now rediscovering the idea of self. For half a minute he seemed to wrestle with it, his face screwing as he tried to get his head round it.

But he hadn't the strength left to punch through to the truth. "It's too hard," he whined, looking away.

Rosie steeled herself. Compassion would undo them both. "Shad, I have news for you. Life is hard. Always: sometimes it's a right bugger. It throws difficult decisions at us, puts us in situations where the only choice is between bad and worse. But there is an answer, it's always the right answer and, as luck would have it, it's easy to remember. It's, Don't give up. Don't give up, don't lie down, don't let it beat you. Don't let the bastards grind you down. Think. Remember. Separate the real things in your mind from the ones that were planted there. I don't care if it's hard – you have to do it. Otherwise the bastards have won."

He tried. She could see him trying. It wasn't enough. He couldn't get through the constructs fabricated in his mind. "It's . . . all real," he managed. He rubbed his temple with the heel of his hand. After a moment he raised the other one as well, clasping his fingers behind his cradled head.

In another moment Marsh realised he was free. He straightened slowly and sucked in several deep, soft breaths. But he knew better than to dive for safety. That knife could reach him before he could reach the door.

Rosie nodded in microscopic approval. "No, it isn't. You didn't kill anyone. That's not who you are. I know, right now you don't know what to believe; but *I* know who you are, I can remember for both of us. You're strong and you're tough and you can cope with this the way you cope with everything – with sheer guts and honesty. I swear to you, Shad, the worst is already over. Come home. You'll never regret it."

At least now there was enough intelligence in his eyes to fuel uncertainty. He lowered his hands, including the one with the knife. Rosie almost dared to think she'd done it.

Then in a sudden, fluid, cat-like movement he'd rocked to his feet, stepped over Marsh and passed her in the doorway, holding her at arm's length with the knife.

Rosie responded as she always responded to threats: with anger. "Wave that thing in my face, Shad Lucas, and I'll break your bloody arm!" It was an empty threat – even without the knife he was both faster and stronger than she – but she felt better for making it.

"Stay away from me." Despair caught up the edges of his voice. "Leave me alone."

"I can't do that. I'm your friend – I can't let you vanish into the night when I know you need help."

"It's too late," he stumbled. "I can't . . . change it. And I can't bear it. What I've done – what I am. Let me go."

In fact she had no power to hold him. He was already outside, keeping her at bay with the knife. He didn't seem to realise he could just turn and run, and neither of them could stop him.

Or maybe, somewhere, he did, and he didn't want to do it. Rosie said calmly, "No."

"It's none of your *business*!" He was looking frantically over his shoulder. Rosie couldn't think what for.

"Yes it is. You're my friend – that makes it my business. I don't have so many friends I can afford to lose one."

Finally he saw what he was looking for: lights moving steadily on a track a hundred metres away. A train being put together. "Nobody needs friends that badly." He began backing away from her.

Harry Marsh had found his feet, appeared in the door beside her. "What's he doing?" Then he saw the train too. "Where does he think he can go on that?"

Rosie shook her head bemusedly. "I don't know." But in the moment of saying it she did. "Oh dear God! He isn't getting on the train – he's going under it!"

Twenty-Four

Marsh snatched the torch and gave chase; but he was pursuing a man half as old and twice as active as himself. He was never going to catch Shad before he reached the track, and if it had been further away he'd only have dropped further behind. If Shad was determined to die, Harry Marsh couldn't stop him.

But he couldn't keep from trying. He ran as fast as he could over the rough ground, hurdling rails when he saw them and falling over one that he didn't. He rolled and came up running again. The noise of the engine was getting louder, the rumble of the wagons on the track coming closer. Even if the driver saw the torch, semaphoring wildly as Marsh ran and only occasionally finding the figure racing ahead of him, there would be nothing he could do now. Only blow his horn, and Shad wasn't heading that way because he thought the track was clear.

In the event the driver saw neither of them – not the running man who reached the track an instant ahead of his first wagon nor the breathless one who ground to a halt when he could achieve nothing more. The half-dozen wagons that would be picked up by the next train through here and borne off to Holyhead, or Manchester or Glasgow, trundled unconcernedly past, and all Harry Marsh could do was bellow in an agony of frustration, "Cunningham's going to get away with murder!"

It must have taken twenty seconds for the leisurely little train to pass him. The driver, shunting from behind, finally saw his torch and raised a hand, mistaking him for a colleague. Marsh let him go. It was already too late.

Puffing along in the rear, Rosie saw Shad eclipsed by the train and the shock hit her like a blow. Wide-eyed, open-mouthed, she froze in her tracks and then dropped to her knees in the cinders. A moan of barely human desolation wrenched from her throat. Now, finally, she didn't care about Cunningham. She didn't care about Jackie. She didn't even care much about the loss to the world of Shad Lucas's remarkable abilities. She cared that she had lost a friend. That they'd almost saved him, but not quite. That all the suffering and all the effort had, in the end, been wasted. She hugged her arms about her and crouched on the ground, rocking in impenetrable sorrow.

Marsh waited for the engine to pass, not knowing what it would leave: a broken body or just a nasty smear on the rails. When it was gone, slowly, reluctantly, he raised the torch again.

There was nothing on the rails. On the far side, hunched and shapeless in the stolen coat, braced to flee again, for the moment Shad Lucas held his ground with his face half turned towards the light.

"Cunningham?" he echoed warily.

Rosie heard his voice and thought it a phantasm. She thought she'd seen him hit. But she had to be sure so, after a moment, nerves clenched against disappointment, she looked.

She saw Shad, afraid and stubborn, ready to run but not running. She saw Harry Marsh edge towards him as if stalking a deer, one step at a time, no sudden movements; saw him extend a hand as he stepped across the rails. And there the drama ended. Shad waited for him.

Rosie clambered to her feet, the heart bursting in her chest. She set off towards them at a cumbrous jog, but when she got there she didn't know what to say. She stared at Shad, the tears coursing down her cheeks, and still no words came; so she just grabbed him and hugged him mutely. He looked surprised, but maybe they'd had that sort of relationship. He couldn't be sure they hadn't.

It was a long way back to where Marsh had parked his car. As they walked, between them they told Shad most of what he'd missed. Some of it he understood; some of it even sounded a little familiar.

"You mean, you remember?" prompted Marsh.

"I don't know. Maybe."

"*What* do you remember? Think, Shad, it's important."

"I remember . . ." He had to stop and check it against the memories that weren't his, that weren't real, and only when he was sure that this one was did he continue. "I was here before. Not the platform – back there, by the fence. I remember climbing the fence. Is that right? Did I do that?"

Marsh nodded. "Yes."

Shad was nodding too. "Yeah, I remember. She was in the last wagon."

"Jackie Pickering."

"I didn't get her name. You don't. People never think their own names. She was so scared. She was dying already, her life shrinking . . . I climbed into the wagon. I tried to stop her bleeding." He blinked at a sudden recollection. "I pulled the knife out. Jesus! I knew I was hurting her, but there was so much blood. I thought, maybe I could stop it. But it didn't help. She died while I was holding her. She disappeared down the tunnel, and the tunnel closed."

Rosie let out an unsteady breath. "Which is how your fingerprints got on the knife and her blood got on you."

"Someone else was there," said Marsh softly. "The killer. Did you see him?"

Shad shook his head. "I felt him, though. Behind me, in the dark. I turned to look but . . ." The memory ended abruptly, truncated by violence. "I suppose he hit me."

So near; so desperately near and still, for all they could prove, Andrew Cunningham would walk free.

"That's the last thing you remember?" asked Marsh, and Shad nodded. "All right. What was the first you knew of all this? Why did you go to Railwayview Street?"

"I told you, I felt her fear. I followed it, like a scent. When I realised they were in the yard I left the jeep with the car and climbed over the wire."

Rosie and Marsh traded a swift and wide-eyed glance, at once astonished and expectant. Detective Superintendent Marsh said, very carefully, "What car?"

"The one beside the wire. The silver one."

The silver car Marsh had sat beside, in front of or behind in more rush-hour traffic jams than he cared to remember. "Make?"

There were so many things Shad Lucas didn't know, even with all his wits about him. But he wasn't bad on cars. "Jaguar XJ8."

Harry Marsh exhaled very, very softly. "Got you, you bastard," he whispered. After Shad's safety, and his own, that was what he wanted most. "He left the way Shad got in, and he knew he was going to. He left the car there ready. So he wouldn't have to walk up the platform if he'd got her blood on him."

Rosie had already got what she wanted. She went on hugging his arm as if he might run away again. "I thought we'd lost you."

Shad had the grace to look embarrassed. "It suddenly seemed . . . rather final. I couldn't cope with what was happening, how I felt – I just wanted it to stop. But then I'd never have known, and I wanted answers more than I wanted out. I thought, if it was a good idea after all, maybe I could come back."

Marsh gave an appreciative chuckle. But Shad's puzzled glance told him it wasn't a joke.

Shad too had what he needed most. He kept checking he hadn't imagined it. "I really didn't kill anyone?"

Rosie shook her head. "No. The only person you hurt was hurting you, and he's all right."

"I couldn't . . . survive . . . in prison."

"You're not going to prison," said Marsh gruffly. "You can quote me on that."

It was Friday morning. Rosie *never* showed her face in the *Chronicle* at nine o'clock on Friday mornings, but she thought perhaps she should make an exception today. If she was going to ask for her job back.

On the way to the editor's office, however, she bumped into Jonah McLeod, the chief photographer, a small sandy-haired Scot with the steadiest hands in the business. Just now, though, he seemed to be having a fit of the vapours. He came out of the lift wringing in his hands the soft yellow duster he used to clean his lenses. Then he mopped his tears with it.

"Whatever you're doing," he managed at last, "it isn't worth missing this. Go up to your office right away."

"Why?" she demanded, intrigued. "What's going on?"

But he wouldn't explain. "Just go. Go now." He went on his way, giggling. Rosie got back in the lift.

Jonah wasn't the only one who'd been enjoying himself. When she opened her door she found Alex and two young men in a similar state of discomposure. One was tall and fair with a blond moustache, the other was small and dark.

The tall one was wearing a floral pinafore and a go-to-meeting hat.

"I'm sorry," said Rosie smoothly, going into reverse, "I thought this was my office." She checked the name on the door then came back. "This is my office." She spread plump hands. "Would anybody care to . . . explain?"

Alex performed the introductions. "Rosie, this is Fran Barclay" – in the dress – "and Jamie Lloyd. Fran, Jamie – this is Rosie Holland. I've been standing in for her for a few days."

She produced Fran's letter and her own, waited while Rosie read them.

They explained something but not everything. "And the reason our senior photographer is reduced to using his best yellow duster as a handkerchief is . . . ?"

Alex blew her own nose, though not on a duster. "We've been having a bit of fun. The boys talked about what they wanted to do – publish that as it stood, or specify the exact nature of their problem – and they decided they couldn't do any better than pose for a photograph to go with it."

"Like that?"

"Like that."

Fran was struggling out of the pinafore. It wasn't his normal attire: underneath he had a perfectly respectable shadow-striped shirt. "Jamie and I had a heart-to-heart about the whole sorry business. This was our idea."

They'd devoted considerable thought and discussion to their dilemma over the last couple of days. As Alex had anticipated, Jamie's first reaction was horror that Fran had considered leaving. His second was fury that his employers had subjected him to a pressure to which none of his colleagues was vulnerable; and his third that he was angry enough now to do something about it.

"You want to see it published?" asked Fran anxiously. "You can cope with the consequences?"

"Cope with them?" snarled Jamie. People who'd known him for ten years had never seen him as angry as this. "I'm going to instigate them. Nine o'clock Monday morning me and the Chief Executive are in conference – no calls, no interruptions. If I haven't got this sorted out by the time we finish, he's looking for a new Senior Clerk (Accounts). He's also looking at a lot of publicity. I'm not taking any more crap from these people. Either they treat you the way they treat everyone else's other half or I give a full, frank and attributable interview to this reporter friend of yours."

Fran blinked back a tear of admiration. "So maybe we should forget about the letter?"

"*I'm* not going to forget it," growled Jamie, "so why should anyone else be allowed to? We didn't start this, they did; but I'm damn well going to finish it." He disappeared next door to ask a favour of their neighbour, a tall Polish woman with a fine eye for a flowered hat.

"And we thought," said Fran, carefully laying Mrs Sikorski's most treasured possession on Alex's desk, "that if we gave Jamie's bosses what they were expecting we'd rather cut the ground out from under them. If it isn't a secret he can't be blackmailed. If they go on treating him as they have, it's obvious why. They can't get away with saying it's a coincidence, that they didn't know about him and me."

"And the hat, and the pinny?" asked Rosie carefully.

Fran grinned. "If we need everyone to know we're a couple of queers, we'd better look the part. At least for the photo."

"Er – you didn't think of shaving off the moustache?"

"There are limits to what a man will do," Fran Barclay said

loftily, "even for love."

Before she asked for her job back Rosie thought Dan Sale had better hear the whole story. He sat in shell-shocked silence while she talked. It wasn't all news to him, but enough was that horror bleached the colour from his thin cheeks and ironed out the furrows on his brow.

"And . . . how is he now?" he managed when she'd finished.

Rosie gave her all-encompassing shrug. "Dan, I really don't know. Better than I'd expected; but he's obviously been damaged, how well he'll recover and how much he'll be stuck with I can't begin to guess. I don't know how his brain works at the best of times, I have no idea how it'll have been affected by an overdose of ECT. There may be long-term repercussions for his normal brain function, or for his ESP, or both; or not. On the basis that what doesn't kill you makes you strong, it's conceivable that his abilities will have been sharpened by a close encounter with the national grid. I don't know. I don't think anybody *can* know at this point. We'll have to wait and see."

Dan Sale nodded. "But how *is* he?"

"Calmer. I'm not sure how much he really understands of what happened, but he's been told, and we'll go through it again, as often as necessary, as he's able to absorb it."

"Does he know who he is?"

"Oh yes," nodded Rosie. "Most of what he mislaid has come back. The last week's a bit of a blur still, but he knows who he is and most of what happened up until the murder. And *we* know pretty much what happened afterwards, so there won't be any gaps to haunt him. If he gets no better he'll manage."

"Where is he?"

"Harry Marsh found a clinic on the far side of Birmingham – he thought it would be better to get him out of Skipley altogether for a while. So do I: better for him, better for everyone. Let things settle down before he comes home."

"But people know now that he wasn't to blame."

"Of course – another man's been charged. It'll be in the papers tonight, then no one in Skipley will have any excuse for thinking Shad Lucas is a murderer." She sighed. "But those who think he's a freak will still think he's a freak. Long term, that'll be harder to deal with. Maybe he'd be better leaving Skipley, starting again somewhere else."

"And waiting for the same thing to happen again?"

Rosie gave a rueful sniff. "That's the problem, isn't it? He can leave everything behind except his own history. When it looked as if he was going to lose that too I thought it was a tragedy. Now I'm not sure it would have been. Maybe forgetting would have been a blessing. Anyway, that's not how it worked out so we'll never know. We can hardly stick his finger in a socket and give it another try. On the whole, we should be grateful things didn't turn out a good deal worse."

"There's still a girl dead," Sale said – as if she needed reminding.

"Nothing can change that. But at least her killer's going to pay for it – and thank God neither this paper nor anyone associated with it was in any degree responsible. Dan, we could be sitting here knowing that if we'd acted differently Jackie Pickering would still be alive. Beside that, almost any result is a good result."

Sale nodded slowly. Since they couldn't change history it was important that it contained nothing they would have trouble living with. He changed the subject. "I suppose you've heard what happened here?"

"The siege? Yes, Harry Marsh told me. Nasty enough while it lasted, I'm sure."

He shook his head impatiently. "Not that. Yes, of course it was, but we were in no real danger. There were nearly as many policemen as there were demonstrators. No, what happened afterwards."

She'd heard a rumour about that too. "You mean Matt putting three of them in hospital? Sounds good to me."

Even that wasn't what he was referring to. "I mean, Alex dumping him *because* he put three men in hospital!"

Rosie's eyes widened incredulously. "You're kidding!" But

she knew he wasn't. He didn't make many jokes; and besides, it sounded like Alex. They'd known one another a long time. Rosie knew Alex searched deep into her soul over matters which cost most people hardly a moment's thought. If this was sometimes inconvenient, it was a major part of who she was. She was an ethical woman, doing things properly mattered to her. If she had cared less, compromised more, she would have been someone other than Rosie's best friend and the woman Matt Gosling wanted to marry.

Though he wasn't, it seemed, making too good a job of it. Rosie was clearly going to have to knock their heads together to get any sense out of them. Rolling her eyes at Sale, she clambered to her feet and headed for the door. "I suppose I'd better go and sort them out."

The editor raised an eyebrow. "Before you do, wasn't there something you wanted to ask me?"

Rosie had forgotten. "Was there?"

Sale sighed long-sufferingly. "About The Primrose Path?"

"Mm? Oh – yes! Please, Dan, can I have my job back?"

That snort was the editor of the *Skipley Chronicle* biting back a laugh. "Of course you can, Rosie. The place isn't the same without you."

Her grin, vanishing round the closing door, was all the thanks he got; and all that he required.